EL

THE
Player's
CLUB

ELNIE

♡

THE Player's CLUB

FALLON
GREER

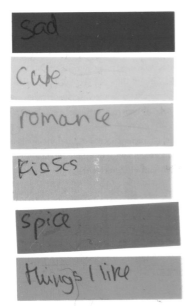

sad

Cute

romance

Kiosks

spice

things I like

THE PLAYERS CLUB
Edited by: Nancy Smay
Proofreading by: Jenny Sims
Cover Illustration by: Mayhara Ferraz
Cover designer: Sommer Stein
Formatting: Elaine York, Allusion Publishing
www.allusionpublishing.com

The *Player's* Club

It was supposed to be a simple assignment: stake out the golden boy hockey player Cole "Mac" Mackenzie as he exited the arena after a Los Angeles Blades game.

Follow him.

Get dirt on his personal life—something salacious to please the money-hungry gossip rag I worked for.

But I missed the moment Mac left the building. Or so I thought...

Twenty minutes later, I saw actual Mac exit after the media left. Apparently, he'd used a decoy to throw off the press—waiting until everyone left to make his getaway in private.

I started following the real Mac, and got more than I bargained for.

He led me to a mystery building tucked away in the middle of the suburbs.

Turned out, he was going to... a private club.

A club that wasn't for the faint of heart—as I'd soon find out after sneaking in.

I wasn't expecting to connect with Mac inside. Nor did I anticipate him to invite me back as his personal guest.

What started as a simple assignment turned into something much more—my biggest fantasy I never knew I had.

This wasn't about the tabloid story anymore. I lied to my boss, told him there was nothing to see.

Meanwhile, I kept returning to the club.

I was addicted to unraveling the mysteries of Mac's world.

Addicted to the man who lit a fire inside me.

But—with my own secret—it was only a matter of time before I got burned.

Chapter 1

Elodie

"I don't get why you're acting like San Francisco is that far away. It's not like I'm asking you to move to the moon."

I scowled at no one in particular. My boyfriend, Todd, loved to throw that dumb line into our arguments about me moving with him for his new job.

It's not that far. It's not that different. It's still in California.

"We've had this conversation already," I said for what felt like the millionth time.

"Baby, come on. You're just being stubborn. You don't even like your job."

"I like my job just fine."

Todd sighed. As he began listing all the reasons I was, in fact, being unreasonable, I tuned him out. Because I was actually trying to do my job—namely, follow famous people around to scope out stories about them.

Yeah, I was basically a gossip columnist. But a girl had to eat, right?

Standing outside Blades Arena, I currently waited alongside an entire crowd of paparazzi for Cole "Mac" Mackenzie to exit, a forward playing for the LA Blades. Mac was one of the biggest hockey stars in the country right now, not to mention he was also one of the sexiest.

He'd just been named the sexiest athlete by *Sports Illustrated*, and he'd recently graced the cover wearing nothing but a hockey stick to cover his crotch. I might've snagged a copy of that and placed it in my nightstand to use for future "inspiration."

That cover photo had proceeded to blow up the entire Internet in the past few days. I'd seen it across all the major social media platforms, usually accompanied with drooling and fainting GIFs in the comments. Females from sixteen to sixty haven't been able to get enough of Mac lately.

The fan frenzy had gotten so intense that some ladies had tried to stand outside Mac's penthouse wearing only pasties and thongs while holding hockey sticks. The shocking thing was that they were wearing anything, to begin with—or that none of them had gotten arrested for indecent exposure.

Then again, this was Los Angeles, a land of excess and self-expression. People wearing little to no clothing was hardly a strange occurrence, especially when the temperatures rarely dipped below seventy degrees during the summertime.

"Baby, did you hear me?" Todd asked me. He sounded annoyed now. "Where the heck are you, anyway?"

"I told you. I'm on assignment."

Todd snorted. "You mean you're stalking some celebrity?"

Once upon a time, I'd been a real journalist, but living in LA was damn expensive. Sadly, writing gossip columns about the rich and famous often paid more than penning exposés on an environmental scandal or, worse, a story about some politician having an affair with a staffer.

At one point, I'd even gotten a book deal with a publisher that'd seemed legit . . . until that publisher had gone under, leaving me with no advance and a book I couldn't shop to other publishers. The parent company of the publisher who'd fucked me over had yet to let me out of my contract, and I didn't have the money to pay for a lawyer. So my poor book just gathered dust and was probably going to keep gathering dust for the foreseeable future.

"I'm on *assignment*," I repeated. "And that means we need to table this conversation for now—"

"Elodie, I'm tired of this back-and-forth. You need to make a decision already. You've had months. I'm moving to San Francisco. Either you can come with me or . . ."

That statement caught my attention. I stepped away from the crowd, which grew larger by the minute. I snapped, "Or what? Are you breaking up with me?"

I loved Todd. We'd been together for five years, and he'd been there for me during many difficult times. And to his credit, he'd never asked me to sacrifice much of anything for him up until this point.

I didn't want to leave LA, though. Despite Todd's assertion that I didn't like my job, it wasn't true. Sure, it wasn't as fulfilling as I'd like, but there was something about getting the big scoop before anyone else that I still enjoyed. Plus, I'd had encounters with some of the biggest stars out there.

How many people could say that Justin Bieber told them he liked their sunglasses or that Kylie Jenner had asked them what the code to the Starbucks bathroom was? Not too many.

"Are *you* breaking up with *me*?" Todd asked.

I almost laughed because this conversation was verging on the absurd.

"No, no," I assured him. "I'm sorry. I shouldn't have said that. Of course I don't want to break up. I love you."

Todd let out a sigh. "Give me a damn heart attack, why don't you?"

"It's not that I don't want to be with you. It's just that my job is here, in LA. I'm on the road a lot. It's not something I can do remotely," I said.

"There are writing gigs in San Francisco, you know."

I scoffed. "What, writing about Silicon Valley tech bros? No thanks."

"There are lots of remote jobs you could do. At least think about it." Now, Todd sounded like he was pleading with me, which made me wince.

The crowd started getting noisier, which meant that Mac must be emerging from the stadium.

"I'll look online again," I said even though I knew there was nothing out there that interested me.

Is it the job, or is it the guy? My brain asked me. The question had been a niggle in the back of my mind for some time now. But I did what I always did and shushed the thought. I loved Todd. I just didn't want to live in San Francisco. End of story. Right?

"I sent you over some job links," Todd said. "Did you get that email today?"

I had, but I hadn't opened it yet. "Yeah, I saw it, thank you. Hey, I have to go—"

"Did you even open the email?"

I gritted my teeth. I was trying to get through the crowd, but considering I was what some people would call a petite flower, I wasn't having much success. A tall man nearly elbowed me in the face, and it was a miracle I didn't land straight on my ass.

"I have to go! Bye!"

I hung up before Todd could respond, knowing he would be pissed later. Oh well. I had a job to do. Even if Todd thought my work was silly and pointless, it was money. And I was too independent to rely on him to support me. I hadn't even wanted to move in with him here in LA when he'd asked. But in the end, it made financial sense.

I saw movement up ahead, followed by the flashes of cameras, but all I could make out was a tall figure with a jacket covering his face quickly exiting the stadium.

"Shit, shit, shit," I muttered. I tried my best to push through the crowd, but by the time I got to the front, Mac was already getting into his fancy BMW and driving away.

Mac was normally pretty friendly with the paparazzi, a lot more accessible than many other celebrities. Usually, he stopped to chat with fans and reporters. Apparently, he'd been in a hurry tonight. The other paps around me grumbled in frustration.

A tall, slender woman who I'd seen around LA before stuffed her phone into her bag, clearly unhappy. "Avoiding the press won't help him," she said to another reporter. "It's only going to piss people off and make them take a bigger swing at him when they finally get more of the story."

"He's probably hoping the speculation will die down," the other reporter commented, shrugging.

"He's not in Idaho anymore. This is LA. It's only going to get worse. People are clamoring for some type of explanation. You don't get to fuck a married woman and then act like it never happened. Especially when your uber-religious parents are out here asking for prayer requests for their son's salvation."

Both reporters snorted.

Mac had always been a media darling. He had more than four million Instagram followers and a million on TikTok. He knew how to keep his audience engaged, both on and off the ice. It also helped that he was handsome, charming, talented, sexy as hell—

I shook myself. So what? I might have a little crush on the guy. It wasn't like I was the only person in America who swooned when he posted a sexy selfie on social media.

Now that Mac had disappeared, the fans and reporters began to leave the area surrounding the exit to the stadium. I was reluctant to take off, though. I didn't know why. Maybe it was because I would be going home to an empty house with only cobwebs in the refrigerator.

Maybe I should get takeout on my way home, I thought, finally making my way to my car. I began scrolling the various apps, trying to find coupon codes because I was a cheap bitch even though I was also a lazy bitch who didn't want to cook. I finally decided to order sushi from one of my favorite places near my house when I saw someone leaving the stadium through a nearby door.

At first, I didn't recognize him. But then I noticed the very obvious dragon tattoo on his left bicep, and I blinked in surprise.

It was Mac. And I watched as he bypassed the players' car lot and walked toward the spectators' parking lot instead.

I didn't hesitate. I got out of my car and followed him. Maybe I was mistaken—hadn't Mac already left? At least that was what the hoard of people waiting around seemed to think. But it wasn't out of the realm of possibility that the first Mac had been a decoy.

That tattoo was unmistakable. *You should know. You stared at it in that cover photo for long enough.*

If it really was Mac, someone should tell the dude he really needed to wear a jacket. Otherwise, why bother going to the trouble of having a decoy? That tattoo was too damn recognizable not to cover up. *Then again, he probably thinks everyone who cares has already left the stadium.*

I watched in amusement as Mac went to the dingiest car in the lot, an old, beat-up Corolla that had seen better days. I was half convinced the poor vehicle was older than I was. *What the hell?*

As I stood there staring in disbelief, he turned the ignition on and began to drive away.

"Shit!" I'd followed him and hadn't even considered that he'd drive away. I sprinted back to my own car, fumbling with my keys, and peeled out of the parking lot.

Nearly out of breath, I called Roy. "He uses a decoy!" I yelled into the phone, scanning desperately for Mac's car up ahead.

"What the hell are you hollering about, woman?" Roy yelled back. Although my boss had lived in LA for nearly two decades now, he still retained his Southern accent, especially when he was pissed off or talking fast.

"Mac! He used a decoy. I'm following him right now!"

"Seriously? Are you sure it's him?"

I finally caught sight of Mac's Corolla, two lanes over and a half-dozen cars in front of me. I grinned, probably looking like a totally insane person. "Yes, seriously!"

"Who's the decoy, then?"

"No freaking idea."

I was so focused on catching up to Mac that I didn't see the car in front of me stop. By the time I did, it was too late. I heard the crunching sound of bumper-meets-bumper before I registered what I'd done.

"Elodie? Are you okay?" Roy asked.

I swore a blue streak. "I'm fine, just a fender bender. But I gotta go. I'll call you later." I hung up before he could say another word.

As I got out of my car, the driver in front of me doing the same, I sighed and watched as Mac drove off.

"What the hell, lady? Do you know how to fucking drive or what?" the driver snarled, looking like he'd happily brawl with me in the street.

Why do I want to stay in LA again? I sighed deeply.

Chapter 2

Elodie

A week later, I once again waited in my car at Blades Arena. Except this time, I didn't stand around with all the other paparazzi outside near the door. I waited in the spectators' lot, with a perfect view of the beat-up Corolla that Mac drove. It was a rust color. Or maybe it was red and had faded to that shade. I was so damn confused.

"You're sure that's the right car?" Roy, who was on the phone, asked me. "Because we can't miss him again."

I rolled my eyes, glad my boss couldn't see me right then. "Yeah, it's the right one."

"Because if you're wrong and follow some rando—"

"It's his car! Trust me. But I gotta run, Roy. I think people are starting to leave the stadium. I'll check in with you later."

The fact that the usually unflappable Roy Fink was freaking out about this whole Mac-car situation just made me even more nervous. It didn't help that I'd had to fess up to the fender bender thing being my fault when I'd arrived at work the following morning.

Roy had taken one look at my car, raised one of his notoriously bushy eyebrows, and given me a look that made me want to squirm like a child in trouble for stealing candy.

Don't get into another accident, for the love of God, my boss had warned me just an hour earlier. *I don't want to pay workers' comp because you can't pay attention to what you're doing while driving.*

Well, I wasn't driving right now, was I? I was just sitting in my car, sipping a latte that I'd probably regret later, considering it was already past five o'clock, and waiting for Mac to emerge. But there was a good chance I might need the energy tonight, even if I didn't get any sleep later.

I heard the sounds of the crowd, even as far away as I was in the spectators' lot. Thanks to social media, I watched a livestream of the Mac doppelgänger come out. Once again, a jacket was draped over his head, and he quickly hurried to his car without engaging with any fans or media.

I paused the livestream a few times, scrutinizing the doppelgänger. I'd studied a few different videos of Mac— and his stand-in—over the course of the week, trying to see the minute differences between the two men.

I'd quickly realized that the doppelgänger always wore a pair of white New Balances that the real Mac had never been photographed wearing. Considering Mac had had a brand deal with Nike for years now, you would think he'd have done a better job dressing his decoy. New Balances made zero sense.

"Sloppy, sloppy," I muttered to myself. In this age of social media and recording everything, somebody should pay attention to these details. Then there was the fact that Mac always left with his dragon tattoo on full display.

Whoever had concocted this scheme hadn't really thought all this through enough.

I finished off my venti latte, wishing I'd given in and bought a snack to go along with it since I was now shaky from too much caffeine. I waited and waited, but no *real Mac* came out. All of the paparazzi and fans had left now, and I had a brief panic attack that I had, in fact, pegged the wrong car as Roy had feared.

But then I saw him: Mac Mackenzie, in all his glory, walking up to that junker of a car and sliding behind the driver's wheel. At least this time he wore a jacket that covered up his dragon tattoo. I watched as he glanced around the parking lot, as if he knew someone was watching him, and I slinked down into my seat. A chill ran down my spine as he glossed over my car without even noticing me.

I let him drive away for about thirty seconds before I started following. I knew I had to be extra careful this time. I couldn't afford another fender bender, and I certainly couldn't afford to lose him again.

I had a gut feeling some new story lurked under the surface of this entire thing. Sure, it could just be that Mac had gotten tired of the limelight and wanted a break. But then why had he just done an interview with *The LA Times* a few days ago? And why was he still posting on Instagram and TikTok nearly every day?

Clearly, he wanted to keep a low profile—but only when it suited him.

I followed Mac for what felt like an eternity, although it was only for three whole miles. In LA, going more than a block could take you twenty minutes. I breathed a sigh of relief when we avoided getting on the 101. The last thing I wanted was to try to follow Mac on the freeway.

When Mac parked his car behind what looked like an office building, I pulled in a few rows over and watched him walk in. It was a nondescript, two-level structure surrounded by bushes. There was also a large garage attached. It looked like it could be a warehouse of some kind. I waited and waited, but nothing more exciting than watching Mac's butt disappear into the building happened.

"The fuck?" I scowled after an hour and Googled the address, but nothing too interesting came up. building housed a small marketing firm in one suite and an interior designer's office in another.

Was Mac getting his place remodeled? I glanced at the time. It was nearly seven o'clock now. Why would he have an appointment this late?

I wasn't sure what to do, but over the next half hour, a few cars started trickling in. It seemed odd that people would be arriving at an office building now, but what the heck did I know? When a car carrying three women wearing tight, slinky dresses and stiletto heels rolled in, my curiosity perked up. *Ohhkay, what's this now?*

I was seriously confused. These people weren't dressed to meet with contractors or freelancers. They looked like they were going out to a club.

"Welp, I guess I better go see for myself," I said. I applied another coat of mascara and lipstick, suddenly wishing I was wearing something other than jeans and a boring white blouse. At least I hadn't worn Vans—though my ballet flats weren't much of an improvement. If I'd known there was a wardrobe code for this assignment, I would've dressed for the occasion.

As I approached the front door, I realized there was a security guard inside, stopping people who entered. He was huge, looking more like a bouncer than your standard mall cop. I had to tilt my head back to make eye contact with him.

"Password," he grumbled, sounding bored.

Uh. Crap. Think. I let out an awkward laugh. "I'm meeting someone here—"

"Password," he repeated.

I stared at him. He smelled like Old Spice mixed with cigarettes. It reminded me of the way my grandfather used to smell before he passed. I thought about making a joke to that effect, but based on this guy's stance, I could see he was serious. And I wasn't about to get around him by batting my eyelashes. When a couple came up behind me, seeming annoyed I was holding up the line, I apologized and ducked back outside. That was when I realized I could hear music thumping from somewhere. *What the heck is going on inside?*

My heart pounded, and sweat beaded on my forehead. But I hadn't gotten this far in my line of work by giving up easily. Sometimes you had to suck it up and do things that made you uncomfortable. You didn't get the scoop on big celebs by being a shy wallflower.

I returned to the security guard and asked, "What is this place, anyway?"

He folded his arms across his massive chest. "If you don't already know, then you should go."

"Well, that sounds ominous." I giggled and flashed a flirty smile, but the guard was not impressed. "You're really not going to tell me? What's the big secret?"

"Like I said, if your name isn't on the list and you don't have the password—" The guard motioned to the parking lot. "You can either turn around and leave, or I can escort you from the premises."

This guy could probably flick me across the street with just his fingers, I thought in panic. I racked my brain for some kind of excuse about why I didn't have a password, but at that moment, my imagination failed me.

I returned to my car, feeling stupid and defeated. Inside, I gripped the steering wheel.

"Think, Elodie, think!" But my brain wasn't being the least bit cooperative.

Sure, if this were a movie, I'd go back and charm the security guard, but I'd already botched that attempt. Besides, I had a feeling that guy was immune to feminine wiles. He seemed about as interested as a brick wall.

Yet I couldn't just let this chance to get a story on Mac pass me by. I had to get into this place. It wasn't somewhere that was accessible to the public. And given that Mac went to all the trouble of using a decoy, he obviously didn't want anyone to know he was coming here. That was suspicious, wasn't it?

I drove around to the back of the building, unsure what I was even looking for. But what I found was a small loading dock, along with an overflowing dumpster. A couple of squirrels took off when I parked my car near their trash piles, their gleaming eyes flashing as they scampered away.

Two more cars pulled around the back of the building and stopped near the loading dock. A woman got out of each car, wearing nothing but skimpy lingerie covered in trench coats that were wide open for the world to see.

Another hulking security guard stepped out. This one seemed quite taken with these two women, and they were let inside through the back without delay. I could practically see the man drooling as the ladies sauntered in front of him.

Which gave me an idea . . . Reaching into the back seat, I grabbed the duffel bag I'd left in my car and riffled inside. I'd forgotten it was still there since I'd packed it two weeks ago when I'd been staying overnight at Todd's. It had been his birthday—*Yes!* the bra and panties set were still in here. Bingo! What luck.

"Now, how do I get changed without getting arrested?" I drove around and parked my car behind a large SUV in the corner of the lot, then climbed over into the back seat. I managed to get the lingerie on without exposing myself, although I was sweating by the time I'd accomplished that task. I honestly had no damn clue what I was doing or what I was getting myself into, but my heart raced waiting to find out. So I took a few deep breaths to calm down and gathered my courage to waltz outside wearing only a bra and panties. It didn't help too much, but I put on my best game face before walking to the back door and knocking. The security guard opened the door, his eyes widening.

I fluffed my hair, my lids lowering in what I hoped was a seductive expression. "You gonna let me in or not?" I asked. "It's a little chilly out here like this."

The guard, though, blinked and said, "ID?"

I laughed and tilted my head coyly. "Where exactly do you think I'm holding my driver's license?" Then I added a slow twirl, giving him a nice view of my cheeky panties.

He smiled. "You new?"

"Can you tell because my butt is shiny? Do I need to powder it?"

He chuckled and, to my immense surprise, stepped aside to let me in. "Your butt looks A-okay to me."

So much for the tight security. This one hadn't even asked for a password! I had to restrain myself from giggling like an idiot. I was so damn excited.

The urge to giggle was stymied, however, when I realized that I had no idea where the hell I was supposed to go. I waited to see another person, maybe one of the scantily clad ladies who just came in, but the building seemed all but deserted. My only recourse was to follow the sound of thumping music, which meant going down a bunch of rather creepy, dimly lit back stairs.

"If I get murdered, I'm coming back to haunt you, Roy," I muttered to myself as I reached the last level of the building. The music was even louder now. I opened the door . . . to yet another bare hallway. This one had a few people milling about, so I followed them through another door, trying to look like I belonged. But my steps faltered when I got a look at where I was. It felt like I'd stepped through a magical wardrobe and into another world. Whereas the hallways and stairs were all gray concrete and beige walls with fluorescent lights, this area was lit like someone's boudoir.

The foyer was gorgeous, with velvet walls, a huge chandelier overhead, and delicately patterned tiled floors with lush rugs. Multiple settees were right at the entrance, and both men and women lounged about. Some were wearing lingerie, some slinky dresses. A few of the men had their shirts off, while others looked like they'd come from board meetings, loose ties the only sign that they'd left work.

I felt multiple gazes on me, but despite my scantily clad appearance, I wasn't underdressed. Not at all. I fit in perfectly here. As I passed by, one man eyed me, giving me a lurid wink.

I shivered and kept going straight ahead, expecting someone to stop me and demand why I was here, but no one did. And as I made my way farther into whatever this place was, I realized it wasn't just some underground bar or club. There was more going on here.

I approached a large glass window where a few people milled around watching something on the other side, and my eyes nearly bulged from my head. A woman—completely naked—was draped over the back of a chair. A man stroked the woman's ass for a moment before he knelt and began eating her out.

Holy shit. This is a sex club.

Chapter 3

Mac

"Want another?"

I shook the empty bottle back and forth. "Nah. Maybe later."

The bartender, who'd been working here at The Scarlet Rope for a long time, gave me a once-over. "You doing okay, man?" He raised a brow. "Sorry about the loss today, but you guys always bounce back."

I grimaced. I wasn't about to admit that I'd already forgotten about our loss tonight against the Seattle Speedhawks. "Yeah, I'm good. Just a tough loss."

Before the bartender could turn into a pseudo-therapist, I excused myself. The one good thing about this place was the level of discretion. Even though many people here knew who I was outside of the club, everyone signed an NDA. It was the one place I could be myself without worrying about anything getting leaked to the press.

I wandered from room to room, trying to find something to catch my attention. But nothing did, and I suddenly wished I'd gotten that refill. When a server with a tray of shots passed by me, I grabbed one, then another, downing them quickly.

Normally, being at The Scarlet Rope never failed to get my blood pumping. How could it not, with wall-to-wall sexy women? Everyone was here for the same reason, so it didn't take too much effort to get one—sometimes two, three, four—to come over. Hard to get wasn't one of the games people played in this type of place.

A beautiful woman wearing red lingerie and matching lipstick caught my eye. She smiled and licked her lips, her gaze dropping from my eyes down to my dick unapologetically.

Normally, that would've gotten me to go over to her.

Tonight, though—tonight, my head was all fucked up.

I meandered around the club like a pathetic, lost puppy. *Snap out of it, dude! Look where you are!*

I wasn't exactly sure what was going on with me. Maybe I was feeling the loss tonight harder than I'd thought. We'd been having a streak of amazing games, but tonight, we'd had our asses handed to us. Worse, I'd played one of my best games. That should make me feel better, but thinking about it only pissed me off. It felt like I'd wasted energy on a losing battle. Plus, one of the newest guys on the team—Riley Gibson—had fucking blown multiple chances to score just to show off. I couldn't stand guys who did that shit.

I forced myself to stop thinking about punching Riley in his big, stupid face. Instead, I grabbed a glass of wine off a tray and considered going to find a good watch room.

Some of the play rooms were open for anybody to view, while others only allowed select members to watch. Those members paid more, usually if they liked specific kinks or fetishes.

I personally had a thing for watching orgies. One lady's tits getting sucked by a redheaded woman while a guy in a suit fucked her from behind with his pants around his ankles. Nothing was better than watching some two-on-one action. It was even better when there were eight or ten in the room, all moans and squeals bouncing off the walls, filling the room, the slapping sound of flesh against flesh—

My dick stirred. I was about to go check out my usual watch rooms when I caught a server sidestep *Handsy Paul*.

Handsy Paul had gotten his nickname because he was—you fucking guessed it—handsy. Sure, this was a sex club. Touching was encouraged here, generally speaking. But Handsy Paul liked to get handsy with women who didn't want to be touched, often the staff.

Why he hadn't gotten banned yet, I didn't fucking know. Maybe he knew the owner or something. But I'd stepped in more than once when I'd seen women looking uncomfortable around him.

"Aw, come on, baby, don't be shy," Handsy Paul whined in an obnoxious singsongy voice.

The server looked like a total deer in headlights. I'd never seen her before, probably a newbie. Sometimes I wondered what the people who did the hiring here told employees to expect. From the looks of things, it didn't seem like this woman knew what she was getting herself into when she'd agreed to work here.

"I can get you something to drink—" she said, but Handsy Paul took hold of her forearm, and her tray of drinks nearly fell to the floor. I moved quickly to step in, steadying both her and the tray.

The server's eyes widened. But I wasn't done with Handsy Paul yet. I gave him a restrained shove, yet the scrawny asshole went flailing backward.

He scowled up at me, his bushy eyebrows turning into a fully formed caterpillar on his forehead. "What the fuck? You pushed me!"

"You're lucky that's all I did. This is the last time I'm telling you. Keep your hands to yourself unless you have permission to touch." I thumbed to the server. "And definitely leave this lady alone. She's not here to play with you. She's just trying to do her job."

Handsy Paul's face turned red. "And I was just helping her do her *job.*"

The server visibly bristled. I had to stifle a smile because she looked pretty fierce right then. Despite her tiny size, she looked like a girl you didn't want to mess with.

"I'm not here for *that*," the server snapped. She glanced down at her lingerie-clad self and added, "Despite how I may be dressed."

Handsy Paul seemed to consider trying another tactic. But I was over this whole fucking scene. Backing the guy up against the nearest wall, I spoke in a low voice, "If I see you harass another woman here, I'll throw you out myself. You don't want that, trust me. I'm not as nice as security. And wipe that fucking smirk from your face before I do that for you, too."

His smirk vanished. Grumbling obscenities, he pushed me away and scurried off, metaphorical tail between his legs.

The server sighed. "Thanks for the help." She took in my appearance, and asked, "Do you work here?"

I wasn't used to not being recognized. I didn't know whether to be offended or amused. Based on the woman's expression, she genuinely didn't seem to know who I was.

I glanced down at my clothes: T-shirt and track pants. "Do I look like I work here?" I asked, amused.

She let out a laugh. "Well, I didn't want to say it . . ."

"What? That I look like I live in my car?"

She giggled, and the sexy sound made my dick twitch. Maybe even more than the watch rooms did. Despite the low lights, I could tell she was gorgeous, with eyes shaped like a cat's, high cheekbones, and luscious, full lips. And that was all before my eyes dropped to the banging body below. She looked like a Victoria's Secret model in her bra and panties. *I wonder if there's a set of feathered wings she could wear . . .*

Man, what I would give right now to strip those bits of material off her body to see the entire package. I couldn't help but wonder what color her nipples were. Red as berries, or brown like the warm shade of her eyes?

Fuck, I'm getting hard just standing here with this woman.

"I . . . I should get back to work."

I offered a curt nod and let her go even though I wanted to find an excuse for her to stick around. *She's not here to partake*, I reminded myself. She was just trying to earn a paycheck.

As she walked off, she almost upended her tray a second time, this time without any reason. She clearly had zero waitressing experience. I just hoped she didn't spill those drinks on someone who'd get her fired.

I watched her from a distance as she tried to take down drink orders, but eventually I had to force myself to stop staring like a creep. I was going to turn into another Handsy Paul if I wasn't careful.

I went back to wandering around, considering if I still wanted to go to a watch room. I figured I could use a distraction from the off-limits Victoria's Secret angel, so I decided I'd view my usual one. The guy at the door let me in with nothing more than a nod.

The room was plush, though it was as dimly lit as the rest of the club. The furniture was all velvet—couches, settees, and sofas. At the back was a fully-stocked bar.

The only rule in watch rooms was that patrons weren't allowed to approach and touch the participants. If they wanted to have fun, they'd have to either book a room for others to view them or pay for a private room.

Opposite us was a two-way mirror where we could watch the scene unfold. This room was specifically for orgies, and I watched as two different women pleasured a man. A blonde sucked his cock, while a black-haired woman kissed him. They were spread out on a lush silk bed, and all kinds of accessories were scattered about the room: whips, chains, handcuffs, dildos, vibrators, butt plugs, and a couple of things I didn't think I'd ever seen used before.

The black-haired woman spread her legs wide, showing the pink of her bare pussy. I accepted a pint of beer from a server, taking in the scene and letting every other thought disappear from my mind.

The blonde sucked the guy's cock faster now. The man wrapped a clump full of her hair around his fist and pulled her head down until she choked. I felt the sound deep in my balls. When he let her up for air, she gave him an adoring gaze while saliva dripped down her chin. Meanwhile, the other woman inched in, climbing on top of his lap while the blonde moved to sit on his face. The raven-haired woman threw her head back, riding the guy's cock hard, her full breasts bouncing. And my mind wandered back to the server. She'd had black hair, albeit it had been neatly pinned high up on her head like a ballerina. What would she look like with her hair down? I could imagine it falling to her waist, how easy it would be to use as a handhold as I fucked her from behind—

I gritted my teeth. *Leave her alone.* There are plenty of women here for playtime. She's not one of them.

But even as I tried to separate my thoughts of the server from the scene in front of me, I couldn't. The black-haired woman let out a scream as she orgasmed, and I wondered if the server ever let herself get loud during sex. The guy grabbed a leather crop and spanked the blonde until her skin heated red, and I wondered what my hand-print would look like on the server's bare ass.

I was so lost in my head, I didn't even notice that the trio had finished. They were kissing and caressing now, the man's cock starting to go soft.

I placed my empty beer down on a table and head-ed out, hard as a fucking rock. I was tempted to find the first woman—or women—I could and fuck them all un-til I got whatever this was out of my system. But despite my best intentions, I found myself looking for the pretty, black-haired server. It didn't take long for me to find her. She was behind the bar, a handful of men vying for her attention. It wasn't surprising patrons gravitated toward a newbie, even when she wasn't here to play. Couldn't say I blamed them. Something about her had hooked me from the moment I looked into her eyes.

I couldn't even say she was the most beautiful woman here. Yet something about her was captivating. Perhaps it was that she seemed strangely innocent in a literal den of iniquity. There was something so hot about that.

When I approached the group of guys drooling over her, they stepped aside without me saying a word. Every-body—except this pretty little server—knew who I was. That was a rare find.

She raised an eyebrow as the other guys scattered in opposite directions.

"Did you just get rid of all my customers?" she asked, sounding a little annoyed.

I shot her a grin, placing a nice stack of bills on the counter. "Don't worry, angel. I'll make sure you're well tipped tonight."

She snorted, but I detected a blush crawl up her cheeks.

When was the last time I saw a woman blush? I couldn't remember. The women I spent time with were never shy. They'd been around places like this for too long to ever be embarrassed. She was definitely out of her element.

Caroline had always told me that being shameless in the bedroom had given her confidence, and even calm, with the other parts of her life. *I never get frazzled,* she'd said more than once. *What's to get frazzled over when a man whipped and pegged me only last night?*

"Do you want something to drink?" the server asked, forcing me to push the memories away.

"No thanks, but I would like your name."

She wrinkled her nose, then glanced down at her bra. "I guess this getup doesn't work with a name tag."

"I think the getup is just perfect the way it is."

"My name is Elodie." She shot me a shy glance. "Now, do I get to ask you a question?"

Elodie. I rolled the sound of the name inside my head. Pretty. It suited her.

"Ask away," I replied, leaning against the bar.

"What were you doing—" She nodded toward the back of the club. "Back there?"

I stilled. You'd think in a place like this I wouldn't give a rat's ass about talking about my predilections, but it was an old habit. I'd been so used to judgment, even disgust, that I preferred to keep shit vague until I knew somebody understood. You don't necessarily talk about what you do here. You just do it.

Besides, this woman seemed like an innocent little lamb compared to the other patrons here.

"I like watching," was my vague reply.

"Watching? Watching what, exactly?"

Her eyes were wide, her tone a little breathless. She was adorable—and naive. "Have you ever been in a place like this before?" I asked.

"Is it that obvious?"

Considering she seemed to be struggling to turn on the tap for a patron's beer . . . "A little bit," I said gently.

"Well, pretty sure it'll be my last day here. While you were watching Netflix in the back—"

I snorted.

"—I spilled a drink on one guy, and nearly dropped a plate of fries on another woman. I think some cheese got on her shoes, too." Elodie grimaced. "But don't tell her it was me."

"Your secret is safe with me." I let Elodie finish pouring her beer before continuing, "What do you think of the place, though?"

Elodie seemed flustered. "Um, I don't know. It's distracting."

"Distracting? What, like you enjoy what you see?"

Elodie fumbled with a mixer, vodka spilling onto the counter. "Um, sure, maybe."

"Hey, can you make me my drink instead of talking to this guy?" a man demanded, giving me an annoyed look.

Shit. I didn't want to get her in trouble. I put up my hands, then mouthed to Elodie, "Good luck."

I slanted my eyes to the impatient patron. "Be nice to her." Then I stood, making sure the guy took in my full height, how much I towered over him. The guy quickly broke eye contact with me. *Smart move.*

I wandered around again, stopping to talk with a few people I recognized. One woman, Layla, who was often in one of the BDSM/punishment rooms, took my hand and squeezed it.

"I'm going to a room now," she said. "Will you come and watch?"

I lifted her hand, bringing her knuckles to my lips and kissed the top. "If you're going to be the star of the show, of course I'll watch."

Making myself comfortable in another watch room, I watched as Layla was bound, gagged, and blindfolded. Three men were involved in her punishment tonight. One man tied her so she hung from the ceiling, while another whipped her—softly at first, but with more force as she cried out in both pain and ecstasy. The third man fingered her pussy, but only enough to keep her perpetually on the edge.

Despite my best efforts, I couldn't help but wonder if Elodie would like to be dominated. *Here I go again, thinking about the server.* Although I enjoyed watching others, my personal kink was being a Dom. I loved having a woman at my mercy, controlling her every cry and every movement of her body. I loved when I could bring a woman to the edge of climax over and over until she begged for release.

Seeing a woman covered in welts and then kissing those welts during aftercare as I held her close—it was strangely beautiful.

I'd only spoken to Elodie for a few minutes, yet something told me she'd balk at something like getting whipped. Sure, some women were into light bondage, but the few times I'd tried to up the ante, those same women had run in the opposite direction. One woman had called me sick in the head when I'd told her I wanted to put a ball gag in her pretty mouth.

Not Layla, though. She was panting now, the trio of men inflicting pain to bring her pleasure. Layla's muscles were taut, her nipples pointed and dark, and I could tell she was about to come. But they wouldn't allow it so soon—not for a while yet.

I drank and watched, letting my thoughts drift away, the sounds and sights filling my senses. When I was younger, I'd have to stifle the urge to stroke my cock while watching a scene like this, but now I simply let my own body grow painfully hard without any stimulation.

In the years of learning and becoming a master at the intricacies of bondage and discipline, dominance and submission, sadism and masochism, I'd also learned how to control my own body. I could bring it to the edge and keep it there, never giving in to orgasm.

Layla screamed as she came, her body convulsing, the orgasm lengthening as one of the men pumped in and out of her pussy and the other fucked her in the ass. The moans and wet flesh slapping created an erotic symphony of noise.

It was a heady scene, one I could immerse myself fully in, and by the time I exited that watch room, I felt a little dazed. Yet I went looking for Elodie once again. The woman was like a magnet, drawing me near without even trying.

I found her beside a table, shattered glass, and a pool of whatever used to be inside at her feet. Serena, one of the owners of The Scarlet Rope, was yelling at her.

"Who even hired you? Because it wasn't me, that's for sure." Serena rubbed her temples. "It doesn't even matter. You're fired. Go home."

For her part, Elodie didn't seem too upset at getting fired.

I raised a brow. "Rough night?"

Elodie sighed. "You could say that."

She started toward the exit, but a sense of panic hit me. I reached out, touching her arm, something I was usually careful not to do without permission. "Wait. Where can I see you again?"

"Um, I don't think—"

I released her arm and stepped in front of her. "Would you consider coming here just to enjoy yourself?"

That made her still. I watched as the wheels turned in her brain, her pupils dilating. "I don't know . . . maybe."

Adrenaline coursed through me. "Well, if you ever want to come here again . . ." I leaned down, my lips only a breath away from the curved lobe of her ear. "Give them the name Raven Blackwood. That's my private password. They'll know you're a personal guest of mine and let you right in."

Elodie took in a deep breath. "Okay," she whispered. Her skin turned crimson again. I loved the effect I seemed to have on her. It had nothing to do with my hockey-star status, either, which was refreshing. She was simply affected by *me*.

And damn if I wasn't affected by her.

Chapter 4

Elodie

I woke up freezing. Wrapping myself up in blankets as I shivered, I looked around, confused about where I was.

Then I remembered. I'd come to San Francisco to visit Todd. The nights—and early mornings—were always too cold for my delicate LA sensibilities. Todd liked to tease me when I went out all bundled up when it was all of fifty-five degrees out.

Speaking of Todd—I reached out to his side of the bed, but it was cold. So I grabbed my phone to check the time and sat up. It was only a little after seven. How long had he been awake? He'd mentioned he didn't have to go into the office until closer to ten today, and Todd had always liked to sleep in.

The bedroom door creaked open. Todd came in with a mug of what smelled like green tea. He was shirtless and smiling as he sat down on the bed. "You awake yet?" He sipped his tea, raising an eyebrow.

My eyes fell to his toned chest. My boyfriend was a handsome guy—blond, lightly tanned, and muscles in all the right places. He took good care of himself, going to the gym regularly and making all kinds of green smoothies when he felt like he needed a detox.

"I'm awake," I stretched and replied groggily. I started to push the blankets aside, but it was so cold in the damn bedroom that I couldn't commit and pulled them up to my neck instead.

Todd laughed at me. "It's not that cold, baby."

"Is the heat even on?" I muttered.

"I'm not turning the heat on in the summer." He patted the back of my hand. "How about I make you some hot tea to warm you up instead?" He kissed my forehead, not waiting for a response before getting up and heading to the kitchen. I grumbled, a little annoyed, mostly because Todd knew I wasn't a tea drinker. At least he should have known that by now. I liked my morning beverage to be coffee—preferably an extra-large Americano with an extra shot of espresso. No cream, no milk, no fluff.

I braved the morning tundra to grab my bag from the closet and rifled around to find long pants and a jacket. The cold hardwood floor under my bare feet felt like ice, and I rushed to dress so fast that I nearly fell on my face. God, how fucking freezing was it in here?

When Todd returned with my tea, I drank it without complaint. At least it was steaming hot.

He picked up a balled-up piece of clothing that had fallen from my duffel bag and shook it out. *The sexy lingerie I'd worn to The Scarlet Rope.* I blushed, and then blushed harder when Todd chuckled at my expression.

"Now, why didn't you wear this last night?" he asked.

"I forgot it was in my bag." Which was true, to an extent, anyway.

"That's a damn shame. I would've appreciated seeing you in this."

After my adventure at the sex club, I'd gone home in a daze, but not before changing out of that bra and panties. I'd rolled them up and stuffed them into my overnight bag without a second thought.

Well, I hadn't thought of the *outfit* again, but I had thought about the evening, mostly about a certain gorgeous man and the way he looked at me. How could I *not* remember the heat that blazed in Mac's eyes while I wore those fabric scraps? I'd had a number of dreams about the hockey star, many of which had been so sexual that I'd awoken throbbing and desperate for a release.

Worse, I'd gotten myself off, imagining what Mac would do to me in bed. I'd told myself that everyone had fantasies, even people in long-term relationships. Fantasies were harmless. You literally can't stop your imagination, only your actions.

Yet my guilt must've shown on my face because Todd's expression changed to frustration.

"Did you hear a word that I just said?" He tossed the lingerie back into my bag. "I feel like you've been distracted since you got here last night."

That was an understatement. I hadn't told Todd about going to The Scarlet Rope. Or about Mac, beyond mentioning that I'd been assigned to write a story about him. Normally, I'd be inclined to tell Todd all the juicy details about a celebrity encounter, even though Todd was rarely interested in it. But this? This had felt like a dirty little secret from when Mac first approached me. The mere mention of his name would surely send my guilt into overdrive. Todd would be able to tell by the look on my face that this entire thing wasn't exactly innocent.

I grimaced. "Sorry, sorry. Work has just been crazy, and I haven't been sleeping well."

"Have you been going to that yoga place I got you passes for?"

When I shook my head, Todd sighed. "I don't get you, Elodie. I try to help you, but you never let me. You can't sleep, so I offer solutions to your problems, but you refuse to do anything. And then the cycle continues—"

My phone buzzed from the nightstand. Todd and I stared at each other as if waiting for the other person to break first. But I knew that ringtone. It was Roy, and I'd been dodging his calls the past few days.

I wasn't about to answer it when I was already accused of being distracted, so my phone kept buzzing and buzzing. It finally stopped, only to start all over again thirty seconds later. Roy wasn't going to leave me a voicemail. He would haunt me until I picked up.

I finally caved and answered. I mouthed, "*Sorry,*" to Todd before heading outside to talk alone on the balcony,

"Andrews!" Roy's voice boomed in my ear. "Where the hell have you been?"

"Sorry—"

"Whatever, don't care. Do you have an update on Mac, or am I wasting my fucking time again?"

I hesitated. A seagull cawed and swooped toward a nearby roof, causing a flock of crows to burst into flight. The skyline was foggy and dreary, as usual at this time of day. When it was clear, you could see the Golden Gate Bridge on the horizon.

"You're not wasting your time," I hedged, my mind racing. "I followed Mac again, but I didn't get anything interesting. Sorry."

Wow. I'd been going back and forth on if I should tell Roy about Mac or not. Apparently, I'd made my decision. This discovery was going to be *my* little secret. With Roy on the phone, I didn't have time to contemplate my true intentions.

My boss growled. "I thought you said you weren't wastin' my time, Andrews."

"I'm not." I stood straight, refusing to let Roy's bluster make me feel guilty. "I tried to get into the building Mac went into, but it was locked up tight. It was an office building, so I'd guess Mac was there for a business meeting."

"A business meeting? Great scoop." Roy's tone was, of course, sarcastic. He sighed. "So are you saying there's still something worth chasing, or should I reassign you?"

No! Panic burst inside my chest. "There's definitely something going on. The fact that Mac was there late at night, and people coming and going from the building at that time of day . . ." I paused, not wanting to reveal too much but also not wanting to be reassigned. Meanwhile, the seagull on the roof across from me was joined by three other seagulls, who all started screaming at each other. One held what looked like half a loaf of bread in its beak. Bits of bread began to fall into the street like snow as the gulls fought over their bounty. I stared lost in thought.

"Fine, keep digging," Roy finally said. "But you need something good for me next time. Otherwise, we're just wasting our fucking time. I'm gonna have to take you off the big assignments if you're not producing anything, Elodie."

"Yeah. Okay. Got it."

After I hung up, I wasn't ready to go back inside just yet. I didn't know why I was lying to my boss. I'd never felt protective about the celebs I'd been assigned to write stories about before. Sure, sometimes I felt a little guilty if the story was extra scandalous. But famous people understood the symbiotic relationship they had with the press. They hated us, but they also needed us. It was the same thing for journalists.

So why had I not wanted to tell Roy about The Scarlet Rope? Maybe I was just embarrassed that I'd let myself get swept up into the strangeness of it all. Or maybe I was embarrassed that I'd liked what I'd seen—

I shook myself. I had a job to do. It didn't matter that my brain seemed obsessed with Mac and liked to dream about him in the dark of the night. It didn't matter that he was oddly sweet and protective toward me and that I'd fantasized how that might translate into other situations.

"Babe?" Todd's voice broke through my thoughts, making me jump a little in surprise. "Did you hear me?"

I had definitely *not* heard him, and I was sure the guilt was written on my face. I could see Todd's frustration return immediately in his expression.

"Look, I need to go into the office. Something came up." His voice was flat, his gaze not even meeting mine now.

"I thought you had the morning off, and we were going to hang out?" I asked.

"So did I." The remark was pointed. *I thought you wanted to spend time with* me, it seemed to say.

Todd dressed and was out the door before I could convince him to stay. What was worse was that I didn't *try* to make him stay. He was in a bad mood, and I didn't have the energy to break him out of it. He was often in a bad mood lately. I knew he was frustrated with my not wanting to move to San Francisco, but the constant bickering about it was tiresome, too. And it sure as hell didn't make me want to spend time with him.

After Todd left, I poured the rest of the mug of tea he'd made me down the sink and ventured across the street for some actual caffeine. Once at the café, I decided I might as well get some work done. It was better than moping around Todd's tiny apartment all day alone while waiting for him to come home. Finding a corner where nobody would look over my shoulder, I started searching for answers about the mysterious Cole Mackenzie.

What made him tick? What had driven him to seek out a place like The Scarlet Rope? Sure, lots of famous people in Hollywood had eclectic tastes. That didn't surprise me in and of itself. But Mac had always come off as squeaky clean. "Which is probably why he wants to keep this secret," I muttered.

I started looking at Mac's various social media channels, but I already knew they wouldn't give me anything new. I laughed at his latest video on TikTok, though, where he danced to a viral song with a charm and irresistible lack of reserve. The comments were filled with heart-eye emoji—at least the PG comments were. Some of the more R-rated comments made me blush a little in my chair. Couldn't say I disagreed with them.

When I googled Mac's family, I only found a few bits of information floating around the Internet. Apparently, Mac had been raised in Northern Idaho. His Wikipedia article listed Coeur d'Alene, Idaho, as his birthplace, but no articles came up about his time living there. I found a number of articles about Mac's time at the University of Minnesota, where he played college hockey, but very little about his childhood and adolescence in where I presumed was Idaho.

I frowned, tapping my chin. There was no way that his high school, for instance, wouldn't be proudly claiming

Mac as an alumnus. Yet there was no mention of Mac being a graduate of any of the high schools in Coeur d'Alene.

After looking at Google Maps, I began looking up smaller towns near Coeur d'Alene. I barely noticed that my Americano had gone cold as I searched and searched online. My stomach rumbled as I realized I hadn't eaten either.

I finally found a hit in the tiny town of White Rock, some fifty miles from Coeur d'Alene. And that was when I discovered there was a prominent pastor by the name of Robert Mackenzie. When I found his photo on the church's website, I nearly fell over in my chair because he looked just like Mac. *His father.*

Well, I guessed Mac was a preacher's kid. I couldn't help but smile. Everybody knew preachers' kids always ended up the wildest. I remembered one girl in my high school who got pregnant at sixteen, and her dad had been a leader in their local church. It had been quite the scandal in Los Angeles, even back then.

Robert "Bob" Mackenzie was a mega-church leader that boasted tens of thousands of members despite being located in a tiny community. I watched a few YouTube videos of their services, blinking in surprise when they even had people zip-lining down to the stage, like some Vegas act.

Bob Mackenzie had a booming voice and an intimidating presence. As he spoke of thunder and brimstone, I shivered, feeling a bit like I needed to go to church and repent right away.

I discovered that Mac had two sisters and a brother. His mom, Judy Mackenzie, was a homemaker. She was on stage with her husband a lot, her hair blond and perfectly coifed, looking not a day over forty despite being in her midsixties.

I eventually found a copy of a yearbook from Mac's high school and smiled as I flipped through the digital files. Mac was just as handsome then as he is now but in a sweet, boyish way. His hair was long in a lot of the photos, which I had to imagine his dad probably hadn't liked.

He was pictured more than once with one girl, including at prom. *Dawn Morrison,* the caption said.

My curiosity led me down another path, and it didn't take long to find out where this Dawn Morrison had ended up. She'd moved away from Idaho soon after high school and now lived in Malibu. She owned a pottery studio and was married to a woman now. *Interesting.*

I noted the pottery studio website, wondering if Dawn would talk to me about Mac.

The morning inched into afternoon, and I forced myself to take a break to eat lunch. But I was quickly back in sleuthing mode, going through old newspaper articles from Mac's high school days.

I discovered that both of his parents were in photos at his hockey games, but by the time Mac had reached his senior year, his parents had disappeared. Then looking at his college photos and his current photos at various Blades games, his parents were nowhere to be found.

That's strange, I thought. Sure, Idaho was far from LA, but I had a hard time imagining that his parents just stopped attending his games entirely, never lending their support to his amazing career.

But when I read through Bob's biography on the church's website, there was no mention of Mac's accomplishments. Just that Bob and Judy had three children—

I stilled. *Mac had three siblings. So they had four children, right?*

I wondered if it was just a typo, but something tingled deep inside my brain. The fact that his parents had seemingly stopped attending his games, acting like their eldest son no longer existed . . .

You don't know that for sure. The idea was solely based on conjecture. For all I knew, his parents had tried to attend as many of his games as they could, but it was probably expensive to travel that much. And the church website bio could just be a typo. Sometimes my imagination went a little wild.

I returned to Todd's apartment, feeling strangely energized. I didn't know if what I'd dug up was enough information to keep Roy happy, but it was something at least. And if Dawn would talk to me, well, that'd be amazing.

I started dinner, mostly because I felt guilty that I'd been ignoring Todd earlier that morning. And because I needed to stop thinking about Mac and his mysterious history.

Todd arrived home with a bouquet and a smile on his face. And I felt happy to see him. He kissed me, turning the kiss into something long and slow, and I let myself enjoy it.

"Sorry about earlier," I said when we parted, taking the flowers from Todd to put them in a vase. "Did you handle whatever you needed to get done today?"

Todd shrugged. "Mostly. One of my coworkers is on maternity leave—Julie, remember?—and it's been a clusterfuck since she went offline. I get that she's on leave, but she can still answer critical emails, right? She's the only one with the data we need—" Todd kept talking, only needing me to nod and cluck when appropriate. By the time we sat down to eat, it seemed he had purged himself of work and looked more relaxed than he had since I arrived.

When he asked what I'd spent today doing, I explained, "Just researching Cole Mackenzie. You know, the hockey player?" I swallowed the lump in my throat.

"Never heard of him," Todd said.

I gaped at him. "Seriously? He's one of the biggest players in the league right now."

Todd laughed. "Since when do you care about hockey?"

I grumbled, but he had a point. I didn't care about hockey last week—and neither did Todd. So instead of trying to explain away why anyone would care about a wholesome forward with a hidden dark side, we talked about other things.

Todd kissed me when we went to bed, whispering in my ear, "How about you put on that lingerie I found earlier?"

A panic came over me. Normally, I'd be happy to wear something sexy to bed, especially if Todd wanted me to. But the thought of wearing that lingerie, the same bra and panties Mac had seen me in, devoured with heat in his eyes—I swallowed. "I need to wash them. Besides, they're all wrinkled up now."

"Then I'll just get you naked," was Todd's reply. "Even better."

I let him caress me and kiss me even as I struggled to stay focused on the moment. But when Todd reached for the waistband of my pants, I pushed his hands away.

"What's the matter?" he asked.

"Um. I forgot. I started my period today," I lied.

Todd was quiet for a long moment, but then he just sighed and rolled away from me. He grabbed his iPad and started reading without another word.

I felt guilty. But not guilty enough to have sex with Todd. My mind was too far away.

I apologized and turned onto my side, my back to Todd, but my thoughts kept finding their way to Mac again. I decided right then and there that I'd accept Mac's invitation to attend The Scarlet Rope a second time.

It's for research, I reassured myself. *No other reason.*

Chapter 5

Elodie

My best friend Hannah wrinkled her pert, perfectly sloped nose. "You look like you're going to a PTA meeting." She laughed.

I looked down at my outfit: a black skirt, tight blouse, and heels. "What kind of PTA meeting are *you* going to wearing skirts this short and painted-on tops?"

"Dearest, that is not short. That's just . . . normal." Hannah unceremoniously pulled up my skirt so it was a centimeter from covering my crotch. "Now, that's short. Much hotter."

I batted her hands away, rolling my eyes. "Okay, okay, fine. What are your suggestions?"

"It's a sex club. Are you supposed to wear anything at all?"

I shot her a look, but Hannah just laughed at me again.

Hannah was LA gorgeous—auburn hair, tall, leggy, with big boobs, and tan. She always had men looking at her, and I couldn't remember the last time we were out at a bar when some guy didn't try to hit on her. So it was pretty shocking that she worked as a nanny. What sane woman would let someone as beautiful as Hannah near her husband, I didn't know. But Hannah's current family adored her.

"How are the kids?" I asked Hannah, wanting to get the attention off my sartorial confusion. "Is Maverick still trying to get himself killed?"

Hannah lounged across my sofa. I'd invited her over to help me figure out what the hell I was going to wear to my second visit to The Scarlet Rope. Strangely, I didn't want to wear just lingerie this time. Maybe I wanted to be subtler. Or it could be that my *one* set of sexy lingerie was the one I'd already worn.

"Did I not tell you that Maverick tried to climb off the balcony yesterday?" Hannah asked.

As Hannah liked to say, Maverick was the family's completely insane two-year-old son. The kid had already broken both arms, given himself multiple black eyes, and had just recently bashed his forehead against the family cat. I couldn't fathom how the kid had managed that last one.

I whirled around, aghast. "Seriously?"

"He somehow got around not one, not two, but THREE baby gates." Hannah slapped her forehead. "I went to go pee—seriously, it was all of thirty seconds—and he was playing downstairs. Then I hear a shout, and he's about to get over the second-floor balcony."

"I guess you caught him in time?"

Hannah gave me a look. "Duh. And he screamed in my ear so loudly I think I have permanent damage." She rubbed the ear in question. "Anyway, he has to sit in the bathroom with me from now on whenever I go. I'd rather he ripped open a box of tampons than break another arm or leg. Or his head. Plus, the hospital asked a lot of questions last time I brought in the little maniac. It's not a good look when a nanny gets investigated by CPS."

Hannah went on to tell me all about the older daughter—Stella—who was an angel who could do no wrong. Hannah groused that she'd had a false sense of security since she'd started nannying when it was only Stella. Hannah had made the mistake of thinking the second born would be just as easy a child as the first.

"I saw that Emma and Ryan went to Aruba for their anniversary," I said, reaching for another appalling bright orange top.

"If you're sniffing for intel," said Hannah, "you'll get nothing from me." But her eyes still sparkled as she said the words. "And yeah, they did. They were hella drunk when they got back home. I heard the bed creaking even before I left the house."

Emma Terrance and Ryan Foster were among the most prominent celeb couples and #couplesgoals on social media. Three years ago, Roy had given me an assignment to find any dirt on the two, which was how I ended up meeting Hannah.

When Emma and Ryan hired Hannah as Stella's nanny, the Internet was agog, assuming there was no way Ryan would stay faithful to Emma with a gorgeous woman like Hannah around.

So I'd started researching, getting to know Hannah in the process. I talked to multiple members of their household, including both Emma and Ryan's chef and personal trainer. I'd watched the family's comings and goings for weeks.

And guess what? That assignment had been a miserable failure because there was no dirt on Emma and Ryan. They were shockingly boring—and stupidly in love with each other. And Hannah was just their employee who they paid well and respected. She just happened to be beautiful, a fact that didn't bother Emma since she was so confident in her marriage.

Roy had been pissed at the lack of dirt, but I'd found a new friend in Hannah. She'd quickly become my bestie.

"I wish I could go with you," Hannah lamented, tossing me a dress she'd brought from home. "I've always wanted to go to a sex club."

I shimmied into the dress, wishing I had Hannah's curves. Where she was an hourglass, I was just a rectangle. I also had tiny boobs. But when I was about to take the dress right off, Hannah made me stand in front of the mirror for a moment.

"Damn, I love this on you," she said. She turned me to the side. "Look at this juicy booty!" She even squeezed said booty to emphasize her point.

"I look dumpy." I crossed my arms across my belly. "You look way better in this dress."

"No way. If we just shorten it a bit—" Hannah raised the hem a few inches. "And voilà. You look stunning."

I wasn't sure *stunning* was the right term, but I also knew Hannah was always honest. If I looked terrible, she'd tell me. I took off the dress so Hannah could put some double-sided tape on the bottom to create a faux hem.

I'd confided in Hannah about everything I'd uncovered about Mac, swearing her to secrecy. When I told her I was going to return to The Scarlet Rope Saturday night, she'd insisted on coming over to figure out what I was going to wear. I hadn't thought it necessary, but now I was glad she did.

"I just hope I can get more info about him," I said, pacing across my small living room. "He's just such a mystery. He's all over social media, yet it took me days to figure out the most basic information about him. What makes him tick, what drove him to get involved with a place like The Scarlet Rope . . .?"

Hannah raised an eyebrow. "This is all for your *story*?" she asked, sounding skeptical.

I blinked. "Yeah. Of course. What else would it be for?"

"I don't know, but you seem especially interested in him."

I blushed, hating that my skin betrayed me. "He's my assignment. Of course I'm interested in him."

Finishing up the hem, Hannah placed the dress on a hanger before hanging it from my mantel. "I'm just saying. It sounds like you're getting personally involved."

Now I felt defensive. "I have a boyfriend."

"Oh yeah. What's his name again? Rod?"

I threw a pillow at Hannah. "Don't be annoying. I know what I'm doing."

"Then again, Mac won't be there tonight since he has a game in Vancouver."

"Exactly." I downed the last of the wine I'd been neglecting. "If this were about me being obsessed with Mac, wouldn't I want to make sure he was actually going to be at the club?"

After giving the password Mac gave me—Raven Blackwood—I was half expecting to be laughed out of the club. But the bouncer just ushered me inside without another word. Before I was allowed to mingle among the guests like last time, an impeccably dressed woman had me follow her into a room that was well-hidden behind a wall near the entryway.

"This way," she said, very businesslike. She wasn't dressed like she was going to enjoy herself at the club. She was dressed almost demurely, but I could tell by the cut of her jacket and the shine of her heels that her outfit was expensive.

"Have a seat."

I sat across from her in a room that could only be called an office. It was . . . boring. At least compared to the rest of the club. It looked like your average techy office. It was only missing the huge panels of windows overlooking the bay, as in Todd's office.

The furniture was luxurious but not gaudy. The woman sat at her desk before pushing a stack of documents toward me.

"As I'm sure you're aware, The Scarlet Rope is all about our patrons' privacy," she said. It sounded as if she was going through a script for the millionth time. "That entails going over and signing a contract with the club."

I started to go through the papers, my gaze catching the phrases NON-DISCLOSURE AGREEMENT and PATRON RULES AND REGULATIONS, among a few others.

"Uh," I said, feeling overwhelmed, "do I need a lawyer?"

The woman tittered. "You can consult one if you wish, but these are all standard contracts. Basically, keep the knowledge of our existence to yourself and behave appropriately. Meaning, everything—and I mean *everything*—must be consented to. If someone comes to us to tell us that you violated their boundaries, we'll investigate and have you out on your ass in a second if you're proven liable."

I felt a little ill. Not because I disagreed—but it all felt so . . . intense.

But I'm not really joining. So what did it matter if I signed?

Then again, that NDA made me rethink everything. I'd already told Hannah about The Scarlet Rope. If I wrote about the club in my story about Mac, they could sue me if they wanted to.

I chewed on my lower lip.

"I need to speak with a lawyer first," I said finally, knowing Roy would strangle me if I signed anything without handing it straight over to legal first.

The woman didn't seem fazed. "You can do that, of course, but I can't admit you without signing these papers either."

Torn between wanting to stay and being cautious, I decided to sign the papers with a fake name. They hadn't asked for my ID, which had surprised me. Maybe me having the password from Mac had automatically made me a little more legit.

Or maybe all of this was just a bunch of theater to scare people into keeping quiet.

Once I finally gained admittance to the club, I desperately needed a drink to calm my nerves. I kept looking over my shoulder as if the woman would discover I'd given her a fake name and throw me out on my ass.

I grabbed a shot of something and, after drinking it, nearly coughed it back up again. "What the hell was that?" I hissed between wheezes. A few people near the bar shot me looks. A woman wearing a black leather getup and a mask covering her face flashed a wry smile.

"Those are called fireballs," she said, raising a beautifully waxed eyebrow. "First one?"

"What's in them? Gasoline?" I grabbed a glass of water to wash down the acidic taste of whatever that had been.

"Pretty much." The dominatrix—because she looked almost exactly like what I'd expect a dominatrix to look like—gave me a once-over. "I haven't seen you here before."

"It's my second time," I explained. Looking down at my dress, I realized I was actually overdressed this time. "Do I stand out that much?"

She smiled and held out a hand covered in a lacy glove, bright red nails shining from underneath. "Delilah. Nice to meet you . . .?"

"Roxy," I said, realizing I'd been stupid not to give a fake name when I'd met Mac the first time.

I glanced around the bar, watching everyone mingle and drink together. Or if they weren't talking, they were touching—kissing, caressing, their hands moving into dark unknowns.

"Do you have any tips?" I asked, feeling awkward watching a couple nearby get hot and heavy as if it were totally normal to hump in public.

"For one, don't look so freaked out." Delilah's smiled. "Try to relax. You look like you're about to get into trouble." She leaned toward me. "And don't feel guilty about liking whatever it is you like. When I first started coming, I used to feel ashamed, but life's too short for that kind of bullshit. Just go have fun. You're in a safe place with no judgment."

I wanted to believe Delilah. And I hoped I could grow comfortable—but I was clearly out of my depth. I felt especially out of place as I wandered around, watching different "shows" through the glass.

One was a BDSM experience between five different people: three guys and two women. As I stopped to watch, one of the women was being whipped. The other was gagged and bound while the two men fucked her in her pussy and her ass.

I felt my body respond to the scene, my nipples peaking against the fabric of my dress. When I caught the heated glance of a masked man nearby, I nearly ran in the opposite direction—because I wanted to respond? Or because this entire thing scared the bejeezus out of me?

I watched a few other shows, including one that seemed to be a role-play room based on the woman wearing what looked like a Catholic schoolgirl outfit. The man wore a sports jacket with elbow patches and horn-rimmed glasses. It must've been a role-play of student and professor.

I watched as the professor took off his tie and used it to bind the student's hands as she kneeled on the desk. He flipped her skirt up, revealing that she wore nothing underneath, and spanked her for her naughty behavior.

The moans the woman issued made goose bumps litter my skin. I felt like I was drunk and floating far away. Everything about this place was intoxicating, like a wicked dream I couldn't believe was happening. I could almost swear I was drunk, although I'd only had that one terrible fireball shot earlier.

When a couple tried to get me to join them, I demurred and made my way back to the bar. Delilah was still there, but now she was surrounded by people, like a queen holding court.

Delilah spotted me, ushering me to sit beside her. "Now, boys, behave yourselves," she purred, patting my knee. "Roxy here is new, and she's a little shy."

I could feel the men's gazes on me, hungry and interested. But at the same time, I didn't feel intimidated. Sitting there with these men watching me was strangely empowering, knowing they couldn't do anything unless I gave them express permission.

"Did you go have some fun?" Delilah asked. She ordered me one of her favorite drinks, handing me the pink-colored cocktail with a smile. "You look a little flushed."

"Just taking it all in." I glanced at the men, who'd given us some space but were still watching. "Why do I feel like a gazelle about to be pounced on by a leopard?"

Delilah laughed. "They're all bark and no bite. Believe me. But if you're interested in any of them, you'll have to be obvious about it. We don't play hard to get around here. Either you want something, or you say no. And if you say no, the other person has to respect it."

Her eyes darkened. "If some guy gets handsy with you," she continued, "yell the safe word. You'll have a dozen people coming over to pound the guy and throw him out."

I raised an eyebrow. "The safe word?"

"Did you not read the contract?" Delilah clucked her tongue. "It's 'turkey.'"

I nearly choked on my drink. "Turkey? Like a Thanksgiving turkey? That's not very sexy."

"That's the point. Scream the word TURKEY, and nobody will mistake that for screaming from an orgasm." Delilah stirred her drink. "Then again, everybody has their kinks. I'm sure some people here are into role-playing some weird-ass, gobble-gobble shit." She winked.

"So," Delilah said, "who invited you here?"

"Hey, I found this place on Google just like the rest of you," I joked. At Delilah's look, I admitted, "Mac Mackenzie."

"Oh really? Now, that's a scrumptious hunk of a man. I've wanted to get my mouth on that man since I first saw him here."

I felt myself growing hot. With jealousy? "Have you ever—?"

"With Mac? No, he mostly just watches. Besides taking the occasional woman home afterward, I can't remember the last time I've seen him participate."

My stomach twisted. Which was stupid because Mac could take home anyone he wanted. *So why do I wish he'd take me home?*

"Do you know what he is? I mean, what he's into?" I asked.

Delilah smirked. "Now, what would be the fun in me telling you that? You'll have to find out for yourself."

Delilah's words ran through my head as I wandered a second time, letting myself mull them over. I found it interesting that Mac preferred to watch more than participate. Was he into just voyeurism? From what Delilah said, it sounded like he enjoyed watching other people but wasn't interested in people watching him.

A few of the men surrounding Delilah found me, flirting with me and plying me with drinks. But when one of them asked me to go to a room with him, I declined. To my relief, he nodded, saying he hoped he'd see me again soon.

When I got back home, I knew I wouldn't fall asleep anytime soon. Besides, I was still aroused, like I'd been edging myself all night long. Strangely, the thought of getting out my vibrator didn't appeal to me. In my mind's eye, I saw Mac. Closing my eyes, I could imagine him taking my arm, pulling me close, his hand large and warm on the small of my back and—

And you have a boyfriend. Guilt assailed me. But even as I got into bed, wide awake, my thoughts were about anyone but Todd.

Chapter 6

Mac

Although the sounds of moans and flesh slapping against flesh-filled the room, I could barely pay attention to any of it.

Elodie had come back. She'd used my password.

When Serena, one of the owners of the club had told me that just five minutes ago, my entire body felt like it was on fire. My nerves pulsed; my blood raced. I'd barely heard anything else even though Serena probably had some questions for me. I'd given out my password only twice since joining, and it hadn't happened in the past two years.

Elodie had come back. Why? Had she been looking for me? Or was she mainly curious about the club?

Anger bit me at the thought that she'd been here without me. Anger—and jealousy.

Maybe she'd come back for other reasons. Perhaps she'd come back to enjoy herself with other people. My password had just made her life easier.

I didn't want to think about her with another man or multiple men and women. *She'd seemed so innocent.* I had a hard time imagining her getting into some orgy right off the bat. That didn't seem like her at all. The thought of her watching made me hard. It was what I did most of the time. I wondered if she liked to watch, too. I could see myself taking it a step further with her, though. And I hadn't thought about that with anyone for a very long time.

I gritted my teeth, forcing my attention back to the show at hand. This particular orgy was all women, and they were all sexy as fuck. Watching one pair make out while another woman ate another's pussy was always immensely erotic. The pair that were making out moved to start scissoring each other while the third woman went to sit on one of the woman's faces.

But despite the lascivious display in front of me, I couldn't help but think about Elodie—again. I couldn't believe I'd missed her.

Her dark eyes, her curvy little body. I'd been obsessed with the thought of her since I'd met her, which wasn't like me. I was always around gorgeous, alluring women, and it didn't take much to take one home either.

But Elodie—she'd been different. It hadn't just been her innocence either. I couldn't even name why I'd found her so alluring. But I knew myself well enough to admit that I wanted her. If she showed up again, I was going to get her to agree to let me fuck her.

Movement caught my gaze. And then, as if I'd conjured her out of thin air, Elodie sat next to me.

I blinked. The room was dim, but it was her. I nearly reached out to touch her but held back. I didn't want to spook her, so I held back the exhilaration that felt ready to burst out of me.

She gave me a shy smile. "Hi," she mouthed. She wore a tight little black dress, her dainty feet in strappy heels.

Fuck, I wanted those legs wrapped around my waist as I plunged inside her, my cock filling her until she could only scream my name—

I took her arm and guided her out of the room. I found us a quiet corner booth where we could talk in private.

"I looked for you last time I was here," she admitted. Suddenly, she looked shy, which was fucking adorable.

"Serena told me," I said, my voice gruff.

"Serena?"

The note of jealousy in her tone made me grin. "Serena is one of the owners. You should've met her. She handles all of the paperwork for new folks."

"Oh." Elodie let out a laugh. "I'm not sure she told me her name when she made me sign away my firstborn."

"That's her, all right. Don't worry, she intimidates the fuck out of everyone. I probably should've warned you about that. Nobody gets in here without that initiation."

Elodie shot me a surprised look. "She intimidates even you?"

"Me? Hell, yes. And she's not even a dominatrix. She's actually asexual."

Elodie blinked, then burst out laughing. "That's amazing. She owns a sex club but has no interest in sex? I guess that'd make it easy to keep things professional."

"It's a bit like a baker being allergic to sugar, but sure, I guess so." I leaned closer, letting myself inhale the scent of citrus and honey that seemed to cling to Elodie's skin. "But what about you? You're not . . . allergic to sugar, are you?"

She sucked in a quick breath. "Nooooooo."

"Did you have fun the last time you were here?" Although I wanted to know, a part of me also didn't want to hear the answer. I clenched my fist under the table as I waited for Elodie's reply.

"I just wandered. I also got some advice from a dominatrix named Delilah. She was really nice," said Elodie.

"That's it?" I let my fist unclench. "You didn't let yourself indulge?"

"I mean, I watched a few rooms." A blush crept up Elodie's cheeks. "The ones anybody can watch."

"Tell me."

She squirmed in her seat, which was fucking adorable. I turned her face back toward me since she kept looking everywhere but at me.

"You're not in trouble," I joked, stroking her jaw. "Unless you want to be," I added, my voice dropping low.

"Oh. No. Of course." She played with a strand of her hair. "Um, let's see, I saw a few different things . . ."

Elodie then gave me a detailed account of every room she watched, including one with professor/student roleplay that I had the sudden, desperate urge to try with her. I got the impression that she liked to be dominated. This felt too good to be true.

A fantasy played out in my head. The thought of Student Elodie bemoaning her low grades, with me telling her there was an easy way to make that nasty F go away. She'd blush and pretend not to get it, but when I reached under her skirt, I'd find her wet. It wouldn't be long before I was bending her over a desk, her skirt bunched to her waist, her pussy dripping with desire as I thrust into her . . .

My cock was as hard as iron at the mere thought.

"What was your favorite?" I asked.

"Favorite?" She licked her lips, which made my cock twitch. "I don't know, but the BDSM probably caught my attention the most."

"Because it was strange?"

"Yes but no. Something was extra sexy about seeing another person in complete control of someone. There has to be a lot of trust built there to surrender yourself like that."

God, it was like she was speaking a language only I understood. It was intoxicating. *Does this mean she'd be interested . . .?*

It was too much to hope for. There'd been other women I'd thought would want to be my sub, but when push came to shove, they'd balked.

Getting loosely tied up and spanked a few times was one thing. Getting hung from the ceiling while you got whipped, your nipples clamped, and your body aching with pleasure? That was another thing entirely. And with Elodie, I could see wanting it all.

But first things first. Just because I was attracted to her didn't mean she'd make a good partner. I reminded myself that I knew fuck-all about her.

"The thing I like about this place," I said, "is that privacy is extremely important. Serena doesn't fuck around with the NDA."

Elodie smiled wryly. "Yeah, I could tell that."

"It's also important to me, being in the public eye."

Elodie's expression didn't change. If she knew who I was and was acting like she didn't, she was doing a good job of hiding it. I studied her. Eventually, she looked away, and she seemed uncomfortable.

"Are you a celebrity or something?" she asked finally.

My lips quirked. "To some people, I suppose. I'm a hockey player."

"Oh." She finally returned her gaze to mine. "Can I confess I've never watched a hockey game?"

"You wouldn't be the first person to say that to me," I said wryly.

"I know LA has a hockey team . . ." She shrugged. "That's about the extent of my knowledge."

Considering her gaze kept moving to various parts of the room, I had to admit, I wasn't totally convinced by her right now. *Maybe I just want to believe she's telling the truth.*

Maybe I just wanted to believe that somebody would want me for me, not for my fame. But based on how attracted to her I was, I wasn't sure it would change anything for me if she did somehow know who I was.

"So what do you do?" I asked. "And don't tell me you're a professional server because we both know that's a lie."

Elodie spluttered. "Rude!"

"How many times did you almost spill drinks on somebody last time you were here?"

"Maybe I'm just trying to change careers," she asserted.

"Well, you'd make a great professional drink spiller."

She laughed. "You're probably right."

"Sweetheart, we both know you aren't a server. You're too—" I hesitated, which was a bad idea.

Elodie rolled her eyes. "Don't finish that sentence. No, I'm not a server. I'm a writer."

When she didn't supply any more details, I raised an eyebrow. "And . . .?"

"And what? I write words for a living." Now, she seemed flustered. Why? Did she not want to talk about her work?

Living in LA meant I knew writers galore. And they all seemed like they wanted to tell everyone about what they were writing, especially if it was for TV or film. More than one screenwriter had propositioned me while living here. Not for sex—no, they wanted my connections even though I was an athlete, not an actor or producer or some assistant fetching coffee for a movie set's actors.

"What kind of words?" I finished off my drink, wondering if I wanted a second one. Then again, with Elodie, I should probably keep my wits about me. If she decided she wanted to play, I wanted to remember every second of the experience.

"I'm writing a book." Elodie shrugged. "It's not very interesting. I'm not writing dinosaur erotica or anything."

I nearly choked on air. "Dinosaur—?"

Elodie grinned. "Oh, you don't know about dinosaur erotica? You're missing out. All kinds of books out there about being pounded in the butt by a T-rex."

I gaped at her. "You're fucking with me."

To prove me wrong, Elodie whipped out her phone, typed in a few choice words, and then showed me all the T-rex porn available. And there was . . . way too much of it.

"Now I know what you like," I commented.

Elodie laughed. "Getting pounded in the butt by a gigantic reptile does not sound appealing in the least." Her eyes sparkled. "I'd prefer a centaur. At least they're half man."

"I'm not even going to go down that slippery slope." I ran my knuckles down her arm, loving that goose bumps rose on her skin as I traced my fingers along a vein in her forearm on the way back up. "So you're saying you don't want to be pounded in the butt? Ever?"

That question might've been a bit direct, but hey, she'd opened the door to it, so I took the opportunity. *She'd opened the back door, I supposed.*

Elodie shivered. "Um, uh, what a question."

"Or maybe you'd like to pound somebody else in *their* butt."

She looked around. "I think we're going to win a Guinness World Record with how many times we've said, 'pounded in the butt' out loud."

"We're in a sex club. That phrase is as tame as it gets around here."

"True." She watched as I kept stroking her arm, but soon enough, she shifted to give us a little more space.

I didn't want space. "Are you seeing someone?" I asked.

She blinked. "I have a boyfriend, yeah."

My chest tightened. Not what I wanted to hear, although I wasn't sure it changed anything for me.

"So why are you at a sex club alone?" I didn't try to hide the growl beneath my words.

"It's . . . complicated." She began playing with her hair again. "Todd wants me to move to San Francisco. I don't want to leave LA. I think we're at a stalemate, and neither of us wants to make the next move."

She looked so sad right then that my anger faded quickly. I took her hand and squeezed it.

She's not your type anyway, I reminded myself. *She's too innocent. She'd run in the opposite direction if she knew what you wanted to do to her.*

"What about you? Are you seeing anyone?" she asked.

I smiled. "Not at the moment. That's why I'm here at the club. It's helpful for meeting people."

"People like you, you mean."

"What does that mean . . . ?"

"People who like a certain type of sexual excitement," she clarified.

"You could say that, yeah. It helps to know that some-one won't be freaked out about it. If they're here, they ob-viously aren't."

"And how many people have you met? Here, I mean," asked Elodie.

"There have been a few." At her widened eyes, I laughed. "Is that so shocking? I'm not here just to watch. I'd like to connect with someone at some point and enjoy myself with them here. But I haven't met the right person for that yet."

"But you must've taken women home . . ."

I explained to her that I rarely took women home with me, preferring to enjoy women in the rooms here at The Scarlet Rope. Taking a woman—or multiple wom-en—home complicated things. More often than not, they'd want more or expect a relationship of some sort. Or worse, they just wanted a chance to get some dirt on somebody like me and then run straight to the tabloids to spill what they'd learned.

"It's not really about adding notches to my bedpost," I added. "That's never been a problem for me, especially with my celebrity status. I could go to a bar for that. Or take up with any of the dozens of women waiting outside the arena. For me, it's about finding people who enjoy the same things as I do."

"They don't have apps for that by now?" asked Elodie.

"Oh, they do. But I like to vet people in person. It's too easy to get catfished online. And the club itself vets the members, too. Online dating is too much the Wild West for me, personally."

I kept Elodie's gaze. "But it's all about exploration. And trust. Trust is paramount because there's no shame here. Just enjoyment." When Elodie seemed puzzled, I put out my hand. "Let me show you."

She froze, which made me chuckle. "We're just going to watch," I explained. "Watch and learn. I promise."

I could see her hesitate. But when she placed her hand in mine, triumph burst through me. At that moment, my mind could only repeat the word, *mine.*

I took her to one of the BDSM rooms. This scene was just two people, a man and a woman. The woman was the dominant, with the man on all fours in front of her. She placed a ball gag over his mouth and went to choose a whip from the vast array hanging from a nearby wall.

I watched Elodie out of the corner of my eye. She was transfixed, her cheeks turning bright red when the dominatrix began to whip her sub. The man whimpered and moaned, which only made the dominatrix whip him harder.

"Make any more noise, and you'll pay for it," she said.

The man shivered. But when the woman yanked him up by his hair, he let out a sound of pleasure/pain that resounded throughout the room. Soon, he was being tied up to hang from the ceiling to serve his punishment for disobedience.

The whipping continued, from hard to soft and everything in between. Red marks littered the man's body.

I only had eyes for Elodie. It took all of my self-control not to touch her, but these rooms weren't for touching other people. They were just for watching.

When the dominatrix thrust a large glass butt plug into the man, Elodie shivered. She caught my gaze, and she licked her lips. "I need a breather," she mouthed.

I escorted her out of the room, internally freaking out. Had I pushed her too far? But when I had her drink a glass of water, she let out a little laugh.

"Sorry," she kept saying.

"Was it too much?" I asked, feeling like a complete piece of shit. When was I going to stop being ashamed of something I enjoyed?

Her eyes widened. "No. I mean, it was a lot to take in, but . . ." She looked at a loss for words. "I don't even know how to explain it."

"Try me."

Her dark eyes flashed with something that made my own body respond. "I think it was sitting there with you," she finally whispered. "I didn't have this kind of reaction the last time I was here."

It was me. I was the reason for this reaction. I was affecting her, which was everything I'd hoped for. I wanted to kiss her. I wanted to push her against the nearest wall and fuck her mouth until she was putty in my arms. What I wouldn't give to hear the sound of her choking on my cock.

But I restrained myself. I clenched my jaw until it ached. "So you liked it?" I finally ground out.

"I'm not sure. I think so."

She thinks so.

"I'll take that as a yes," I said.

Her lashes fluttered. "So are you like that guy?"

It took a moment for my brain to compute what she was asking. Then I let out a chuckle. "Do you mean a submissive? No. Far from it." I touched her cheek. "Baby, I'm a dominant all the way."

Chapter 7

Elodie

Roy stared at me, looking as disgruntled as ever. "Wholesome? The guy who likes to screw married women?"

I had to restrain myself from squirming. "Apparently, Mac's turned over a new leaf."

Roy got up from his office chair and went to pour himself a cup of coffee. His coffee maker was probably older than I was, an ancient dinosaur of a machine that made the bitterest, blackest coffee you could imagine. I once tried a sip of whatever noxious brew Roy enjoyed and nearly blacked out. It was so gross.

"You're sure there's nothing interesting about him?" Roy repeated. He drank a long sip of his coffee, his mustache twitching. "Nothing at all?"

I refused to break eye contact, even as my palms started sweating. Could Roy tell I was lying? Considering Roy had worked at getting the truth out of people for decades now, I knew he was no idiot.

But he also had no reason to distrust me. I was normally very honest. Too honest, really. He'd reamed me more than once for being a Goody Two-shoes who needed to pull the "stick from my ass."

"Nothing," I replied.

Roy grunted. "Fuck. Well, I can give you another assignment, then. We don't need to waste any more time on this guy."

Relief washed over me. I no longer needed the assignment to get closer to Mac. I had my ticket into the club whenever I wanted. And now that I was part of that whole story in my own way, I wanted nothing to do with an exposé on Mac Mackenzie. At this point, I mainly wanted to protect him. That was the one thing I definitely knew. As for anything *else* I wanted? I couldn't be sure.

I also knew that if Mac ever discovered that I'd wanted to meet him because of my job, he'd never trust me again, let alone talk to me. We'd be over and done with.

The thought of Mac hating me made me feel sick. It was one thing if he just got tired of me. It was another if he could never trust me again.

Why do you care so much if Mac trusts you?

I shook myself. Right now, I needed to think about when it came to my relationship with Todd. Because if I wanted to experiment with Mac, I would need to break up with my boyfriend first. I'd toed the line so far. But if I ever crossed it, I wouldn't be able to look Todd in the eyes.

Roy returned to his desk and shuffled some papers around, finally handing me some stained with coffee. "Spilled some this morning," he explained, "but you can still read them."

I scanned the pages. "Trevor and CJ?" I looked up in surprise. "The morning news anchors?"

"Ayup. Apparently, they're screwing." Roy put his feet up onto his desk, looking smug. "Just got the tip last night.

Somebody saw them coming out of Le Château together after getting real cozy."

"Damn." I shook my head. "Didn't Trevor just have a baby with his wife?"

Roy nodded. "Exactly."

Disgusted, I shoved the documents into my briefcase. "I guess I'm going to Malibu, then?"

"ASAP. Follow them out of the news station, see what you can get." Roy's bushy eyebrows narrowed. "And don't come back here tellin' me that you couldn't find shit. Otherwise, I'm gonna think you're fucking with me, Andrews."

Unfortunately for me, Trevor and CJ had already left the station by the time I'd arrived. *Damn LA traffic,* I groused. I'd left with plenty of time to run into them, but then I'd gotten caught on the freeway after an accident. I didn't arrive in Malibu until after lunchtime.

I didn't want to go straight back to the office. I got some lunch and did some people watching while hoping to see some celebs. Lots of them lived in Malibu, and it wasn't uncommon to see celebs getting mobbed outside the most popular restaurants in the area.

It was after I finished my salad that I remembered that Mac's old girlfriend—Dawn Morrison—had her pottery studio here in Malibu. Looking up the address, I realized it was only a few blocks away.

And wouldn't you know it, it was open, too.

The studio was small but well-maintained, with lots of plants and natural light filling the space. Words of affirmation were written across the walls, along with a few puns about throwing clay. There was even a painting of the famous scene from *Ghost* on one wall.

"Are you here for the beginners' class?" a woman asked me as I wandered.

I blinked, my brain working overtime. It took me a second to realize the woman was Dawn herself.

She didn't look at all like she had in high school, mostly because her hair was short and she was covered in tattoos now. She also looked like she worked out. I could see muscles bulging through her tight T-shirt, a six-pack peeking through the thin fabric.

"Uh, yeah," I said on impulse. "Is there still room?"

"Sure thing." Dawn waved me over, and before I knew it, I was sitting in the studio at a pottery wheel, learning how to make a ceramic bowl.

The class consisted of me and three other women. Dawn was an enthusiastic, fast-paced teacher. I could tell that she loved what she did. She made lots of jokes that kept the class from seeming too serious.

As I was trying to make a bowl that didn't fall apart, I racked my brain. How did I get Dawn to tell me about Mac? Their high school had been too small for me to lie and say we'd both attended there.

When my bowl collapsed a third time, Dawn came over to lend a helping hand.

"You gotta keep your hands on it at all times," she explained. "And keep the wheel spinning. Yeah, there you go. Don't let up. But try not to hold it too hard either. Mold it into what you want. Don't force it." She winked at me.

I let out a nervous laugh. "I guess I'm thinking too hard. Or I'm just distracted."

"Lots of people come in here when they're stressed about work."

"Oh, it's not my work," I hedged. I shot Dawn a glance. "I'm actually meeting an old boyfriend for dinner tonight. We dated in high school, and he wanted to see me again."

Dawn raised an eyebrow. "You sound terrified."

"Just nervous." I gave her a small smile. "Sometimes I think he's the one who got away, you know? We reconnected online, and when I realized he lived in the area . . ." I shrugged. "And now we're having dinner."

"And what about him? Is he single?" Dawn asked.

"As far as I know. But would it be weird to hook up with my high school boyfriend?"

I felt a little guilty for making up this story, but it seemed to be doing the trick. Dawn sat across from me, only occasionally making sure the other attendees didn't need her assistance.

"Weird? Nah. As long you're both on the same page." She chuckled. "If I were to see my high school boyfriend, well, we wouldn't be on the same page." When I looked confused, she explained, "I'm gay. Married to a woman and everything, and my ex was—well, very much *not* a woman." She pointed at the ring on her finger.

"Oh. Well, yeah. That might make things awkward." I hesitated, finally asking, "Did you know, back then?"

"That I'm gay? Oh, fuck yes. We both knew. He was my beard, and I was his. Our relationship was for the benefit of others." Dawn's expression turned nostalgic. "We were best friends, but after college, we kinda stopped talking. It's funny. At that age, you think you'll be friends forever with certain people, but more often than not, you drift apart."

What did Mac need a beard for? Was he into BDSM back then and felt he had to hide it?

"Then again . . ." She chuckled. "My ex is pretty famous now. I doubt he'd be interested in having dinner with his old beard."

"Is he an actor?" I asked innocently.

"Nah, an athlete." When I waited, Dawn laughed. "And no, I'm not telling you who he is."

I added some water to my pottery clay. I needed to know more. "You said you were his beard," I said. "Is he gay, too?"

"Definitely not." She chuckled. "His family was just uber religious and way fucking intense."

My heart sped up a little. "But he was hiding something?"

Dawn's eyes narrowed a little. "Yeah, he was. But that was a long time ago." She got up and proceeded to help me finish molding my bowl, the subject of Mac's secrets officially closed for discussion.

I returned home with my lopsided bowl, wondering if I'd made a mistake in going to see Dawn. If I wasn't going to turn this into a story for Roy, why was I so interested in discovering more about Mac?

The answer was that I found something about him enthralling. Seductive. I thought of his heated gaze on me as I'd watched that BDSM scene, and it felt like he could've flayed me alive just with his eyes.

How could he make me feel naked without taking a single bit of fabric off my body? I didn't understand it. It was like he could burrow under my skin and discover all my deepest, darkest secrets if I wasn't careful.

My phone started ringing. I ignored it, not recognizing the number. But as I listened to the voicemail, I realized it was for my car payment.

The voice droned on, telling me that if I didn't make a car payment soon, my account would be delinquent and turned over to the collections department.

I swore. I checked my bank account, and to my dismay, there was one overdraft fee after another. I hadn't been paying attention to my money situation in the past two weeks, and I realized that I hadn't gotten paid in a month because I hadn't written any new stories. I thought I'd had enough to tide me over, but now . . .

"Fuck," I muttered, sitting down at the kitchen table with my head in my hands. Living in LA, I couldn't go without a car. I could trade it in for something cheaper, but I'd still have a car payment. And even worse, I wasn't sure if I could make rent, either, not with all these overdraft fees hitting my account.

As I scrolled mindlessly on my phone, trying to figure out a game plan, I saw that the Blades were playing tonight. And because of the Mac story, I still had a press pass to any games I wanted to attend.

I grabbed my bag and headed for the stadium, desperately needing a distraction.

I knew hockey was a rough sport, violent even, but my jaw dropped as I watched Mac, his teammates, and the rival team get into multiple fights. Mac himself was the instigator on more than one occasion, getting his ass landed in what was basically hockey time-out.

I watched as his coach yelled at him. Mac stood, gesturing, his expression ferocious, and I had to fan myself. *Damn, why am I so turned on right now?*

Mac looked like he wanted to toss his coach onto the ice. Despite being half Mac's size, his coach didn't back down. Mac finally scowled, sat on the bench, and took his punishment, but not before giving a few air kisses to some fans in the stands.

I didn't fully understand the game, I had to admit. I'd never been a sports girl, and hockey was as foreign to me as somebody speaking French. But I found something about it enthralling.

Maybe it was the way the guys managed to maneuver across the ice, pushing the puck with their sticks like they'd been born with it in their hands. It was smooth and graceful, almost . . . balletic.

Mac would kill me if I used that description, I thought in amusement.

But the pushing, shoving, and fighting were the opposite of balletic. It was all rough and tumble, pure masculinity on display and for consumption. And consume was all I could sit there and do.

I'd never understood the appeal of this sport. Until now.

It helped that Mac was clearly a talented, savvy player. He easily skated across the ice, scoring multiple goals throughout the game. The stadium erupted into cheers and yells every time he smacked the puck into the net. Numerous women had seats nearest the ice, holding signs, flowers, and God knows what else. I half expected some of them to take off their bras and throw them onto the ice.

I was sitting up in the nosebleed section, which was fine by me. I didn't want Mac to know I was here. Not yet, at least.

The game was a close one, with the Blades scoring the winning goal in the nick of time. Mac and his teammates let out a rousing roar of excitement after their win, gathering together and hooting and hollering like crazy people. I laughed out loud at their antics.

After it was over, I went straight to the locker room, my press pass giving me quick access to behind the scenes. The players came filing in, clearly high off their win, the smell of sweat clinging to them. The guys began taking off their skates and then stripping off the heaviest parts of their gear.

Mac's gaze caught mine within moments. His eyes darkened. I imagined he was shocked to see me, and I realized I needed an excuse for why I was there. I couldn't tell him I was with the press. That would pretty much be the end of things. I stuffed my badge into my pocket and hoped against hope that he hadn't seen it.

"How'd you get down here?" he asked, approaching me with a towel around his neck.

"Oh, you can get anywhere with a little flirting and some cleavage." I laughed nervously.

Mac glanced at my blouse, which showed a grand total of zero cleavage. "Cleavage, huh?"

I shrugged. "I buttoned it up before you guys came inside."

"That's a shame." His eyes sparkled.

I realized people were staring at us. I cleared my throat, putting some space between us.

"Can we go somewhere to talk? Privately?" I asked.

Mac nodded. "Give me twenty minutes. I'll meet you outside in the parking lot. My car is near the south end in lot C, row five."

"I'm impressed you remembered exactly where you parked," I joked. "I swear I can never remember that the second I walk away from my car."

Mac, though, just shrugged off my comment. I could tell his mind was already elsewhere.

He then returned to the bench, now giving the press his full attention. I watched him for a bit, enjoying his answers to their questions. He never failed to have a witty quip or rejoinder. When more than one journalist probed him about his affair with a married woman, Mac managed to say something clever and avoid the subject entirely.

I hated that I couldn't use my press badge without giving myself away. I just had to stand there and watch, feeling awkward. Eventually, I decided to wait in my car.

I let myself relax once I was safely inside, pushing the seat back so it would recline. I'd been so full of energy during the game and after, but the post-adrenaline crash left me feeling extrememly tired. I'd experienced it on more than one occasion, usually in the midst of chasing a story and doing something that was borderline illegal.

But I soon regretted leaving the locker room because now my brain had returned to the voicemail on my phone. I needed money, and I needed it quickly. Did I tell Roy about my predicament?

I chewed on my lip. Considering I was lying to my boss about Mac, I doubted Roy would feel inclined to help me out.

I could suck it up and write a story about Mac. That was what I'd been assigned to do, anyway. And I had a big, juicy story to tell, NDA or not. I couldn't imagine how the public would react to the story of Mac going to a sex club. Or his predilection for BDSM.

The world might be more accepting than it was even twenty years ago, but it wasn't that accepting.

I chewed on my lower lip until it was sore. I sighed, rubbing my temples. As much as I knew the money would be great, I could never do it. Even though Roy would probably risk the lawsuit from his employee violating an NDA, the thought of writing about Mac felt like a betrayal. Maybe it was because he'd been so upfront about wanting privacy. And I also knew that The Scarlet Rope probably had the resources to sue me personally for breach of contract if I spilled the beans. Though . . . I hadn't signed the NDA. Technically, Roxy had. I wasn't even sure if that made a difference or if I was bound to the terms by my actions anyway.

I heard the distant sounds of cheers, which alerted me to Mac's exit. Or rather, his decoy's exit.

Fifteen minutes later, I saw Mac walking to his beat-up old car parked only a few rows from mine.

Chapter 8

Elodie

I waved over at Mac. When he caught my gaze, his eyebrows rose.

"How did you know it was me?" he asked ruefully.

That's a great fucking question.

"You're pretty recognizable," I lied, not wanting to admit that I knew about him using a decoy whenever he left the stadium.

Mac took me to his car and opened the passenger door for me to get into the front seat. "Sorry for the wait," he said. "I have to use a decoy whenever I leave."

I raised my eyebrows, trying to look surprised. "Seriously?"

"He's my brother." When my eyes widened in real surprise, Mac chuckled. "Yeah, I know. But he does get paid for it in free tickets. And access to lots of women." Now Mac sounded annoyed. "Some of them married."

"Your brother, then . . ."

Mac shrugged. "Is having an affair with a married woman? Yeah. Not me. That nice little story bit me in the ass, though. And I told Brian to cool it because his behavior was fucking me over. He did, but it was too late. The damage was done."

Now that was a juicy bit of intel—except it was only juicy to me. If I went to Roy and told him that Brian Mackenzie had been the one fooling around with a married woman, Roy would kick me out on my ass.

Who the fuck is Brian Mackenzie, and why do you think I give a rat's ass who he's screwing? I could hear Roy's growling voice in my head.

"Don't tell anyone that," said Mac, his tone serious. "The press hasn't caught on yet."

Now, I was confused. "Don't you want to set the record straight, though? That rumor hasn't done you any favors."

"And admit to everyone they were excited to see my brother, the insurance salesman?" Mac smiled wryly. "I doubt it. Besides, it's not the worst thing the press has written about me. It comes with the territory."

Guilt made me feel a little nauseous. It'd been easy to tell myself that following these celebs and writing stories about any dirt I could find on them was just part of the game. The celebs understood that. If Mac learned I was a reporter, he'd never trust me again.

You're getting attached, my mind warned me.

"I think you might have to dock your brother's pay," I joked. "Or maybe fire him."

"I tried. The man is relentless. It's why he makes an excellent salesman. He can sell anything—even himself." Mac rolled his eyes. "I've been buying his shit for twenty-five years."

I could hear fondness underneath the frustration, though. I so desperately wanted to ask more about Mac's family. I'd assumed he was estranged from all of them, but apparently not. Did Brian know about Mac's going to The Scarlet Rope? I wondered if Mac's understanding of Brian's behavior was due to his not wanting to seem hypocritical.

Then again, having consensual BDSM sex wasn't exactly the same as having an affair with a married woman.

"Let's get out of here," Mac suddenly said.

"Umm . . ."

"Come on, I won't bite. At least not unless they take too long to bring my food. I'm freaking starving."

I smiled. "Okay."

We drove to a greasy diner far enough from the stadium to avoid fans but not so far that Mac couldn't drive me back to my car easily. When we arrived, Mac stuffed his hair into a baseball cap and added a pair of thick glasses to his face.

"Does that always work?" I asked as we sat down, gesturing to his disguise.

"Usually. It also helps to take off my Blades sweatshirt," he said with a wink.

I blushed. He'd stripped off his Blades shirt in the car, changing into a nondescript red sweater instead. It'd taken all my self-control not to ogle him. He'd laughed at me, teasing it was okay to peek, which had only increased my embarrassment.

We ordered pie and coffee. According to Mac, this place had the best apple pie in the area. As I dug into my slice, I had to agree. Even the coffee was decent, at least by diner standards.

"I love this place," Mac said.

He practically shoveled his pie slice into his mouth in one bite. Yet he somehow managed to seem downright sexy doing it. Maybe it was because he ate with such confidence, not giving a shit what anybody thought about him. Or perhaps it was because he made little groans of pleasure as he ate.

What the hell is wrong with me? I'm getting turned on from this guy eating pie. I had to mentally shake myself.

We ate in companionable silence. All the things I wanted to ask him were forbidden, or I didn't have the courage to say them out loud.

As if reading my mind, Mac said, "I can't stop thinking about you."

My entire body reacted to those words like a match lit a fire. I slowly set my coffee mug down because my hands started shaking.

"Me too," I admitted, my mouth dry.

Mac's heated gaze seemed to see straight through me. "I thought so," he said in a low voice.

I swallowed. My heart pounded like crazy. "So what do you want, then?" I asked.

"You saw what I liked at the club. I want that. With you."

The thought of letting Mac tie me up, whip me, gag me, punish me—and then bring me to the heights of pleasure? My brain didn't even know how to compute that information. My body, on the other hand? It felt ready, even if it truly didn't know what it was getting itself into.

"You want me to be your submissive, then?" I asked.

"I want to explore things with you, yeah. But there aren't set rules. We can make our own. I know what I like, but I want you to like it, too." A seductive smile crossed his face. "Not just like. Love. Want with your entire being."

"What if I want to tie you up?" I quipped.

He chuckled. "I wouldn't be against it, if you really wanted to. But like I told you before, I prefer to be the dominant in a relationship. Do you think you could handle being a submissive? I take it that it's something you've never done before. "

"No, I haven't." I shook my head. "And I'm not sure I could handle it, to be honest."

"Does it appeal to you? At all?"

I lowered my gaze to my coffee mug. "Yeah," I said softly.

"Our relationship would be discussed extensively before anything happened. I'd draw up a contract—"

"Seriously?"

Mac didn't laugh this time. His face was dead serious. "Yeah. I don't fuck around with stuff like this. Anyone who says they're into BDSM but doesn't iron out every detail has no fucking business in the community. That would be extremely risky. The contract protects both parties."

I licked my lips. "I guess that's reassuring."

"As my submissive, you'd submit to whatever I wanted. But we'd discuss what your limits would be, along with a safe word." His lips quirked up. "It's all about pleasure in the end. Nothing is actually supposed to feel bad, even if you experience a little pain. Although submissives submit, they actually call all the shots. They get to say when they're done or when they don't want to do something. And aftercare is imperative after every session."

I had to admit I was intrigued. Combined with my intense attraction to Mac, I was tempted to . . . well, submit.

Besides, if I wanted out, I could leave, right?

What about Todd?

That thought was a dash of ice water spilled over my head. Fuck me, how could I forget about my *boyfriend?*

Sure, lately we hadn't been acting much like a couple. We'd barely texted since I'd returned to LA after our disastrous weekend in San Francisco.

Worst of all, I hadn't missed Todd at all. I'd been so focused on Mac that Todd's lack of interest hadn't even fazed me.

"And just as important," Mac was saying, "your privacy and mine. Neither of us would talk to anybody about our arrangement. The only reason people talk in the BDSM community is when somebody behaves badly. Otherwise, discretion is paramount."

"That makes sense," I replied. Lord knows, I certainly didn't want anyone finding out about this.

I felt torn between what my body wanted and what my head thought I should do. And what would it mean for my heart if I gave in to this temptation? Would I be able to walk away unscathed?

"So?" Mac took my hand. "Thoughts?"

"I don't know. I mean, I do have a boyfriend."

Mac released my hand. "Right." His expression turned grim.

"Though things aren't going great right now. I told you I don't want to move to San Francisco, and he wants me to." Seeing Mac's expression grow darker, I said hurriedly, "Never mind. It doesn't matter."

"Well, if you are interested, then the ball's in your court. But I won't pursue you if you're in a relationship with someone else. I'm not about that."

That last statement from Mac caused him to clench his jaw. Was he thinking about Brian? Maybe he wasn't as forgiving of his brother as I'd initially thought.

We eventually exchanged numbers, Mac assuring me that I would need to be the one to reach out if I wanted to pursue things further. He drove me back to my car, not touching me the entire way, even as I wished he would.

Even as I wished he *wouldn't*, because I knew the second he touched me, I'd be a goner.

Hannah's eyes widened so far that she looked like an owl. "He seriously propositioned you?"

"I mean, I guess so."

I'd driven straight to Hannah's place after talking with Mac, needing to discuss this with somebody. Although I knew I was breaking all kinds of promises, along with the NDA I'd signed at the club.

But Hannah was my best friend. She wouldn't spill the beans. And I couldn't keep this whole thing to myself. I needed to make sure I wasn't crazy for even pondering it.

"What should I do?" I asked her

Hannah shook her head and then refilled both of our wineglasses. "Girl, you know I'd ride that pony to pound town. Or to the stable. Whatever. How could you even think about hesitating?"

"But what about Todd?"

Hannah grimaced. "Shit. I forgot about him."

"You know what's worse? I forgot about him, too."

That made Hannah burst out laughing. I laughed, too, even as I felt like a terrible person. How could I forget my own boyfriend?

"You should just break up with him already," Hannah said. She leaned back into her chair, completely relaxed. "He's a total bore."

"He's a nice guy," I said, feeling defensive.

"So nice that he's been trying to guilt-trip you into moving to a city you don't want to move to."

"You have to make sacrifices for your relationship."

Hannah's eyes narrowed. "Then why haven't you moved already?"

I groaned and collapsed onto the couch, the wine already going to my head. I wished I had an easy answer for that. Then again, I already knew what I should do. I should break things off with Todd.

"You know what my philosophy is?" Hannah asked.

"I'm almost afraid to ask . . ."

She smiled. "If you're even considering being with a second man, dump the first one. Because you wouldn't be if he kept your attention."

Fuck. She had a point. "But what if I'm just caught up in this because it's exciting? Todd is reliable."

Hanna feigned a yawn. "Boring. You know I've never been a fan of his."

I blinked in shock. "What? Since when?"

"Since forever! He's boring as fuck. He probably gets turned on whenever the Dow Jones goes up or whatever. Full-on jizz in the pants excitement." Hannah rolled her eyes. "You deserve a guy who'd jizz in his pants just looking at *you*, not his stock options."

I started laughing so hard tears rolled down my face. "That's not fair," I countered, even as I couldn't really disagree. "And Mac would never jizz in his pants."

"Fair enough." Hannah smiled wickedly. "He'd definitely make sure to jizz on your face instead."

I tossed a pillow at her. Though she wasn't wrong, was she? Well, maybe about Mac jizzing on my face.

But as far as my relationship with Todd...that had grown stagnant a while ago. It had grown routine, and not in a good way. But I was too much of a coward to admit it to myself because that would mean breaking things off. I hated conflict, and even as much as I was tired of our relationship, I did care about Todd. I didn't want to hurt him.

"You need to make a decision," said Hannah. "This dillydallying isn't helping anybody."

I sat up, scowling. "That's easy for you to say. You're not in my position."

"Oh, poor Elodie. She has the hottest hockey player around wanting to bang her silly."

I gave her the finger. It only made Hannah cackle.

I gave her all the details about signing a contract with Mac, which widened her eyes. She asked me so many questions that my head spun by the end of the conversation. I also ended up writing some of her questions down because they were definitely things I needed to ask Mac before I signed anything.

Now I'm thinking about this as a when, *not an* if. That thought alone made me shiver in excitement.

"Do you think I'm insane?" I asked.

Hannah raised a perfectly manicured eyebrow. "I mean, yeah. But not in a bad way." She leaned forward, pointing a finger at me. "You need to stop doubting yourself and let yourself have fun."

"Have you ever done BDSM?"

Hannah laughed. "Me? I'm not the submissive type. I'd probably take that whip and break it over a dude's head before I'd let him tell me what to do." Hannah shot me a look. "Do you think you are? I never got submissive vibes from you."

"I mean, I think there's something kind of appealing about not having to make any decisions . . ." I shrugged. "At least in the bedroom anyway."

Hannah was the type of person who reveled in being independent. She'd lamented that trait, mostly because she had a tendency to intimidate any weaker-willed men. Hannah had inadvertently chased off a guy more than once because she hadn't shown that she'd "needed" him.

I'd never had that problem. I didn't mind having a guy wanting to feel needed while dating me. But I'd also pretty much been on my own since I was eighteen when my mom had died. I'd had to take care of myself because there hadn't been anyone else to take care of me.

Hannah had the choice to be independent. I hadn't. So the thought of giving over the reins to somebody else, especially a man as capable as Mac . . . Yeah, it definitely held an appeal.

It helped that I was attracted to him, dreamed about him constantly, thought about him as often as possible, fantasized about what he'd do to my body if I gave him a chance—

"Elodie? Hello?" Hannah poked me with her foot. "I asked you a question."

I shook myself. "Sorry. What?"

Hannah waved a hand. "It doesn't matter. But you do need to make a decision, you know that, right? Whatever you decide, I'm here for you. Especially if it's getting some amazing BDSM hockey dick." She winked at me.

When I arrived home, I still wasn't sure what I wanted to do. The thought of hurting Todd because I was already attracted to another man didn't sit right with me.

Was I just feeling this way because I didn't want to move to San Francisco? I didn't know anymore.

Or was this thing with Mac for real? Would I regret it if I didn't let myself have some fun for once?

Chapter 9

Elodie

The following weekend, Todd came to town. He took me out to one of our favorite Mexican places in West Hollywood, where we'd had our second date.

Todd had been the consummate gentleman when we'd first started seeing each other. He hadn't demanded sex by the third date like other guys I'd gone out with. He'd been patient, letting the relationship develop at a slow pace. He'd taken me out on the town, bought me flowers, and told me I was beautiful.

We'd met when I'd been writing my book. He'd been encouraging, always asking me questions about it, marveling that anyone could write an entire book.

"Writing college papers was bad enough," he'd lamented. "But an entire book? No way."

He'd been there for me when my mom's extended family had tried to reinsert themselves into my life. I hadn't wanted anything to do with them, considering they'd abandoned my mom when she'd gotten pregnant with me out of wedlock. Even after she and my dad married, they judged her. Then my dad had run off, and they'd let a single mother struggle when she shouldn't have had to.

Todd had been a good boyfriend. So when he took my hand, his expression open, and he said, "I'm moving back to LA," I should've been overjoyed.

"What?" I gaped at him. "Why?"

"Because you don't want to move to San Francisco." He squeezed my hand. "And our relationship is more important than anything else. I realized after you left the last time that I was letting my ambition get in the way. I'm sorry. And I'm sorry if you felt pressured."

I slowly took my hand back. I struggled to find the words to respond. Shouldn't I be excited? Relieved? But I mostly felt . . . annoyed.

"You can't give up this job opportunity," I said. "You've worked your ass off."

Todd raised his eyebrows. "There'll be other positions, and don't worry about my apartment. I signed a month-to-month lease because I felt I wouldn't be staying there long."

Now, I just felt horribly guilty. "You said it yourself. The company is moving away from LA. There won't be many positions based here, and you had your heart set on this job."

"But it doesn't matter. *You* matter, Elodie. That's what I want you to understand."

I still felt perturbed—at Todd? At myself? At the world? I didn't know. I shoveled some chips and salsa into my mouth because I didn't know what to say.

"I just don't know," I said, shaking my head. "I'd feel terrible for making you give up this job."

"But not enough to move to San Francisco," said Todd quietly.

"God, why did shit get so complicated?"

When the server brought out our dishes, I was relieved by the reprieve from this discussion. Fortunately, Todd seemed to sense that I didn't want to talk about this anymore because he changed the discussion to lighter topics.

He told me about his trip to a local Chinese place in San Francisco that served the hottest noodles in the city. Todd and a few of his coworkers ate the noodles, initially enjoying them despite the mouthwatering spice, only to go home and regret that decision all night.

"I think I broke the toilet." Todd laughed. "Babe, it was the most painful experience in my entire life. I felt like I was giving birth."

My lips twitched. "Todd, I'm trying to eat here!"

"Sorry, sorry. But the noodles were so good that I kept eating the leftovers, but I had to eat it on the toilet because, well—"

We finished our dinner in a good mood. Todd came over to my place, and before I'd even shut the front door, he took my face in his hands and kissed me.

The kiss was deep and slow, and I felt a burgeoning heat in my belly. I kissed him back. I wanted to see if what I'd felt was real.

But as Todd maneuvered me farther into my house, I suddenly felt stifled. I had the urge to push him away from me even though I'd been so turned on all the time lately.

Maybe it was the way his tongue kept snaking in and out of my mouth. Or the fact that he tasted like onions from his burrito. Any eroticism I might've felt was extinguished when he grabbed one of my breasts and squeezed a little too hard.

I broke the kiss. "Todd," I said, breathing heavily.

"What?"

He started to unzip my jeans, but I batted his hands away. He gave me a confused look like a lost puppy, which only irritated me.

"I don't think this is a good idea," I said.

He stilled, then stepped back. His expression shuttered. "What's wrong?"

"Nothing. Everything." I sat down on the edge of my bed, sighing deeply. "This isn't working anymore."

"You're going to have to be more specific."

I gritted my teeth. "Our relationship. I think we need to go our separate ways."

Todd just stared at me, but I didn't back down. I felt strangely relieved, saying the words aloud finally.

"I told you I wasn't going to take the job," he said finally.

"But you should take it. It's a huge opportunity. I don't want you to stall your career for me."

"I just told you that I was fine with it."

"Are you?"

When he looked away, I had my answer. I patted the spot next to me on the bed, and he eventually sat down next to me.

"We just aren't compatible. Not anymore, at least," I said quietly. "I think you feel it, too."

"Maybe. But what I said earlier was true: our relationship is more important than my job."

"I believe you, but at the same time, it shouldn't be this hard. I think you'll regret giving up that job in the long run. And I don't want to move to San Francisco. I'm okay with you needing to move on."

Todd looked sad yet not devastated. He pushed his fingers through his hair. Had he been considering whether breaking up was a good idea, too?

"So does this mean we're breaking up?" he asked.

I nodded. "Yeah. Don't you think it's for the best?"

"I don't know. But if it's what you want, I won't fight you on it."

Todd left soon after. He didn't kiss me goodbye, but his expression looked resigned. I felt guilty, but I also had no interest in calling off the breakup. Especially with what I had waiting for me around the corner. Something I knew I'd regret passing up.

I felt free. I felt like I could live the life that I wanted without worrying about Todd. He'd been a good boyfriend for the years we'd been together, but we'd outgrown each other. I'd always have a place in my heart for him.

This wasn't a bad thing. It was just . . . life. And life had a way of forcing your hand sometimes.

When I drove to The Scarlet Rope the next evening, I didn't think too hard about why I wanted to go there. Maybe I just wanted to distract myself.

Or maybe I wanted to run into Mac.

I used Mac's password, wandering inside without any plan. I immediately got a drink from the bar, needing a bit of liquid courage for tonight.

I was continually surprised at how busy the club was, even during the week. Did none of these people have nine-to-five jobs? Nobody was tired after spending over an hour commuting to their office?

Then again, I had a feeling the people who had the money to be patrons here weren't worried about getting to the office on time in the morning. They were probably athletes like Mac, or actors with mansions in the hills, or billionaire CEOs with plenty of employees to do the real work for them.

A man in a black mask started flirting with me, and I let him for a while. When he asked me what I liked, I just shook my head.

"I'm still figuring that out," I admitted.

"Well, this is the perfect place to try things out." He raised his glass. "If you want somebody to experiment with me, ask for me. I'm Viper."

"That's your legal name, then?" I joked.

He winked. "Spend some time with me to find out."

I politely declined his offer, which he took in stride. I wandered to watch a few different scenes, including one that was some role-play. A woman nearby had to whisper in my ear that it was apparently a monster/captive roleplay.

"Monster?" I whispered, confused. "What, like Frankenstein?"

"This guy is an alien. He's abducted this woman to his spaceship."

I marveled, shaking my head. It also said a lot that I wasn't horrified and merely intrigued. It was like nothing could surprise me anymore. The Scarlet Rope had apparently pushed way beyond my boundaries. Where once I would've scurried in the opposite direction, now I was just curious.

I watched for a little longer until deciding to move on. When I entered the BDSM private room, I found a chair near the back and made myself comfortable.

This scene was a man and a woman. The man was the dominant this time. He was clad in black leather, a mask on his face, while the woman was already naked.

The man was all muscles, and I couldn't help but see a resemblance to Mac. I swallowed hard when he bent the woman over a table and began to spank her so hard that he left red handprints on her ass.

"Get on your knees," he commanded.

The woman complied, gazing up at the man with wide eyes.

"Take out my cock," he then said.

She did so, his cock large and veiny. She could barely fit her hand around its girth. She licked it up one side and down the other. The man, though, took hold of her hair and pushed her down so she swallowed his entire cock.

He fucked the woman's throat until he finally pulled away to let her breathe. She gasped, saliva running down her chin as she licked her lips like she couldn't wait for more.

I felt sweat bead on my upper lip. I glanced at the other people in the room, but when my gaze caught a handsome man's eye, I quickly looked back at the scene in front of me.

The woman choked on this man's cock, but she still moaned in disappointment when he told her to go lie down on the bed. He went to the wall of whips, chains, and other instruments, taking down a few items and going to the bed.

"Beg me," he said to the woman as he lightly traced down her spine with a crop.

"Please, Master." The woman got on her hands and knees.

The man whipped her ass until it was bright red. "Keep begging," he said.

She begged and moaned and begged again until he'd covered her body in welts from the whip. Then the man got onto the bed, pushed her down, and thrust his cock into her as she screamed in ecstasy.

As I watched, I floated between time and space, paying extra attention to this since it involved submitting to a Dom. In many ways, this was practice. It was strange, watching this while no one was touching me. I wished suddenly that Mac was here.

I also suddenly wished Mac would do these things to my body. I trusted him. I'd always played by the rules and was tired of it. What would it be like to do something completely out of my comfort zone? To experience sex unlike I'd ever experienced before?

I left The Scarlet Rope in a haze. I barely registered that a man was standing outside, his arms crossed, leaning against a beat-up Corolla I'd recognize anywhere.

"Elodie," Mac said, his deep voice making me shiver.

My heart lurched. His hand was outstretched. Without a second thought, I took it, and his eyes flashed with a heat that made me nearly melt into a puddle right at his feet.

Chapter 10

Mac

"I thought you had a game tonight," Elodie said, her forehead creasing.

I rubbed her fingers. "It was a home game. I told the staff here to call me if you showed up again."

She took a deep breath. Then another. I could feel her body practically vibrating with energy. Her pupils were dilated, her cheeks flushed. When she licked her lips, my cock jumped. How was it this woman could drive me insane with such a small gesture?

"Oh." Her voice was faint, yet she didn't seem unnerved. She seemed . . . excited.

"Why did you come here tonight?" I asked.

She licked her lips again. *Dammit all to fucking hell.* She was going to kill me.

"I broke up with Todd," she said, surprising me again.

"I'm sorry to hear that." I forced myself to say the words even though we both knew how hollow they were.

Her lips quirked. "Well, it'll be okay. He was nice about it. We've grown apart, and we wanted different things."

Fucking *Todd*. I didn't want to hear about Todd. Because then I thought about finding the guy and beating the shit out of him for letting a woman like Elodie get away from him. Was he a complete fucking moron? He'd had paradise in his hands, and he'd let it slip through his fingers.

Then again, Todd's loss was my gain. Maybe I should be thanking him. I touched Elodie's jaw, tucking a strand of hair behind her ear. When she tilted her head toward my hand, triumph filled me.

"That sounds very mature of you both," I said gruffly.

"Mature, sure." Her eyes sparkled now. "But boring. And it also told me that Todd wasn't the type of guy who'd fight for me."

"He's an idiot," I growled.

"Maybe." She inhaled. "Or maybe I am." Now, she wouldn't look me in the eye. "I do have some questions for you. About that contract and everything."

My dick stiffened. "Do you?"

"I've been thinking about your . . . proposal." Her lashes fluttered. "And I'd like to discuss it."

"Well, then let me take you to my place." When she blinked in surprise, I added, "To talk. That's it. Scout's honor." I held up my hand with my index and middle fingers pressed together.

"Were you a Boy Scout?"

"Would you be shocked if I told you I was an Eagle Scout?"

Elodie gaped at me. "What? Seriously?"

"Once again—Scout's honor." I grinned. "I grew up in Idaho. Being a Boy Scout was pretty much a requirement. Maybe someday I'll even show you how to start a fire."

"Come on. We'll figure out how to get you back to your car later." I opened the passenger door for Elodie, suddenly wishing I'd driven one of my nicer cars tonight. But she didn't seem to mind getting into my Corolla. In fact, she seemed mostly amused that my car was so old that it had both manual windows and locks. She played with the window crank, her grin infectious.

"I think this car is older than me," she joked as we got on the freeway.

I patted the steering wheel. "A lady never discloses her age."

"Love the little tree air freshener, by the way. I feel like this car would be incomplete without it."

"It even has a cigarette lighter. I'm only missing the fuzzy dice." I chuckled.

We drove in comfortable silence. Elodie shot me a few shy glances, making a handful of pithy remarks about my driving abilities as I weaved in and out of traffic.

When we arrived at my place, she'd fallen silent. I put in the code for the gate, and then we were traveling the long driveway toward the multicar garage.

"I think you brought me here just to intimidate me," Elodie joked as I steered her inside. Her mouth was agape as she took in the surroundings, but she started laughing when I led her farther into the house.

"What's so funny?" Now I was just confused.

She flung her arms wide. "This is the most bachelor-y bachelor pad I've ever seen."

I took in my living room: furnished with a large couch, a flat-screen TV, and one rickety side table perfect for setting your beer down.

"It's not that bad," I protested.

She put her hands on her hips. "You have a huge-ass house but don't even take the time to furnish it?"

"There's a couch . . ."

Elodie began wandering around, much to my chagrin. The kitchen was pretty bare, I had to admit. When she opened the fridge, she started laughing at what she saw.

"Red Bull, mustard, and—is that a twenty-pound bag of shredded cheese?" She gave me a confused look.

"Cheese is paramount." I closed the fridge and went to my bar, which was at least very well-stocked. "Wine? Beer? Something harder?"

"Wine is fine."

I decided to take her upstairs. The second floor included multiple bedrooms and was better furnished. The primary bedroom had an adjoined sitting room. I turned on the gas fireplace and had Elodie sit beside me on the couch.

"Okay, this room is better," she admitted, smiling at me. "Did you just run out of money to finish the rest of the house?"

I shot her a glare. "No. I ran out of time."

"Ah. Well. Maybe you'll get back to it someday." She gave me a sheepish grin. "I'm sorry if I offended you. I really was just teasing."

"I know." I finished off my whiskey and went to find another bottle I'd left in this room. "I know this place needs work." I hesitated, then added, "I had some help with the rooms up here."

"Oh?"

How did I explain that Caroline—who happened to be my lover when I was a teenager, no lesshad helped me decorate this room? I didn't even know how to broach that subject. Besides, I'd only just gotten Elodie to agree to come here. I didn't want to scare her away.

I refilled my glass, then snagged a few documents I'd been working on earlier.

"I hired a decorator," I lied, returning to sit next to Elodie. "But then I got so busy I had to put things on pause."

Elodie set her wineglass down. I let myself take in her appearance, shimmering in the firelight. Her hair was a beautiful black, but with the fire reflecting off the strands, I could see bits of red underneath. Her skin seemed to glow, her lashes dark and dusky against her fair cheeks. I wanted to kiss her so freaking badly, but now was not the time.

"So." I cleared my throat. "You wanted to talk?"

"I did."

I handed her the documents. "This isn't the formal contract between us. It's just an example, but I thought it'd be helpful."

Elodie took the papers and began scanning them. "Should I have a lawyer?" she asked.

I almost chuckled but stopped myself. "If you want, but it isn't necessary."

"'If either party is seriously injured beyond the scope of this agreement; maimed, or dies as a result of said injuries, the other party will not be held liable by the maimed/ deceased party's estate . . .'" Elodie's eyes were wide. "Good lord, is that necessary?"

"As long as we have boundaries in place beforehand, there's no reason to worry. But it's for our mutual protection."

"Well, I'll try not to kill you, then." Elodie handed the papers back to me. "I'm assuming this is talking about a civil suit, not a criminal one?"

I nodded.

"I'm sorry, did I freak you out?" I took her hand. "This is just standard contract legalese."

"I know. Pretty sure all those 'terms and conditions' we have to sign just to download an app have the same thing. I think I recently signed away my firstborn to get a new credit card."

I grabbed an empty notebook and began writing. "Now, it's time to get down to the nitty-gritty. We'll go through everything, and you'll decide what you're excited about, what you might be interested in trying, and what you definitely don't want to do."

We started a list. Elodie was uncomfortable at first, especially as things got more and more graphic, but by the end of things, she seemed more relaxed. The second and third glasses of wine probably helped.

"Nipple clamps, yes. Butt plugs, yes. Whips, maybe." I gave her a heated smile. "We can discuss how much whipping you'd prefer."

Elodie squirmed. "Uh, I have no idea."

"There's whipping that doesn't leave any marks. Then there's whipping that does leave marks. Then you can go so far as to draw blood . . ." When her eyebrows rose to her hairline, I chuckled. "Yeah, it's a thing."

"Um, do you do that? Regularly? The drawing blood thing?"

"I've had it done to me."

She blinked like a confused owl.

"But it's been a long time."

We reviewed everything that could possibly be relevant, including what days and times Elodie would act as my submissive. Where she would live, where we would have sex, when we would have sex, how long we would have sex, and everything in between.

"What about feet?" I asked.

"Mine or yours?"

"Yours." I smiled. "Have you ever had your toes sucked? Or given a foot job?"

"Do you want me to give you a foot job?" she asked, confused.

I laughed. "That's not my bag, but how about we put that one under maybe."

"Mmm."

By the time we'd gone through every possible sexual scenario, I was so wound up that I had to start pacing to keep myself from pouncing on Elodie. I had a feeling she'd be receptive, but I'd promised her that I hadn't brought her here to have sex.

It didn't help that the wine had relaxed her. She'd taken her hair down from its ponytail, the dark tendrils framing her heart-shaped face. Her cheeks were slightly flushed, and she kept re-crossing her legs as if tempting me to push them wide and discover all her secrets.

"So I guess this whole thing is separate from the contract I signed with The Scarlet Rope?" Elodie asked.

Her question broke through my hazy brain. "Yeah, this is just between you and me. But like the club, I'd ask you to sign an NDA as well."

Now Elodie looked annoyed. "Good lord, how many NDAs am I going to sign? Can I talk about"—she gestured vaguely—"stuff we do but just not mention you by name?"

"That's fine, as long as you keep out identifying details." I sat down again next to her. "I know it seems like a lot, but believe me, it's all for a good reason. It's to protect us both. And especially since I'm a public figure, you don't want to get mixed up in something that could affect your job or reputation."

"Oh, I get the logic behind it. But it also makes it seem so . . ."

"What?"

She wrinkled her nose. "Businesslike. Dry. Boring. Like you're inspecting a house or something."

I laughed. I turned her face toward me. "I can assure you, sweetheart, you won't be bored. And neither will I."

Her eyes widened, and it was at that moment that my self-control snapped. Not completely, but it wasn't made of steel either.

"Can I kiss you?" I asked in a low voice.

Her lashes fluttered, her voice trembling a bit. "Um . . ."

"Just a kiss. I promise." My hands practically shook with need as I stroked her cheek. "But I don't think I can wait any longer."

When she breathed, "Me neither," I nearly shouted in triumph.

I pulled her into my arms. I was probably not as gentle as I could've been, but when Elodie let out an excited gasp, I didn't let myself feel bad about it.

I kissed her hard, tangling my fingers into her hair. My other arm wrapped around her waist, making sure to keep that hand on her back.

She tasted like the wine she'd been drinking but sweeter. *So fucking sweet.* I pushed my tongue into her mouth, and she let out a little moan. I gripped her harder. She kissed me back, our lips and tongues tangling, the kiss getting so intense that my cock was rock hard in moments. It had been ages since my body had reacted this way to someone.

Christ, she's going to make me come in my fucking jeans, I thought, both amazed and dismayed. That hadn't happened to me in more than a decade, and I'd hoped to die before it ever happened again.

I deepened the kiss. I bent her over my arm, showing her how I'd bend her over any piece of furniture I wanted. Every part of her body, I would claim. I couldn't fucking wait.

I trailed my hand under her shirt, her skin warm and soft. This small sampling of her taste was enough to make me crazy. I didn't know when and didn't know how, but I felt like this woman would be the end of me.

Finally, Elodie broke the kiss, gasping. "Mac," she said, breathing hard.

I'd pulled her into my lap. I wanted her to feel exactly how hard she'd made me. "And that was just a fucking kiss," I said, groaning.

She let out a little laugh. "Wow."

"I have a guest room." The words came out before I could think them over. "You can stay the night."

Elodie sucked on her bottom lip, which nearly did me in. "I'm not sure that's a good idea."

"I won't touch you."

Do you even believe yourself? I pushed the thought aside.

"I know." She stroked my arm as if soothing me. "But I still need to think about this whole thing. So if you could give me a ride back to my car . . ."

"Of course."

But I didn't make a move to get up, and neither did she. She gazed into my eyes, and when I moved to kiss her again, she didn't push me away.

Our lips touched, this kiss softer but just as passionate. She melted into my embrace. I gripped her shirt with a clenched fist, hoping against hope that she'd change her mind and stay the night.

Chapter 11

Elodie

I woke up late the following morning. Luckily, I wasn't expected in the office. I climbed from bed with a groan, feeling hungover yet I hadn't gotten inebriated last night. Maybe I was just drunk from Mac kissing me.

I collapsed back into bed, my mind replaying the night. I didn't know how I'd had the strength to go home instead of staying the night. It hadn't helped that Mac kept kissing me, seducing me with every brush of his lips, every slide of his tongue—

And his throbbing hard-on, which he very intentionally made sure I'd felt? *Gah.* That thing felt huge. I buried my face in my pillow. God, I was in trouble. Despite my insistence that I needed to think about the contract, I knew I was going to sign it. I didn't have the willpower to resist Mac anymore.

And why should I? There was no shame in enjoying this arrangement. Especially now that I'd ended things with Todd. The fact that Mac had been so thorough in drafting the contract showed that he knew what he was doing.

That made me wonder how many other women he'd entered into similar arrangements with in the past. I shook that thought from my head. It didn't matter. This was about us. And I knew deep in my bones that he wanted me to feel safe. Even as the thought of letting him do all those things we'd discussed last night would drag me out of my comfort zone.

I shivered but finally dragged myself out of bed because my stomach was rumbling for food. As I got some food, though, reality smacked me in the face as the stack of bills sitting on my table seemed to scream at me.

What was I going to do about my job? I had an assignment, and to get paid, I had to complete it. Which meant not being honest with Mac about who—and what—I was.

I picked up the bill on top and opened it. It was for my car, again. It warned me that if I didn't make a payment in the next thirty days, they'd start the repossession process.

"Fuck," I muttered, feeling sick to my stomach. I lived in LA. I had to have a car, unfortunately.

I sat down and stared at the bill. My brain whirled in what felt like a thousand different directions. I knew that even if I signed Mac's contract, I couldn't quit my job either.

Was I naive? Thinking that I could figure out a way to have my cake and eat it, too?

After eating and showering, I glanced at my phone. I frowned when I saw a text message from a number I didn't recognize.

Hi, Elodie, this is your uncle Jose, your mom's brother. We're having a party next month at my place. Let me know if you can make it.

The text made me sit down. I hadn't seen or spoken to my mom's side of the family since she'd died. Jose and his wife, Maria, had attended Mom's funeral, along with their four kids, but that had been it. Mom also had a sister back in the Philippines, but I'd never met her.

My grandma Esmeralda hadn't approved of my father. She especially hadn't approved when Mom had gotten pregnant with me outside of marriage. My parents only got married because they'd had to. After, poor Mom had been abandoned and left to raise me on her own.

I picked up a photo of my mom from before she'd had me. She'd been a beauty queen back in the Philippines. In the photo, she wore her tiara and sash. She looked beautiful. Young and hopeful.

She'd never once said that she regretted having me, never acted like I was a burden in any way, but I'd always wondered. She'd ended up alone in Los Angeles, working three jobs at a time to keep food on our table since her family essentially abandoned her.

It's just you and me, baby, she'd say to me all the time when I was a child. *We don't need anybody else.*

I didn't remember much about my dad. He'd left when I was only four years old. For a few years, he'd send a postcard from wherever he ended up, but even that had stopped by the time I was in middle school. I remembered Mom sitting at our kitchen table, her head in her hands and a pile of letters scattered across the table.

Dad had returned all of Mom's letters. When I'd tried to read them, Mom had freaked out, telling me to get out. She'd scrambled to collect all the letters. I'd always wondered what she'd done with them. Had she kept them hidden, or had she destroyed them? I never did find them after she was gone.

Although I was half Filipina, I'd never felt all that attached to that side of my heritage. Maybe it was because I'd been born and raised in the US, or because Mom had never wanted me to speak Tagalog. The few times she'd spoken it around me, she'd get annoyed when I'd repeat the words back to her.

You're American. Speak English, she'd tell me.

I sighed. I was inclined to ignore my uncle's text. He'd tried to mend fences with me since Mom's death, but I hadn't been in a place to let him. I had too much animosity toward my mother's family for not being there when she needed them most.

A random thought hit me. Jose and his family would be horrified that I was talking to Mac about signing a contract to make me his sub. I chuckled under my breath. *They'd probably have me committed.*

As I sat and drank my coffee, my mind awhirl, there was a knock on my door. Not expecting anyone, I checked the peephole before opening it, only to find a courier holding a manila envelope in his hand.

"Elodie Andrews?" he asked, sounding bored.

"Yeah, that's me."

After I signed for it, he handed me the envelope. The return address was a law office here in LA. I knew what it was before I even opened it.

Taking the contract out, I returned to the kitchen to read through it. Seeing my name and Mac's in writing, along with everything we'd agreed to, made my heart race.

On top of the stack of documents, though, was a Post-it that read, *Let my lawyer know if you have any changes or questions. -Mac*

The contract was twenty pages long. I didn't think I had the mental capacity to look at it right then. Instead, I finished my cold coffee and texted Hannah, asking her to come over when she could.

By the time she arrived, I felt like I might burst. I was so desperate to tell her everything. Though I felt a little guilty for spilling the beans, I hadn't signed the NDA yet.

"You look like you're about to explode," said Hannah, giving me a concerned look.

I simply handed her the contract. Her eyes widened.

"Is this . . .?" she asked.

I nodded, feeling a tinge of guilt, wondering how Mac would feel if he knew I'd shared the contract with her.

"Well, shit." She slowly sank onto my couch. Her eyes widened as she began to scan the text. "Damn. Well, he is thorough. I'll give him that." Her gaze caught mine. "No golden showers, eh?"

I smacked her arm. "Come on, now."

"Hey, I'm not here to judge." She snickered as she went through the list of *nos*. "Well, I guess I'm relieved at some of these. Too bad about the choking, though. It can be fun."

I gaped at her. "Wait, you've . . .? You know what, never mind. Do you think this is totally insane?"

"Well, yeah, but that doesn't mean you shouldn't do it." She shrugged and handed me the documents. "Are you going to sign them?"

"I need to read through it all, but . . ." I suddenly felt sheepish. "Yeah, I think I will."

Hannah whistled and stood. "Then this calls for a toast. Elodie is going to get her freak on! It's a miracle."

It wasn't even lunchtime, but I wasn't going to refuse some celebratory wine. Hannah helped herself to a bottle of Cabernet sitting on my counter. She popped open the cork and poured each of us some. We clinked glasses, Hannah's expression amused but strangely proud.

That was when someone else knocked on my front door. "Who is it this time?" I grumbled.

A Blades tote bag sat on the front step. A note was attached, and I recognized Mac's handwriting immediately.

There's a game tonight. Two tickets are inside. And no, I'm not above bribery. See you tonight.

My pulse raced as I brought the bag inside. Hannah and I found two jerseys inside, along with the tickets, two nice water tumblers, wristbands, and signed caps from Mac himself.

"Dang, he really wants you to say yes," Hannah said, putting on one of the caps. "And I, for one, very much appreciate his enthusiasm."

"Since when did you care about hockey?" The question reminded me of when Todd had asked me the very same thing. I had to laugh at myself.

"Since the hottest player on the team wants to get into your pants," she answered.

I looked at the tickets and frowned. "These are for the game in Colorado."

"Wait, did you read the back of the note?" Hannah turned over the piece of paper. "'A limo will be waiting for you at five o'clock to take you to the airport,'" she read. Her eyebrows shot up. "Damn, he's really pulling out all the stops, isn't he?"

I grabbed the note from her. "The game is at eight. How are we going to get there in time? It'll take us an hour just to get to LAX."

"Girl, he probably has a private jet."

To my amazement, Hannah was correct. The limo drove us not to LAX but to John Wayne where the rich and famous took off in their private jets. Instead of getting stripped and yelled at by TSA like regular folk, we were wined and dined the second the limo driver opened the car doors for us.

"Is this real life?" I asked for the thousandth time after the private jet had taken off. We'd already been served champagne and the fanciest appetizers I'd ever seen.

Hannah giggled. Giggled! Hannah *never* giggled. "I sure as fuck hope so." She popped a ball of fancy cheese into her mouth. "This is amazing. Not even Emma and Ryan have a private jet, and they're fucking rich."

We landed in Denver and before I knew it, we were at the stadium. Inside, we were escorted to a private box with an amazing view of the rink. I was wearing Mac's jersey, while Hannah wore the other, along with a cap.

My friend was busy figuring out what kind of scrumptious food we should order from the menu, but I focused on seeing Mac. I couldn't believe he'd gone to all this trouble. Hadn't I already basically told him I'd sign the contract? Then again, he hadn't been able to see inside my head to know just how excited I really was about this, even if I pretended I needed time to think about it.

Was all this effort just to get into my pants? Was I going to owe him big for all this? Or did he actually *like* me?

I felt like a giddy schoolgirl. When both teams began to enter the ice, and the crowd went wild, I found myself hooting and hollering with them.

Simply nothing was more exhilarating than everyone cheering for your man. Technically, he wasn't even mine, but I already felt a certain possessiveness over him, given our impending arrangement.

Mac was the first to enter. He skated the circumference of the rink, stopping near the north end where Hannah and I were sitting. When he looked up, he flashed a smile and tapped two fingers to his forehead in a salute. It felt like one of those moments you read about. Out of all of these tens of thousands of people, he'd sought me out. He was about to play a game, yet he'd been thinking of me.

I could hardly breathe. He hadn't even touched me— he'd just *looked* at me—and I felt like I was going to faint. *Oh God.* A panic attack was coming on. It had been years since I had one. My heart pounded in my chest, and my palms and face began to sweat. Hannah must've noticed something was wrong. She grabbed my arm.

"Elodie, breathe. Breathe, girl."

She kept her hand on my back as I took a deep breath. Then another. Hannah started fanning me with a random brochure, continuously amused at my lack of composure.

"I'm not sure if that was nervousness or excitement. But whichever it was, it's clear you are so far gone," she said, shaking her head. "But I can't even judge you for it."

Luckily, the game started then, and it helped me focus on something other than what would likely be happening soon. I wasn't sure if it was how I felt, but the game was exhilarating. The home team, the Blizzards, was one of the best in the league, and the Blades trailed behind in the beginning. But they soon caught up, especially after Mac scored two goals in a row.

Hannah grabbed my hand, squeezing it so hard that I started to lose feeling in my fingers, but I didn't care. The game was currently tied, with only thirty seconds left on the clock, and my skin tingled with anticipation as I watched the numbers tick down.

Twenty-nine.

Twenty-eight.

Twenty-seven.

Carmichael, one of the wingers, stole the puck and sent it sailing across the ice in Mac's direction. Everyone in the crowd jumped up as Mac took control, racing down the ice while shuttling the puck back and forth.

Eight.

Seven.

Six.

Five.

Mac glided toward the net, swung his stick back, and slammed the puck. Everyone in the arena held their breaths as the tiny puck flew toward the goal. It slid between the goalie's knees and crossed the red line. Mac scored the winning goal of the game!

The buzzer sounded two seconds later, and the stadium erupted. I screamed, Hannah screamed, and then we jumped up and down, hugging each other.

"Oh my God!" I kept saying over and over again. "Did you see that?"

"That was fucking amazing." Hannah shook her head. "Holy shit. Wow. What a game!"

It was the first time I'd truly understood what all the hype was about when it came to Mac's hockey prowess. We were giddy, a little drunk, and near bursting with excitement. The high was still carrying us as a security guard came in and asked us to follow him. Hannah actually *skipped* as we made our way to the locker room area.

Mac was one of the first to walk out, freshly showered and looking triumphant. It was only the presence of other people who kept me from throwing myself at him. It didn't help that his grin was infectious. Every time I saw this man, I wanted him more than the last.

Carmichael, the player who had assisted in the winning goal, came out right behind him, also grinning. Brady

Carmichael was all muscle. Although he wasn't as tall as Mac, he was all angles and strength. He'd recently buzzed his head, and he now looked like he'd come straight out of the Marines. Despite his tough exterior, he was a favorite among the fans, as he tended to say off-the-wall things during press conferences. I'd become a bit of a hockey aficionado lately.

Brady's gaze caught mine, then slid immediately over to Hannah's. Interest flashed across his face. When I glanced over at Hannah, she seemed just as intrigued.

"Amazing game," I said to Mac. "Congratulations."

"I'm glad you were able to come," he replied.

Hannah snorted. "You sent a limo and a private jet for us. Of course we were going to come."

Brady gaped at Mac. "Seriously, dude?"

Mac shrugged and winked at me. "It was short notice. I had to pull some strings."

I was tongue-tied. Feeling embarrassed, I blushed and stared down at my shoes.

Fortunately, Brady came to our rescue. "I need a drink. Let's go back to the hotel." He sent Hannah a warm smile. "You didn't tell me your name, beautiful."

Hannah rolled her eyes, but she seemed amused. "No, I didn't. How about you give me a good reason to give it to you, hmm?"

Mac slung an arm around my shoulder. "I can see why you two are friends already."

The hotel not only had a bar but also karaoke rooms available to rent. To my surprise, Mac was the one who wanted to do karaoke.

Brady leaned down to murmur in my ear, "He's a terrible singer."

Mac gave Brady the finger. "Says the guy who loves to try singing 'My Heart Will Go On' at the top of his lungs."

"That's your song?" Hannah's lips twitched. "Celine Dion?"

"Yeah, and? She's the GOAT." Brady shook his head in dismay. "And she's Canadian. I like Canadians. They know hockey."

Hannah smirked. "Shame. I'm from LA."

"I can overlook that."

Mac and I laughed. Our friends were a match made in heaven, it seemed. The four of us got our drinks and some munchies and headed to our karaoke room. I'd only done karaoke once in college, and it had been at a sleazy dive bar near USC.

"Okay, who's going first?" Despite the question, Hannah began looking through the song selection choices, mic already in hand. "Oh shit, I love this one!" She grabbed my arm and pulled me up to the front of the room.

I tried to extricate myself, but Hannah wasn't letting go. The guys were already laughing at us, and when the beginnings of "Before He Cheats" started playing, I couldn't help but get into the mood with Hannah. Her enthusiasm was contagious.

We sang like crazy people, our voices cracking and squealing, Brady covering his ears more than once during our attempts at the high notes. Mac watched with an amused look on his face.

Our gazes met as I sang the chorus, and the heat in his eyes was enough to make my face burn red if I hadn't already been that color from singing my heart out. Brady, for his part, just shook his head and laughed when Hannah pointed a finger at him.

When we finished, Brady said to Hannah, "Never let me get on your bad side."

"I'm perfectly pleasant all the time," she protested.

"You probably make most guys shit their pants."

Hannah wrinkled her nose. "Wow, what a lovely description."

Brady leaned down and whispered something in her ear that made her laugh.

Mac and I exchanged glances. "I'd warn your friend, but it seems like she can take care of herself," he said.

"Oh, don't worry. Hannah is very capable." I shot him a smile. "What's your karaoke song, then?"

"That's a surprise for later." Mac got up and pushed Brady up to the front.

The guys sang "Baby Got Back" as the drinks continued to flow. We were all hammered by the end, laughing like lunatics when Brady rapped Weird Al Yankovic's "White and Nerdy."

Mac had the final song of the night. To my surprise, he chose The Righteous Brothers' "Unchained Melody." Mac had a smooth baritone voice that made me shiver as I listened. All three of us sat enraptured.

Hadn't Brady said that Mac couldn't sing? I glanced at Brady, and Brady just shrugged. He was clearly as confused as I was.

When Mac finished, we all broke into applause.

"I didn't know you could sing!" I said when Mac sat back down next to me. "Brady said you were terrible!"

"I only break out the singing for certain people," Mac replied.

"Shit man, that was something else." Brady smacked Mac on the shoulder. "In case your hockey career goes to shit, you should take up singing."

"And *you* definitely should *not* take up singing." Mac laughed. "You sounded like a dying cat up there."

He and Brady got into a wrestling match, although they were already drunk enough that it was pretty pathetic for a wrestling match between two famous athletes.

I'd never seen Mac this relaxed before. I'd only seen him either playing hockey or at The Scarlet Rope, where he was always in complete control. Seeing him let loose with friends was new, but it was refreshing. I appreciated both sides of him, but I couldn't help but wonder how often he let himself have fun. Did his need for control make it hard for him to be silly like this? Did he need to have the assistance of alcohol to let it happen?

By the end of the night, Brady needed to be taken up to his room, while Hannah was falling asleep on a couch in the hotel lobby. I hadn't had as much to drink as everyone else, and it seemed as though Mac had already started sobering up.

I glanced over at Hannah, who was snoring lightly. "I think we should get her to bed."

But even as I said the words, I had the sudden urge to go to bed with Mac instead. My brain started to put together a plan—we could get Hannah her own room, and then I could go with Mac—

As if reading my mind, Mac gave me a heated grin. "You need to go to bed, too," he said softly.

"I'm not tired."

"Well, I am." He leaned down and pressed his lips to mine. "I have my private jet scheduled to fly you home in the morning."

Disappointment flooded me, even though I knew Mac was trying to be a gentleman. After all, I was pretty drunk. "Thank you," I said.

"Don't look so sad." He touched my cheek. "I'll be back in town soon." His eyes darkened. "And maybe by then, the contract will be signed by everybody."

I swallowed hard. "Yes."

"I hope you'll give this a try."

I wanted to yell that I was desperate for him, that I didn't care about signing a contract, that I just wanted *him*, but I knew he was right. We couldn't sleep together. Not if we were going to do this—whatever *this* was—right.

"Good night, then." I glanced outside, where dawn was beginning to lighten the horizon. "Or good morning, I guess."

Mac kissed me one last time. "Good night, Elodie." He looked over at Hannah. "I'll get you guys a room and help you upstairs so you can get a few hours of sleep, at least."

When Hannah let out a loud snore, Mac and I both laughed and shook our heads.

Chapter 12

Mac

"**D**id you get more furniture?" my agent, Andrea, asked me as she looked around my living room.

"I thought I'd get this place fully furnished."

"Huh."

A tall woman in her midfifties, Andrea Sterling gave off an air of "just try to fuck with me" that often intimidated people. When I'd first met her five years ago, she'd taken one look at me and said that she didn't sign hockey players because they were too much of a pain. I'd somehow convinced her otherwise.

And up until the last few months, I'd kept up that end of my bargain. When she'd found out about the rumor going around about me sleeping with a married woman, she'd given me an earful, to say the least.

Andrea opened my fridge and then gasped. "Cole Mackenzie! Do you have *ingredients* in here?"

Now, I was embarrassed. "I can cook," I protested.

That elicited a laugh. "Since when? Didn't you nearly burn down a hotel trying to make Easy Mac one time?"

I growled under my breath. "That was years ago."

"Try six months ago." Andrea chortled, shaking her head. She shut my fridge, but not before snagging a can of sparkling water. "And La Croix? Who's the lucky girl? And please don't tell me she's married, or I'm going to murder you for real this time."

I wasn't about to tell Andrea about Elodie, and most definitely not about the contract. The contract that had yet to be signed even though it'd been a week since I'd flown Elodie and her best friend Hannah to Denver for the game. I'd been so sure that Elodie would sign it, but she'd gone radio silent since we'd seen each other last. I'd gone out of town for another game and then for a photo shoot on location. We'd texted a few times, but I could tell that Elodie was keeping her distance. I just couldn't figure out why. I hoped like hell she wasn't having second thoughts.

"Mmm, so it is a woman." Andrea sat down at my dining room table with a smile. "Is she the one who was in the VIP box at the Blades game?"

Shit. I should've known she'd be onto that.

I scowled. "How did you know about that?"

"Darling boy, I know *everything*." When I just kept glaring, she shrugged. "You know Hugh. He's got a big mouth."

Hugh was one of her assistants who followed the team to away games on occasion. He also loved to gossip, which I was fairly certain was the reason Andrea had hired him in the first place.

"There might be a woman," I hedged.

"Is she single?"

"Yes, Andrea, she's single." *Thank God she got rid of her boyfriend, at least.*

"Excellent. You dating a nice, unmarried lady would do wonders for your image."

"And last time I checked, you weren't my publicist."

Andrea waved a hand. "Your image and reputation go hand-in-hand with my ability to get you all that nice money you're earning."

I couldn't argue with her there. Andrea was a total shark when it came to her clients. The Blades had tried to lowball me when I'd first been about to sign on, and she'd gone to bat for me with a ruthlessness that I'd never seen any woman display.

Growing up in rural Idaho, women like my mom tended to be softer and less direct. Mom had once described being a preacher's wife as being the neck that swiveled the head of the family back and forth. *Your dad just thinks he's in charge*, she'd said more than once after Dad had huffed and puffed about something.

Andrea, though—she didn't use honey to attract flies. She chased those flies down and smashed them with her fist.

"You do seem preoccupied," Andrea said, studying me. "Which means you must really like this woman."

I groaned. "Give it a rest, will you?"

"I hear frustration in your tone. I'm guessing that means she's giving you the runaround? Oh, I like her already."

To my relief, the doorbell rang, interrupting this line of inquiry. When I opened the door to find none other than Elodie on my doorstep, my brain short-circuited.

"What are you doing here?" That was the first thing that came out of my mouth. *Fucking hell, Mackenzie.*

Elodie's smile wilted. "Um, I thought we should talk . . ."

Her gaze moved over my shoulder, and I realized that Andrea was behind me now.

"Mac, introduce me to your friend," Andrea said in that annoying, sly tone she had. I could also hear the grin in her voice. Meanwhile, Elodie looked like she wanted to bolt.

"I'm so sorry. You have company," Elodie said hurriedly. "I should've called first. Or texted."

Elodie was about to turn tail and run, but I caught her by the arm before she could.

"Elodie, this is my agent, Andrea. Andrea, this is Elodie. She's a friend," I said.

Andrea shook Elodie's hand, Elodie looking like a deer in headlights.

"Lovely to meet you," said Andrea. "Mac, I'll email you later. Have fun *cooking*."

When I shut the door behind Andrea, Elodie's brows dipped. "Cooking? Are you making something?"

I sighed. "Don't ask. Come on in."

I could tell that Elodie was looking around and noticing the changes. After teasing me about living in a total bachelor pad, I realized she was right. And there was zero reason I hadn't finished furnishing the house. It wasn't a priority, but I wanted Elodie to know I'd listened to her. And I also wanted her to feel at home here.

Laying it on kinda strong, my dude, I thought to myself. Though I pushed the thought aside.

"You've been busy," Elodie finally said, her hands on her hips.

"Not really. I paid lots of other people to do this for me."

She laughed. "Okay, well, whoever you hired did a good job." Her eyes sparkled. "Now you've upgraded from a frat bro's dorm room to a bachelor pad."

"Hey, come on now." I pointed at the vase on one of the many side tables. "I have *décor* now."

"You sure do." Elodie patted my arm.

I covered her hand with mine, and she didn't pull away. All the worry about her not signing the contract disappeared. I could see in her expression she was still interested. Thank fuck for that, because I'd only wanted her more with each day that we'd been apart since Denver.

"I did want to talk to you about something," she murmured.

"I figured. I'm also impressed you remembered where I live. And you got through the security gate . . ."

"I might've noticed the code you punched in the night we came here. Sixty-nine, sixty-nine wasn't too hard to remember." Her reply was sheepish.

"Well, I'm glad you found it memorable and made use of it."

She nibbled on her bottom lip. "I wanted to ask if we could do something before I signed the contract."

"What's that?"

"I'd like to have sex with you. Just once."

I froze. My entire body going on alert. The hairs on the back of my neck rose in both dismay and anticipation. "Oh really?"

Elodie put some space between us, again, to my dismay. "I just want to see how we are together without signing anything official."

"Take a test drive, you mean?"

"Something like that. I mean, it'd stink if I signed the contract and sex between us sucked, right?"

I shook my head and pulled Elodie to me until we were nose to nose. "There's no way in hell that'd ever fucking happen," I growled.

Her eyes grew wide, her breathing heavy. She smelled like citrus, and it took all my self-control not to haul her upstairs right then and there.

"You're probably right," she whispered.

"I know I'm right." I brushed my thumb along her jawline. "But if this is what I have to do to get you to sign the contract, then I will."

"Okay." She sighed. "Good. Thank you."

I bent and leaned my shoulder into her stomach, bringing her over my shoulder before standing to full height. Elodie let out a squeal, laughing. "Mac!"

"Did you have somewhere else you needed to be?"

She laughed. "No, but I didn't think it'd happen *now—*"

"Well, then you thought wrong. You can't just walk into my house and tell me you want to fuck me and then expect to traipse your juicy little ass back out the door." I smacked her rear, lighter than I wanted to. "That's not happening."

I slid her down my body and kissed her hard. Elodie responded with an enthusiasm that made my cock harden. So I lifted her again and guided her legs around my waist. *Yeah. Right there.* Carrying her upstairs to my bedroom was excruciating because it was extra seconds of waiting before I could have her sweet body under mine. To think I was ever upset for even a second about this little proposal of hers. Now, it was like I couldn't get inside her fast enough.

"I'm going to fuck you until you can't even remember your own name." I set her down on her feet at the edge of the bed, tangling my hand in her dark hair. "You're mine, Elodie Andrews. Even if it's just for today."

"Yes. Yes, please." She pulled my head down for another kiss. I didn't have the strength to say no to her. Who fucking could? A gorgeous woman like Elodie, telling a guy she wanted him? Christ himself didn't have that kind of fortitude.

I ran my hands up and down her body, enjoying her soft curves, squeezing her ass and massaging it as I rubbed my tongue alongside hers.

She was panting now. To be desired like this was one of the best aphrodisiacs.

"How much do you want me, baby?" I asked, my voice rough.

"Are you going to make me beg?"

"Fuck yeah, I am." My cock was pressed against her belly. "I want you begging for me to fuck you. Is your pussy wet already?"

Her eyes were glassy as her breath hitched. "Mac."

I guided her onto the bed and crawled on top of her, but I needed her naked first. So I stripped her shirt and jeans off until she was left in only her bra and panties. Seeing her like that just reminded me of the first time we'd met. "I wanted to take you into a back room and fuck you raw that first time I saw you," I admitted, fondling her breasts through the lace of her bra.

"Did you?"

"I thought you could tell."

She shook her head. "I had no idea."

That confession just made me wilder. She was somehow both sweet and sensual without even trying. When I pushed down her bra cups and pinched her nipples, she moaned loudly.

"I can't wait to put clamps on these beauties," I said, unable to break my gaze. Her nipples were a light brown, and they were so erect, so hard and swollen. I sucked one into my mouth until Elodie arched under me. My dick was like steel now, begging to be inside her.

"And then what?" Elodie asked.

I shot her a wicked grin. "I'd start you off easy. Nothing too painful or intense. Just some light clamps. But I'd eat your pussy, barely touching your clit, until you were desperate for more."

She was breathing hard. "But you wouldn't give it to me?"

"No. I'd make you almost come but then back off." I hooked a finger under her panties and pulled them to the side. "You'd be so wet that you'd coat my face."

"You seem very sure of your abilities."

I spread her pussy wide and smiled as I felt how wet she already was. I could feel her beautiful mound throbbing as I dragged a finger through her folds. She shuddered just from that light touch.

"Tell me what you want," I commanded.

She shuddered again. "I don't know."

I lowered myself down her body and lightly licked the top of her pussy, just grazing her clit. "I think you do."

She arched off the bed, then swore under her breath.

"Tell me what you want," I repeated.

She squirmed. "Please touch me."

"Where, Elodie? Where do you want me to touch you?"

I had my hands on her inner thighs, staring at her glistening pussy, but I wasn't touching her again there until she asked me to. She covered her face with her arm.

"My pussy!" she finally yelled. "God, please, Mac."

I laughed darkly. "Your wish is my command, sweetheart."

I fastened my lips on her clit at the same time as I thrust a finger inside her. So hot and beautifully wet. Elodie moaned, her hands clawing at the comforter. She kept arching and moving so much that I had to hold her down just to keep eating her out.

"Damn, woman. Hold still so I can do my job." I chuckled over her pussy before kissing my way up her stomach.

She was practically shaking with her need for me to return my mouth to her clit. I made my way back down, spreading her wider. I decided to tease her for a bit, blowing soft breaths between her legs. She finally grabbed me by the hair as I laughed and returned my mouth to her clit, and I devoured her with even more vigor this time. With each second that passed, more of her arousal covered my face.

Elodie was desperate. I kept sucking her clit until she was on the edge of orgasm, my fingers moving faster and more forcefully. I could feel her about to come when I gave her pussy one last long lick and stood.

Her gaze was unfocused, somewhere far away. "Mac?" she whispered, confused.

"Condom," I growled. "Need one. I need to be inside you now."

I grabbed one from my nightstand, used my teeth to rip open the wrapper, and sheathed myself in record time. Thank God she was wet because I plunged in deep and hard. Elodie gasped in ecstasy.

"Fuck, baby, you're tight." I didn't have the self-control to go slow. Not when Elodie was writhing and moaning with every thrust. She wanted it hard, and I was more than happy to deliver.

Her tits jiggled as I pounded her tight little body until I was balls deep. I could feel my orgasm building, but I gritted my teeth, forcing myself to wait until Elodie came. I kept my eyes on hers, enjoying every look of ecstasy on her face.

I raised Elodie's legs so they hooked over the inside of my elbows. With that angle, I was able to brush her clit with my pelvis with each thrust. I smiled as her eyes rolled back inside her head while her mouth fell open. I bit my lip, nearly drawing blood, to stave off the orgasm that felt ready to burst through me at any given moment.

"Mac—" Elodie dug her nails into my biceps. "Oh my God—"

"You gonna come for me, baby? I can feel your pussy getting tighter around my cock." I leaned down to kiss her. "You wanna come for me?"

She nodded. "I do. I need to."

I lifted her a little higher, angling my hips and plunging even deeper. She screamed, coming undone in long, deep shudders. Her pussy clamped around me, milking my orgasm from my body. I saw stars and might've even blacked out for a moment.

Fuck, that was incredible. *So, so damn good.* I kissed her for a while, gliding in and out still fully hard, not wanting the moment to end. Elodie sighed happily in my arms. She looked so content, as if she could snuggle up and go to sleep. But that definitely would *not* happen anytime soon.

Instead, I abruptly flipped her over. Elodie gasped.

I hooked an arm around her waist and hoisted her to her knees. "Up on all fours, sweetheart. We're just getting started."

I woke to the smell of bacon but found my bed empty. I glanced at my phone. 7:00 a.m.

I was about to get up and go find Elodie when she came into my bedroom holding a tray. Atop it were two plates, along with a couple of mugs of coffee, and a glass of orange juice.

"Did you seriously make me breakfast?" I asked, amazed.

"Well, I made *us* breakfast. I was starving, and since you just restocked your fridge . . ." She shrugged, smiling.

"I'm starving too." I winked. "But I suppose food sounds good, too."

Elodie looked especially gorgeous this morning. Her hair was down and messy, her cheeks rosy. I could see multiple hickeys on her chest and neck, which only made me want to add a few more to her collection. Those tiny bruises were like foreshadowing in the best way.

It didn't help that she was wearing only a tank top and boy shorts either, her nipples hard against the thin fabric of her shirt. My stomach rumbling was the only thing that kept me from tumbling her back into bed a third time. How the hell had I gotten so lucky?

Elodie settled onto the bed next to me, the tray in front of both of us. She'd cooked us eggs and bacon, even going so far as to put a flower in a vase. But I was mostly interested in the folded papers under my plate.

I slipped them out to discover the signed contract. There was what looked like a red wine stain on the corner. Had she been pondering it while buzzed?

"You'd already signed them when you came over?" I asked.

Elodie smiled. "Maybe. Does it matter?" Her smile was infectious.

I pulled her into a hard kiss. "You won't regret this," I vowed.

Chapter 13

Elodie

A week later, I couldn't help but notice that Mac seemed distracted. I'd stayed over, but when I'd woken up in the middle of the night to pee, Mac had been awake downstairs.

"Can't sleep?" I wrapped my arms around him from behind.

He jumped a little. "Shit, Elodie. What are you doing awake?"

"I could ask you the same thing. It's the middle of the night."

He hadn't turned on the TV, and he'd left his phone in the bedroom. Had he just been down here alone in silence?

"Go back to bed," he said, turning to kiss me.

"Only if you come with me."

"I will. Just give me a few minutes."

I wanted to protest, but a yawn stopped me. I was too sleepy, and it was cold downstairs. I tried to wait for Mac to come back to bed, but sleep claimed me soon after.

When I awoke in the morning, Mac was in bed, his back turned to me. I cuddled against him, enjoying how warm he was.

He swore under his breath when my cold feet touched his calves. "Jesus! Baby, your feet are frozen. How are they so cold?"

I grinned. "Sorry. I must've stuck them out from under the covers without realizing it. You'll just have to warm them up for me." I tucked my feet between his thighs, which just made him swear again.

He turned over to face me. "Sleep okay?" He kissed my forehead.

"Yeah. You? When did you come back to bed?"

He shrugged one shoulder. "Not sure. Three o'clock?"

"Why were you downstairs?"

He seemed to want to talk about anything else, but he also didn't know how stubborn I could be.

"I have an away game tomorrow," he finally admitted.

I raised an eyebrow. "Okay. Are you going to North Korea, or . . .?"

He chuckled. "Not that intense. I'm going back to Coeur d'Alene. It's in Idaho. It's not my hometown, exactly, but close enough. I haven't been back there in a long time." He rubbed his chin.

I froze for a moment and realized I had to act like I'd had no idea where he was from, that I hadn't intensely researched him and his family just a few weeks prior.

"And you don't want to go?" I asked, curious now.

He rolled onto his back. "I don't know. It's complicated."

There were so many things I'd yet to learn about this man. I propped myself up on one elbow and raised an expectant eyebrow.

He laughed at my expression. "You know, you should've been a cop. Or a lawyer. You're good at getting people to talk."

You have no idea. "Go on."

"It's just weird going back. Lots of memories, you know? I always leave tickets for my parents. But they never come to my games."

I winced. "I'm sorry. That sucks."

"I don't even really want to see them. They're judgmental. We always get into arguments. They've never approved of me." He gave me a confused look. "Is this the definition of insanity? Continuing to do the same thing and hoping for a different outcome?"

"If it's insane, then it's totally understandable. I think everybody wants their parents' approval in the end."

I couldn't help but think of my extended family, how they'd kicked out my mom but now suddenly wanted to communicate with me. They surely wouldn't approve of my current plans, that was for sure.

"What about you? What are your parents like?" Mac asked me.

I felt an emptiness in the pit of my stomach. "I don't have any parents. My mom died when I was eighteen, and I haven't seen my dad since I was little."

Now Mac looked sad. "Shit, Elodie, I'm sorry. I shouldn't complain."

"Eh, it's not a competition. My mom and I were on our own, and since she had to work so much, I knew how to take care of myself. I miss her every day, of course. But I'm grateful she taught me as much as she did before she passed."

Mac took my hand and squeezed it. "How did she die?"

"Cancer. Lung cancer, even though she never smoked. Crazy, right? She died a year after she was diagnosed."

The memories of Mom's diagnosis, the chemo, radiation, her shedding hair, losing so much weight, her disappearing before my very eyes . . . But what was saddest was that, by the end, I was relieved when she'd passed. Because it meant she was no longer in pain. Her death definitely taught me that life was unfair.

"Do you want to go to Idaho with me?" Mac asked.

I stared at him, surprised. "Are you sure?"

"Yeah, I'm sure. And don't worry about meeting my parents. They never attend." His smile was grim now.

"Tell me about them."

Mac blinked. "My parents? Why?"

"I'm just curious. You don't have to talk about them if you don't want to, though."

Mac sighed but proceeded to talk a bit about his parents. He told me about how his dad was a preacher and his mom a homemaker. How they'd had such high expectations for their oldest son, and he'd dashed them to pieces by the time he'd entered high school. Oh, they were proud he was a professional hockey player, but he wasn't a "man of God," as Mac termed it.

"I didn't get married at twenty and start having a thousand children," Mac rolled his eyes. "I also stopped going to church once I went off to college."

I grimaced. "I'm sure your parents loved that."

"They almost called the cops when I said I was an atheist." Mac snorted. "Man, that was a huge fight. My dad nearly punched me in the face when I said God didn't exist. The weird thing is that I didn't even know what I believed at that point. I just wanted to piss him off. It's what I seem to do best." Mac sighed. "Anyway, enough of that."

He rolled on top of me, his smile seductive now. "Let's take our minds off this very boring topic, hmm?"

The night of the game in Coeur d'Alene, Idaho, I was cursing myself for not wearing warmer clothes when I stopped in my tracks. Inside the private box were two people, a man and a woman. Mac had told me I'd be by myself. I realized the two people already inside were none other than Mac's mom and dad. *Holy shit.*

They both turned at my approach. I felt my knees get watery when Bob Mackenzie's intense gaze landed on me. He looked just like Mac, despite the silver hair and wrinkled visage. And Mac's mom was gorgeous, her gray hair immaculate. A large diamond ring flashed on her hand, and I could tell her clothes were designer, custom fit for her perfectly.

Bob and Judy stared at me blankly. "Can we help you . . .?" Judy asked me kindly.

I scrambled for a reason I'd be there. *I'm your son's lover. We signed a contract even. Did you know he's into BDSM?* I nearly burst into hysterical laughter. Shaking off the insane thoughts, I squeaked out, "I'm a friend of Mac's. I'm Elodie." I held out my hand. "You must be Mac's parents? I can see the resemblance."

Bob and Judy exchanged glances. Bob eventually took my hand in a firm grip. Judy got up and gestured for me to have a seat.

"It's lovely to meet you. Melody, you said?" Judy asked. Her voice was kind, and her expression full of curiosity.

"It's just Elodie. No 'M.'" I sat down with a wry smile. "My parents liked to make things complicated with choosing my name."

"That's pretty. Elodie." Judy turned to her husband. "Don't you think, honey?"

Bob grunted. "You said you're a friend of Mac's?"

I forced myself not to squirm under his intense scrutiny. "That's right. I'm from LA, and Mac invited me up here. I've never been to Idaho before. I had no idea how pretty it was." Now I felt like I was babbling.

"We live in White Rock," Judy said. "Although we come to Coeur d'Alene often. Did you grow up in Los Angeles?"

"For the most part, yeah," I replied.

"If you have time while you're here, you should go to Silver Beach. It's the best spot near the lake," Bob said. To my surprise, he even smiled.

I didn't know how to reconcile the estranged, judgmental parents Mac had described with these people in front of me. They seemed like your average, supportive parents who wanted to get to know their son's friend.

"We're hoping to take Mac out for his birthday dinner after the game," Judy said. "Would you like to join us?"

"It's his birthday?" I blurted.

Bob chuckled. "Indeed. But it's no surprise he didn't tell you. He's never been a big fan of parties or the attention that comes along with birthdays."

"Just like his father," Judy said. She shook her head. "The men in this family act like birthday parties are torture."

"Getting people to sing to you *is* torture," Bob groused.

I felt a little hurt that Mac hadn't told me it was his birthday. I also felt strangely guilty, like I should've known when his birthday was already. I was sure I'd come across it when googling him way back when, hadn't I? But if what Bob said was right and the apple hadn't fallen far from the tree, perhaps Mac was intentionally trying to forget about this day.

Fortunately for all three of us, but mostly for me, the hockey game kept us from having to keep making small talk. When Bob went to get Judy a soda, he asked me if I wanted anything. Although I declined, he still brought back some popcorn that all three of us could share, making sure we had our own bag to eat out of. At one point, Mac spotted us. He flashed me an apologetic look. It felt like an out-of-body experience—me sitting here eating popcorn with Mac's parents. I could've never predicted that this would be how I'd spend the day.

After the game, Mac's parents and I were brought to a spot near the locker room to wait for Mac to appear. I was nervous with anticipation. How would Mac react to seeing his parents? Would he want me to join them all for dinner? Did I even mention his birthday if it would only upset him?

As far as I knew, Mac hadn't had any intention of telling his parents of my existence. And how did we explain our relationship? I'd simply described us as being friends, but if Mac said he was my boyfriend . . . I shook myself. We weren't dating. Not really, anyway. I highly doubted Bob and Judy would understand our arrangement.

When Mac saw the three of us standing together, his eyes widened. I could see the shock on his handsome face. But that mask he was able to take on and off for the press quickly slipped into place. He approached us warily but not unkindly. He shook his dad's hand, then hugged his mom before his gaze landed on me. His expression was hard to read, almost apologetic.

"We got to know your friend here," Judy said before I could speak. "We wanted to take you both out for dinner to celebrate your birthday."

"Oh, Mom, you don't have to do that," Mac said.

Bob frowned. "Don't act like that."

Mac tensed. "I don't want to put you out."

"Sweetheart." His mom rested a hand on his chest. "We haven't seen you in so long. Let us take you out."

Mac and Bob seemed to have a staring contest, which I could only describe as similar to two dogs circling each other, waiting for the other to show weakness. I grew tense just watching them. I became more and more interested in the true dynamics of this family when no one else was around.

But then Mac nodded tightly, even as I could tell that he didn't seem remotely excited about having dinner with his parents.

This will be one hell of an interesting evening, that's for sure.

Bob and Judy drove us to a local steakhouse. Mac and I sat in the back, so we didn't get a chance to talk privately, except for a few exchanged glances. Inside, the restaurant was crowded, and for some reason, I got the feeling it was a place Mac might've frequented back when he lived here.

He leaned down to whisper in my ear as we exited the car, "Sorry about this."

"Don't worry about it. It'll be fine." I made sure his parents were far enough ahead as we walked to the restaurant from the parking lot before adding, "I also said you were just a friend. I didn't know what else to say."

"It's fine. They probably don't believe you, though." Mac's eyes sparkled. "But maybe don't tell them about how I spanked your ass last night either."

I smacked his arm, rolling my eyes, and Mac smiled for the first time since walking out of the locker room. But when we were seated in a booth near the back of the restaurant, the mask from earlier was firmly in place.

Bob started grilling Mac with questions even before the server took our orders. Did he overpay for his place out in LA? Was he still driving that fancy car? Had he been to church lately? Judy interjected on occasion, but for all intents and purposes, it was almost like we women weren't even present.

When Mac ordered a salad and a chicken breast, his father remarked, "How do you keep your strength up eating bird food like that?"

"Since when do birds eat chicken?" Mac countered.

"Honey, you know Mac has to be careful about what he eats. He's an athlete, after all." Judy smiled and put a hand on her husband's arm. I got the feeling she was trying to get him to ease up.

Bob shook his head. "You know Eric? Steve White's son? He ate a steak every day and played football. Was the strongest player on the team, too. Probably never ate a salad in his damn life."

"His poor gut," I said jokingly. Mac's parents turned and stared at me. So I added, "I mean, you gotta eat fiber at least sometimes. Right?"

"Dad, I'm pretty sure last I heard, Eric just had his second heart attack." Mac's tone was dry. "That's where all that steak got him."

There was a strange tension between Mac and Bob that I didn't fully understand. Judy didn't seem to be a part of it. She seemed more like the peacekeeper. And here I was, a total third wheel, almost wishing I'd stayed in LA. *And miss this possible scoop of Mac's family?*

I began cutting my own steak, suddenly wishing I'd been smart like Mac and had gotten something lighter to eat. The red meat and baked potato sat heavily in my stomach after just a few bites.

"It was a great game tonight," Judy said. "I really enjoyed watching you play."

"I'm glad you finally decided to come," Mac replied, wiping his mouth with a napkin.

Judy looked embarrassed. "You know we've been busy, what with running the church and whatnot—"

"We never asked you to put tickets aside for us." Bob folded his arms across his chest.

Mac's jaw ticked. "No, but I wanted to all the same."

"That's just how you are, isn't it? You just do what you want, no matter what else anyone thinks." Bob downed some of his water.

Despite Judy's attempts to hush him, Bob wasn't deterred, and Mac looked pissed. His jaw was rigid, and his expression grim. I wondered if the two men would come to blows. My cheeks heated as I suddenly grew uncomfortable to be in the middle of what was clearly a long-standing, private family matter.

"I'm not going to apologize for how I choose to live my own life," Mac said through gritted teeth. "Because it is *my* life."

"Even when it's immoral? Even when it goes against what God wants for us?" Bob's voice gentled, which made things strangely tenser. "You know you'll always be welcome in the family, but not without letting go of these . . . delusions."

Now, I was confused. I caught Judy's glance, but she just shook her head slightly as if to say, *Keep quiet.*

"Delusions?" Mac shot back. "You're the one who's delusional—"

Judy interrupted, "*Stop it,* you two. We came out to celebrate Mac's birthday and to spend some time together as a family for once. Plus, we have a guest. So either you two shape up, or I'm going home and taking Elodie with me."

Bob and Mac scowled, which would've been funny if the situation weren't already so tense. We sat in silence for a long while, and I played Bob's words back in my head. *Not without letting go of these delusions.* What was he referring to? Did he somehow know about Mac's sexual interests? I suppose it didn't take much to disappoint a rigidly religious man, so perhaps, it was something else.

The dinner continued, and Bob and Mac barely spoke to each other. Judy and I tried our best to keep the conversation light, but by the time Bob got the check, we'd all fallen into awkward silence again.

"We're just going to grab an Uber," Mac said as we stood out front. He typed into his cell and let out a relieved breath. "It'll be here in two minutes."

"Uber." Bob shook his head. "Whatever."

The four of us stood out front waiting. Thankfully, it really was only two minutes before a black SUV pulled up. Mac glanced at the license plate.

"2ZGE857. This is us."

I said goodbye to Bob and Judy, and Mac opened the door for me to get in the car. He took a moment to say his own goodbyes before joining me in the back seat. The man could walk out of the locker room after playing an intense hockey game and not look tired, but right now he looked like he'd been run over by a semi.

"Christ, I'm sorry about that," he said, dragging his fingers through his hair. "I never thought they'd show up. This is the first time they have in five damn years."

"Lucky me, I guess . . ." I wrapped my arm around his bicep and nuzzled. A long moment later, he put an arm around my shoulders.

"Yeah. Not the greatest timing for them to finally decide to come."

"Why did you keep putting tickets aside if they haven't shown up in so many years?" I asked.

Mac let out a sad laugh. "I don't know. Stubbornness? Not wanting to be the first one to give in and say our relationship is officially over? Or maybe not wanting to admit that my parents hate me?"

"Your mom doesn't hate you." That I knew for certain. *But his father?*

"No, but she'll never really stand up to my dad either." Mac looked down at me. "But I'm tired of thinking about them."

"I mean, it is your birthday. How about we take this back to the hotel?" I smiled seductively. "You can do whatever you want to me. Maybe that'll make up for tonight."

Mac's eyes darkened, but this time, it wasn't from anger. It was from desire. "Anything? You're playing with fire, baby."

"I'm okay with getting burned then, birthday boy."

He groaned and hauled me from my seat onto his lap. I giggled, loving how much he wanted me. *Me,* Elodie Andrews. It still felt like a dream that a man as sexy as Cole Mackenzie desired me when he could have practically any woman he wanted.

"We'll go slow tonight," Mac said. But I got the feeling he was saying it more to himself than to me.

I nodded, a little relieved. Although I trusted him, I wasn't sure I was ready to get whipped and bound as he pounded my ass, even if I was certain that would be in my not-so-distant future.

Then again, if it's Mac, I know I'll have a great time.

The hotel was only ten minutes away. By the time we pulled up, I was antsy to get inside and get started. The door to our room was barely closed when Mac's tone changed. "Take off your clothes," he growled.

Every hair on my body lifted. *God, he's so sexy when he takes control.*

I nodded and stripped out of my clothes. Mac's gaze stayed on me even as he went to his suitcase. The way my body reacted to him so instantly, so naturally was seriously mind-blowing.

He pulled out two ties and pointed at the bed. "Get up on the bed."

I nodded again, my gaze on the floor. Apparently, we'd entered the Dom-sub era of this relationship. I'd never considered myself a meek person, but something about Mac's commanding presence made me want to give him full control.

I crawled onto the bed. Mac joined me, still fully clothed, and began binding my wrists behind my back and my ankles together.

He grinned, leaning back to examine his handiwork. "Aren't you a gorgeous sight?"

I squirmed. I couldn't really move, which meant that I was completely in Mac's control. The bindings were tight but not painful. Based on the intricate knots that Mac tied them with, they probably wouldn't be too easy to get out of. But that wasn't exactly a problem, considering there was nowhere else I would rather be right then.

Mac flipped me over so I was on my stomach. He placed a pillow under my chest and near my head. Then he started kissing and licking from my neck down my spine, my skin on fire with every touch of his lips.

His hands massaged the globes of my ass. It felt so good, so relaxing. At least until the first smack came. Then the second, and the third. The burn of his hand stung but was also exhilarating. I squealed. Each loud sound of his hand connecting with my ass made me grow more and more excited.

"Such a naughty girl," he crooned, the spanking intensifying. "Making me want you every second of every day. Who do you think you are, showing up here?"

"You asked me to come," I protested.

That earned me the hardest smack on the ass yet. "I didn't say you could speak, did I?"

I shook my head. Mac parted my ass cheeks and leaned down, licking through the crease. *Oh God.* I wished I could touch him, but I was entirely at his mercy.

"What I wouldn't give to fuck this ass." He groaned, slipping a finger between my cheeks and circling my hole with his finger. "I bet it'd be like a vise around my cock."

Chills ran through me. I'd never done anal. Todd had brought up the subject once, but it'd never interested me. At that moment, though, I would've said yes. I would've said yes to anything.

Mac parted my thighs as much as he could with the bindings on my ankles, feeling my wetness coat his hand. Quivering, I pushed against his fingers, desperately wanting him inside me.

"Patience," he said. I could hear the smile in his voice, but patience was the last thing I had.

I tried to buck against his hand, but that only earned me another smack on my ass.

"What did I just say?" he warned.

I moaned. "But Mac . . ." I barely recognized my own voice. It sounded so desperate.

Mac finally slid his hand between my legs and stroked my pussy. "So fucking wet for me already."

"Yes," I breathed.

He rubbed my clit, making small circles with just the right amount of pressure. I could feel my orgasm building. But he stopped as I got to the brink and abruptly flipped me over again. Grabbing the binding at my ankles, he dragged me to the edge of the bed. I was breathless as he took out his cock, making me watch as he stroked up and down painstakingly slowly. A bead of cum dripped down his shaft, and my mouth watered. His smile was wicked, his gaze heated.

"Do you want me to fuck you, Elodie?" His voice brushed like velvet across my skin.

I nodded. "Please, please, Mac." I kept trying to part my legs, even as I knew I couldn't with the bindings on my ankles.

"Not yet. First, you're going to suck my cock. You'll take it all until you can't breathe and choke for air. Understand?"

I nodded. My entire body tingled with anticipation as Mac climbed onto the bed, hovering over me. He fisted his cock and guided it into my mouth. I licked the head until I could taste more salty cum beading at the tip, then sucked him in with enthusiasm, especially as Mac groaned out my name. I wished I could use my hands, but something was so freaking erotic about only being able to use my lips and tongue on him. And about the way he was unabashedly using my mouth—I wanted to be used by this man.

Mac angled his hips, pressing his cock farther down my throat until it hit the back of it. My eyes watered.

"Breathe through your nose. Come on, baby. You can do it." He stilled for a long moment giving me a chance to get used to the feeling and allow my breaths to even out.

"There you go. Such a good girl," he crooned, stroking my hair gently. "You love sucking my dick, don't you?"

Panting, I nodded. I waited for more, for him to begin fucking my face, but when he pulled back, he pulled all the way out.

I opened my mouth to protest, but Mac shook his head.

"You'll take what I give you. Understood?"

I swallowed and nodded again. Mac flipped me onto my stomach again, moved me to the middle of the bed, and then thrust his cock into my dripping pussy from behind. Thank goodness. I'd had no guarantees he'd even planned to fuck me tonight despite how badly I might've begged. I'd feared maybe he'd deny me as some form of torture.

With my ankles still bound, he felt even larger inside me, filling me so completely. It didn't take long before my orgasm was barreling down again. I cried out, my entire body shaking.

"Your pussy is so fucking tight." Mac wrapped my hair around his fist, yanking until my head came off the bed as he pounded into me. "So fucking tight."

I was entirely at his mercy and loved every second of it. I could feel myself squeezing his cock with every stroke. At the same time, I tensed my muscles in an attempt to stop myself from coming, not quite ready for this to end.

When he yanked hard on my hair, though, I lost control as my climax tore through me. I screamed, not caring that everyone in the hotel could probably hear me. Mac grunted and thrust one last time before he pulled out and came on my back, hot cum painting my skin.

"Fuck, Elodie," he said through heaving breaths.

I collapsed onto the bed, completely spent. Mac gently untied my ankles and wrists, cradling me into his arms, so tight yet gentle.

He kissed my forehead, my cheeks, and then my lips. "Are you okay?"

I could barely form coherent sentences. All I could do was nod. "I'm okay."

"I wasn't too rough? I said I'd go easy on you, but . . ."

"It was amazing." I touched his cheek. "But I think I'm half dead. So maybe ask me again tomorrow."

That made him grin.

"I'm glad it was to your liking. There's a lot more where that came from. But I think you deserve your rest tonight."

He eventually got up, cleaned us both up, and then tucked us into bed. I'd be going to sleep having been fucked better than I'd ever had in my life. Before he even turned off the lamp, I was out like a light.

Despite my pleading, Mac couldn't stay the night with me in my hotel room. Although we'd both fallen asleep for a bit, I was woken up a few hours later to the sound of movement around the room.

"I have curfew," he said, rolling his eyes as he pulled his pants on.

I propped myself up on the bed to watch him. I loved watching him pad around the room as he gathered his clothes, his muscles bunching and contracting with every movement. It was truly a feast for the eyes.

Mac had a lean but muscular build with a smattering of chest hair, along with a few tattoos on his biceps. His hair had grown out in the past few weeks, which made him look even more delicious than usual. There wasn't a moment when I didn't want to run my fingers through it.

He caught me staring and shot me a grin. "Like what you see?"

"Sure do. How about you do a spin for me?"

He laughed but complied. "You good now?"

He was wickedly adorable. I made sure to slap his ass as he passed by. "Now I'm good."

That slap resulted in him pouncing on me and giving me a few firm smacks of my own. He growled in my ear that I'd better watch myself; otherwise, I'd face a much worse punishment one day.

I shivered in anticipation. "Even worse than a good firm spanking while tied up?" I asked.

"Oh, sweetheart, much, much worse." He kissed me hard. "I took it easy on you last night. The fun's just getting started, you know."

My brain struggled to compute how that was going easy. "I think you might end up killing me."

"Only in the best possible way." Mac gave me one last smacking kiss before sighing and putting on his shoes. "I have to get back."

Truly bummed that he had to leave, I sighed. "Fine, fine. Have your wicked way with me and then abandon me."

He got to the door and looked back with his hand on the handle.

"Thank you, Elodie."

"For . . ."

"Everything. Signing the contract, coming, dealing with my parents, being a good girl for me last night."

I smiled. "I had fun."

"Me too, sweetheart."

"Text me, okay?"

"Of course." He winked, and then he was gone.

Chapter 14
Mac

I was working out in the Blades gym when Brady arrived. We started doing reps together before getting on to the treadmills to finish things off. Bastard was in better shape than I was, and I actually found it quite motivating. That was part of the reason I always scheduled my workouts with him.

"So how's Elodie?" Brady asked.

His tone told me that he wanted to pry for more information. "She's good."

"Don't give me that look, dude. I have eyeballs."

"What's your point?"

Brady shrugged. "Just that she's the first girl I've seen at our games. You never bring women around."

Brady wasn't aware of my predilections, and I wasn't about to confess all to him either. *He wouldn't understand.* Besides, Brady had a big mouth. He'd tell everyone on the team before you could say boo.

"How's her friend?" Brady then asked. "Hannah?"

He tried to sound innocent, which just made me

chuckle. "Seriously, dude? That's what you wanted to know about?" I shook my head. "You're fucking annoying."

"When it comes to beautiful women? Yeah, I am." Brady narrowed his eyes. "And you're dating her best friend. So Elodie must've said something."

"Why would she? I've only met Hannah that one time."

Brady grunted. "I tried to get her number that night, but she wouldn't do it. Said she didn't trust athletes not to break her heart." He grinned. "Imagine that?"

I laughed. "A swing and a miss for Brady Carmichael? Now, that's shocking as hell. Has any woman turned you down before?"

"No." Brady was glowering now. "It's not a fucking joke, man. It's driving me nuts. I can't stop thinking about her."

"She's probably just playing hard to get. Women like to do that sometimes."

"Maybe." Brady increased the treadmill speed, probably so he didn't have to keep talking about how Hannah had somehow evaded his legendary charms.

As long as I'd known Brady, he'd always been a playboy. Whereas I'd preferred to keep my arrangements private, Brady tended to flaunt them. I'd lost count of how many times he'd come to a party with a new beautiful woman on his arm. And more than one lady had tried to storm into the locker room over the years to yell at him for not calling her back after he'd slept with her.

"I've never seen you like this about a woman," I remarked after we'd gone to the locker room to clean up.

"I can't get her out of my damn head." Brady toweled his wet hair dry. "It's fucking annoying. Is it just because she told me no?"

"Maybe. Or maybe you might actually *like* her."

"Huh. Maybe. But seeing as though I don't know her all that well, I have a feeling it might be the former."

"I mean, have you ever thought about settling down someday?" I asked.

To my surprise, Brady didn't crack a joke. Instead, he seemed to think it over for a moment. "Yeah, eventually. But I've just never found the right woman." He stared off, seeming deep in thought.

"Something you not telling me?"

"There was someone once who I could've seen myself marrying someday. But she was sort of off-limits." He stopped short of divulging anything further.

"And?"

"And . . . I'd rather not get into it right now." He shook his head. "Doesn't matter anyway. It's in the past."

Hmm.

"Well, if you're looking to meet someone of value, you might start dating women who know that the Earth is round, for starters."

Brady guffawed. "Yelena was a special one, that was for sure. But damn, she was smoking hot, wasn't she? Legs for days, amazing tits—"

"But dumb as a fence post," I replied wryly.

"Fine, fine. Yeah, she wasn't too smart. And she wasn't exactly interested in settling down either." Brady stretched out his legs, looking thoughtful still. "I guess it'd be nice to find a woman who wants to be with *me*, not with a hockey player. Like if she had no idea who I was. Maybe I need to go looking for a woman in Siberia. Somebody who doesn't have the Internet."

That made me think of the club. It wasn't Siberia, but because no one wanted their identities outed, it was a place where I could pretend I was just like everyone else and that nothing about my hockey player status was special.

"You could date someone who doesn't have the Internet, or you could just date someone who isn't shallow," I pointed out.

Brady's gaze focused on me now. "And what about you? You aren't exactly getting married anytime soon either."

I shook my head. Marriage had never been in the cards for me. Hell, a regular, monogamous relationship had never been either.

You could sign a contract for a sexual relationship that had clauses for when to end things. You could control what you both could do and what you both couldn't do.

No messy feelings were involved. Just sex and business. But actual romantic relationships? Those were the opposite of staying in control. You just had to trust that the other person wouldn't fuck you up completely. As soon as the heart got involved, well, that was dangerous territory.

"I'm fine with what I'm doing now," I said.

Brady didn't look convinced, but our conversation was cut short when another player came into the locker room. Brady then tried to get me to ask Elodie for Hannah's number, but I told him to go to hell. He was going to have to figure that one out on his own. I was no damn matchmaker.

When I arrived home later that afternoon, I was surprised to see my mom calling me. Since that didn't happen very often, a feeling of dread hit me right in the stomach.

When I picked up, her words stopped me in my tracks.

"Mac, hi."

"Hey, Mom. What's going on?"

She sighed loudly. "I'm calling to give you some news."

I froze. Did something happen to my father? "What news?"

"Well, there's no easy way to say this, so I suppose I'll just say it. Caroline Bradford has pancreatic cancer. She's dying, Mac."

Caroline Bradford. The woman who'd changed the course of my life, for better or for worse. The woman who'd taught me everything I knew. The first woman I'd ever loved. The reason I'd probably never go down the love path again. There were too many memories to count. And too many memories I'd wanted to bury when it came to her.

Caro. I sat in my living room, staring at the glass of whiskey I'd poured hours ago, unable to sleep. *Caro is dying.*

My mom had explained that Caroline was in the hospital and had been given only a few months to live. *It's stage 4. I'm sorry, Mac.*

Then I'd heard Dad in the background, and the call had ended. It upset me that he might've actually derived some pleasure from this. He wouldn't have wanted Mom to talk to me about Caroline. To be honest, I was still in shock she'd even called me to let me know in the first place. The last time my parents had spoken Caroline's name, we'd had our worst fight ever. That was the day I ended up leaving home.

I almost resented Mom for telling me about Caroline. But that wasn't fair. She was just trying to be . . . I didn't even know. Helpful? Understanding? Compassionate?

I finished off my whiskey and considered going upstairs to bed. But I wasn't tired. Despite the alcohol in my veins, I was awake.

Too awake.

Would Elodie pick up if I called? I stared at my phone screen as if it would tell me the answer.

But if I called her right now, I'd have to tell her why. Did I expect her to understand what'd happened between me and Caroline Bradford?

The mere thought made me shudder. She'd start to read into it and draw the wrong conclusions. Or maybe they'd be the right conclusions. All I knew was that I'd had enough to deal with when my parents found out. Although Elodie had been nothing but understanding since we'd met, I didn't want to give her a reason to run either.

I needed a distraction.

The Scarlet Rope was as busy as ever when I arrived. When the cab driver dropped me off a block away, he'd given me a confused look. There wasn't anything open nearby, given that it was already two o'clock in the morning.

"You sure this is the right place?" he'd asked me.

I smiled wryly. "I'm sure. Thanks for the ride."

The club, with its sights, sounds, and smells, brought a wave of blessed relief to my senses. I nodded at a few women I recognized. Delilah sat at the bar like she often did with a group of men surrounding her like a queen with her subjects. She raised an eyebrow as I passed by, which I took as an invitation.

"I haven't seen you here on a Wednesday night in years," she remarked. "Or I guess it's Thursday morning, isn't it?"

"I've lost track," I admitted.

One guy close to Delilah's elbow looked irritated when I sat near her. Delilah gave him a look that said, *Don't push your luck.*

"And by yourself?" Delilah leaned forward toward me. "Where's the pretty girl you've been hanging around with?"

"I'm alone tonight."

"Hmm. I talked to her, you know. Definitely not the usual type of woman who comes around here. She was like a deer in headlights. It was cute but odd." Delilah's gaze sliced through me. "You don't usually go for the sweet, innocent ones."

"Since when do you know what type of woman I go for?"

"Darling, I've been working this club since before you showed up with your pretty face and tight ass. I know everything that goes on around here."

"Even more than Serena does?" I asked wryly.

Delilah snorted. "I'd say so. I can tell you that guy over there in the gold mask? He begged me to peg him the first time we had a session. And that guy in the orange shirt? He loves when I play his stepmother."

I held up a hand. "Christ, I get it. You know everything. The CIA should probably hire you."

"Who's to say they haven't?" Her grin was wicked. "But enough about me. What's up with you?"

I almost considered telling Delilah everything, but she wasn't exactly my therapist. And she had no reason to keep any information I divulged to herself.

"Do you have any recommendations of scenes to watch tonight?" I asked instead.

"Hmm, well, Ariadne and Tessa are doing an orgy tonight. I think it's up to ten people. I swear it probably started five hours ago."

When I was about to go find said orgy, Delilah stopped me. "That girl. Roxy, right? Be careful with her."

I waited for her to explain herself, raising a single eyebrow.

"She's clearly not one for this world. Whatever you've gotten her to agree to . . ." Delilah shrugged. "She just seems like the type who catches feelings easily. And you and I both know you're the type of guy who women always end up falling for."

"Baby, are you saying you're in love with me?" I joked.

Delilah rolled her eyes. "I'm not your baby, sweetheart. And besides, you're not my type. I don't do Doms, remember?"

I leaned down and gave her a quick kiss on the cheek. "Too bad. Because I'd pay big money to watch your ass get whipped good."

She waved me away, clearly done with me. As I meandered, trying to find some entertainment to watch, Delilah's words stuck in my brain no matter how hard I tried to shake them loose.

Had I made a mistake in getting into an arrangement with Elodie? I hadn't pushed her. She'd signed the contract of her own free will. Besides, she was an intelligent woman. She knew what she was doing . . . right?

The thought of hurting Elodie was like a blow to the chest. How had she already managed to wheedle her way into my life like this? If I weren't careful, I'd be the one catching feelings. Which was preposterous—I *never* got emotionally involved.

Not since Caroline, that is. *Caroline.* My chest ached. I'd come here to forget, and here I was thinking about her. I shook my head as I went in desperate search of anything that would take my mind off her.

I found the right room and sat near the front, taking in the scene: Ariadne and Tessa were making out while three men serviced them. One guy was lying on the floor eating Ariadne out, another fucking her in the ass from behind, while the third guy was fingering Tessa and rubbing her engorged clit. The five other people were fucking around them, the sounds of flesh against flesh intense and arousing.

But even as my body got more aroused watching the scene, my mind kept going to other places. Enjoying the club without Elodie felt wrong in a strange way. We hadn't signed any agreement that we'd be monogamous. For all I knew, Elodie was dating other guys besides me.

That thought alone made me want to punch the wall. Was that possible? Would Elodie date multiple guys at once?

Calm your tits, I told myself. Hadn't she broken up with her boyfriend before she'd ever considered sleeping with me? Remembering that brought me relief. That's right. It wouldn't make sense for her to be taking up with anyone new besides me if she'd just broken up with her boyfriend. Or at least I had to tell myself that.

I drank a few more whiskeys, needing the buzz of the alcohol to tame my racing thoughts. But by the time the club closed, I was ready to return home and sleep.

Unfortunately for me, my dreams were filled with both Caroline and Elodie—thankfully none of them together. That would have definitely fucked me up even worse. By the time I woke up around noon, I was still exhausted and vaguely hungover.

I texted Elodie. *Dinner tonight?*

When she replied within seconds, I smiled for the first time in twenty-four hours.

Chapter 15
Elodie

I could tell Mac was distracted. He wasn't his usual flirtatious self.

Sure, he'd kissed me after we'd sat down in a quiet corner of the Japanese restaurant, but he was too quiet, and his answers to my questions were vague. It was like his head was in an entirely different place.

My insecurities wondered if he was tired of me. Was he finding the courage to break things off? Was this over before it really started? Paranoia began to consume me. The longer he didn't say anything, the more worried I became. Fear of losing him made me realize how much I liked him. How I was actually growing to care for him, even if that was dangerous. Moreover, I still had so much to learn about him. And me, for that matter, too. It felt like I'd just gotten onto this path of self-discovery, and I wasn't ready for it to end so soon.

When I was anxious, I tended to be jumpy. So when the server leaned down to set an appetizer in front of me and my mind was still lost in thought, I nearly knocked over my glass of water. Luckily, the server caught it just in time.

"Whoa there!" He smiled. "You okay?"

I let out an unsteady laugh. "Sorry. Yeah, sure, yeah."

When the server disappeared, I looked at Mac and realized he barely noticed the exchange.

Maybe he regretted inviting me to dinner with his parents? I took in Mac's expression as if I was trying to crack a secret code. But Mac wasn't giving anything away. He looked tired, and when I'd asked him about it, he'd attributed it to not sleeping well the night before. Other than that, he just seemed sort of—far away.

We hadn't seen each other since Idaho. *Maybe his parents called him after and told him they hated me.* Would Mac care about their opinion? Jesus, I was starting to spiral. I was grateful when the server returned with a fresh plate of edamame that could distract us both.

My hunger somewhat abated, I gathered my courage. "Are you okay?" I asked.

Mac smiled, but it didn't reach his eyes. "Yeah, why?"

"You seem like you've got something on your mind. You've barely said a word to me all night."

Underneath the table, I twisted my fingers so hard that I had to force myself to stop. I pushed my hands under my thighs to keep them still. But that only made me dig my nails into the booth upholstery.

"Is it about your parents?" I asked.

Mac sighed. "How could you tell?"

"Well, you all definitely seemed tense around each other. It was clear you didn't want to be at dinner, and I'm getting that same feeling now—that you would rather be anywhere than here."

"Shit, no. I didn't mean to make you feel like that."

"Do you want to talk about how you felt after seeing them?"

"Not really." Mac scraped the meat from an edamame pod with his teeth and tossed the shell into the bowl, looking disgusted. "I told you I've always had tickets for them, but this is the first time they actually attended."

"Yeah, I know."

"And then my dad acts the way he did. Why ask us out for dinner if he was just gonna be an asshole? He's always hated me."

I felt my eyes widen. "Your dad *hates* you?"

Mac looked embarrassed. "Okay, maybe not hate. But he's always treated me like I was fucked in the head. I never was the golden boy he wanted."

Bitterness dripped from Mac's voice. I took his hand and squeezed it. "Your dad is wrong, you know. You're not fucked in the head."

Mac let out a bitter laugh. "You're sweet. But you have no idea. Not really."

I could sense Mac wanted to say more, so I waited, giving him space even though the silence was uncomfortable. When the server came by to serve us our sushi, I nearly shot out of my seat to tell him to go away.

"My mom called me the other day," Mac said heavily. "A family friend . . . she was diagnosed with pancreatic cancer. It's stage 4. She only has months to live."

That was probably the last thing I was expecting him to say.

"Jesus. I'm sorry."

"Actually, she's not a family friend. Not anymore."

I blinked, confused. "Why not?"

Mac dipped his sushi in soy sauce, looking far away again. "My dad became head pastor of our church when I was a teenager. As a kid, he was the associate pastor. The head pastor was a guy named Dave Bradford. He and his wife Caroline were good friends of my parents. Caroline is the one who has cancer."

I moved my eyes from side to side, trying to make sense of where the story was going. "*Were* good friends? What happened?"

"Caroline and I happened."

Whoa. My stomach dipped. *Caroline . . . and Mac? What?*

At my shocked expression, Mac chuckled darkly. "She was twenty-five years older than me, but we had a relationship. She was the one who taught me everything I know. I was her submissive. Caroline was—is—a dominatrix."

Holy crap. I'd known something was missing when it came to the tension in Mac's family. But I could've never predicted this, something more scandalous than I ever imagined. I didn't know how to respond. A pastor's wife had been a dominatrix? And she'd had an affair with the son of the associate pastor? *What the fuck?*

"Yeah, I know. It's fucking insane when I say it out loud. And I know it's strange that I'm upset that Caroline is sick, but . . ." Mac shrugged. "It's complicated."

Jealousy tore through me, even if it was sad to be jealous of a woman who was dying. But I couldn't help it. My throat was painfully dry. "Do you still have feelings for her?" I asked, my voice hoarse.

"What? Christ, no! No, of course not. I just care about her, that's all. And hearing that she's dying of cancer brought back a lot of bad memories."

I forced myself to eat some of the sushi I'd ordered, even as it tasted like ash in my mouth. Or maybe it was to stop myself from interrogating Mac further. I wanted to hear all the details about this affair, but Mac looked pained. Or maybe I didn't want to know. I couldn't quite figure it out. It was more like I *had* to know but didn't really want to be subjected to anything that would make me even more jealous and confused than I already was.

And then I felt guilty because I was jealous of his pain. It hurt that he still cared this much about Caroline. That he was thinking of another woman, even if he denied having any feelings for her.

"Then we should change the subject," I said, trying to sound cheery, even if it felt like my world had been turned upside down.

We talked about the sushi, about the terrible traffic that always plagued LA, and about how it was supposed to get hot this weekend. All inoffensive subjects that seemed to help bring Mac back to the present.

"Did I tell you that my uncle wants to see me?" I asked. Why not replace one uncomfortable subject for another?

"Your uncle? Is he visiting soon?"

I shook my head. "No, he and his family live here. But I've never gone to see them."

Now Mac looked shocked. "Why not?"

"Um, it's complicated. He's my mom's brother. Her family never approved of her getting together with my dad or getting pregnant before they got married. But since she died, my uncle has reached out a few times, but I always ignore it."

"Maybe he wants to mend fences," Mac ventured. "I mean, how old was he when your mom got pregnant?"

I hadn't thought about it. "He was a teenager, I guess. It was mostly my grandparents who were shitty about the whole thing."

"You should reply." Mac looked serious now. "Family is important, Elodie. You know what I'd give to have family who wanted to see me? That didn't always judge me?"

"I mean, my mom's family judged her . . ." I felt defensive now.

"Her parents did. You don't know about her siblings."

I was annoyed now. Mac didn't get to lecture me on how I dealt with my own family, just like I couldn't lecture him on his. "How about we talk about something else?" I said, realizing what a mistake it was to bring up the subject of my uncle.

Mac's smile was wry now. "Probably a good idea."

My initial anger faded away. Damn Mac and his smile. It always got me to do whatever he wanted.

After dinner, we returned to my place. The mood continued to be tense for the rest of the night. My imagination ran wild with images of Mac and Caroline. I wondered what she looked like, what he wasn't telling me. I also pondered the fact that he'd told me he was her submissive. Was his being a Dom now some sort of retaliation for him feeling taken advantage of when he was younger? Or did he truly prefer it? There was so much I wanted to ask him, but I also needed to be cognizant of the fact that he'd just received devastating news about this person. I didn't want to push him over the edge by prying too hard.

A few hours later, I was finally dozing when I heard movement in my bedroom. It was dark, but I could make out Mac's figure in the shadows. When he ran into something and cursed, I winced. And then groaned when he turned on a lamp on my dresser.

After he reassured me he was fine, he padded to the bathroom but hadn't turned off the light. I closed my eyes again, sleep wanting to claim me, when I heard Mac come back into my bedroom.

"Hey, Elodie," he said, "what is this?"

My heart practically dropped to the floor after I opened my eyes. Mac held up a notebook—the same one I'd used when collecting information about him. And at the top was Dawn Morrison's name and number.

Chapter 16

Elodie

My sleepy brain was now wide awake. Pulse racing, I sat up, scrambling for an explanation that wouldn't make me seem like a total stalker. Or like I was a journalist digging for dirt.

"Okay, you caught me," I said, keeping my voice light.

Mac raised an eyebrow, waiting for my explanation.

"I was curious about you, and I found out you went to high school with Dawn. So I wanted to hear about what you were like back then. I mean, can you blame me for wanting to know more about a preacher's kid who gets into BDSM?"

Mac still looked uncertain, but then he let out a sigh that sounded relieved. "I guess I'd be curious, too," he admitted.

I let out the breath I'd been holding.

"Did you talk to Dawn?" he asked, setting the notebook down and climbing back into bed with me.

"Yeah. She lives in Malibu and owns a pottery studio. When I found out she lived close by, I couldn't help myself."

"Well, shit. Now I'm not sure I want to know what she had to say about me." Mac's smile was amused. "I haven't talked to her in years."

"Oh, she was very complimentary."

"We were each other's beards, you know. She was gay, and I was into . . . other things. But she probably already told you all that."

I nodded. "Pretty much, yeah."

"How was she? Dawn."

"Um, she's married now. She doesn't look like she did in her yearbook photos. And she did a great job trying to teach me how to make a vase." I chuckled at the memory. "Suffice to say, my attempt was a disaster."

He chuckled but seemed a little lost in thought. I worried that he was thinking better of accepting my story so easily and that he might've been starting to doubt my explanation.

"I know what I did was intrusive, but curiosity got the best of me. Please tell me you don't think I'm a stalker."

Mac simply smiled, not granting me the satisfaction of an answer. Instead, he got up again and handed me a few bills, which also happened to have large OVERDUE notices at the top.

Now I blushed, feeling humiliated. "I ran a little short paying a few of my bills," I hedged.

Mac picked up three other bills and cocked his head to the side. "Is everything okay?"

I wanted to die. I could tell he was concerned, but it irked me. I grabbed the bills from his hands and stuffed them into my drawer.

"I'm *fine*. I'm just a little behind. I had a book deal that fell through, so I've been doing extra freelance work that hasn't paid yet. Don't worry about me."

Mac sat down on the bed next to me. "Do you need money, Elodie?"

I froze. I also bit my tongue nearly in half to keep from saying something I'd regret. *He's just trying to help*, I reasoned.

"I don't need your money," I replied.

"Everybody needs help sometimes."

"Well, I don't." Realizing how bitchy I sounded, I added, "Sorry. I'm fine. Really. Thanks for the offer, though. It's just been tricky, too, because Todd and I were going to move in together, and obviously that didn't happen . . ."

Mac's expression was grave. *Was he blaming himself for me ending things with Todd? Or was he still weirded out about the Dawn thing?*

I glanced at my phone. It wasn't even midnight. "Do you want to go to the club?" I blurted, desperate for a distraction once again.

"What? The Scarlet Rope? Now?"

"Sure, why not?" I went to my closet to find something to wear. "We haven't been there together in a while. I feel like we could both benefit from blowing off some steam tonight."

Mac eventually agreed, to my immense relief. I put on my sexiest little black dress, which I could tell Mac appreciated. He slipped an arm around my waist and pulled me in for a heated kiss.

The Scarlet Rope was bustling with people tonight, but I had only eyes for Mac. He'd been quiet on the ride over, but he seemed to relax the moment we'd been admitted inside the club.

Feeling guilty about both the Dawn thing and getting snippy earlier, I whispered in Mac's ear, "How about we go to a room? Where *we're* the participants this time."

Mac stared down at me, clearly surprised. "Seriously?"

I nodded, a thrill going through me. "How about it, then?"

He didn't say anything. Then he touched my cheek and said, "I'm not sure I want to put our relationship on display. We only just started. You're probably not ready for something like that."

I was both touched and annoyed now. I wouldn't have offered if I'd known he hadn't wanted to do it. But I also wasn't going to push Mac to do anything he didn't want either.

"We can go watch a room together," he suggested. "Then maybe we can get a private room to enjoy each other in."

I nodded, following his lead. He took me to the BDSM room. There was a woman and a man this time. The woman had a collar around her neck, with the man holding the attached leash. She wore nothing but a tiny thong and a blindfold while he was still fully dressed in a suit and tie.

Despite what was happening with just a thin wall of glass between, I fixated on Mac. Did he consider our relationship more serious than I thought? I would've guessed he would've jumped at the chance to up the ante of our play.

Yet it seemed like he wanted to keep things private. Was it because he was concerned about me? Or was it that he just didn't think I had the balls to let other people watch us have sex? When the scene ended, Mac took my hand. I followed him silently to a private room in the back of the club. To my surprise, I shook, but it wasn't from fear. It was from anticipation. My nerves were on fire, my entire body desperate for Mac's touch.

He cradled my jaw. "You ready?"

I could only nod and follow him inside.

The room had a bed, and along the walls were all kinds of instruments and toys. Some I recognized; some I couldn't begin to fathom the uses of.

"What's the safe word?" Mac asked me, startling me out of my thoughts.

"Uh, turkey?"

He smiled. "That's right. Remember, you can say that word whenever you want me to stop."

I nodded.

"Are you ready?" he asked.

I nodded again. My body was tense with anticipation. I glanced at the variety of whips and floggers on the wall, Mac following my gaze.

"Not tonight," he said. "But soon."

I shivered. Mac gathered a few things, but not before telling me to strip out of my clothes.

I stood naked in the middle of an unfamiliar room, my nipples hard as steel, when he came and blindfolded me. Darkness enveloped my vision, and it sent a thrill through me. Mac's fingers brushed across my shoulder as he brushed my hair aside. He kissed my neck gently.

"Put your hands together in front of you. Just like that," he said softly.

I obeyed. Then I felt him tie my wrists, the bindings tighter than when he'd bound me in the hotel room, but still not uncomfortable. It seemed like an eternity as he tied the knot around my wrists. I was about to ask what the hold-up was, but then he stepped away.

I stood there, waiting, listening intently, but Mac didn't say a word. I could only make out his footsteps, and the air moving around me.

"You're so fucking beautiful," he said reverently. "I love the way your nipples tighten every time I speak."

I could feel my traitorous nipples do just that, and Mac chuckled. He rearranged my hair so it fell down my back, then he was on the move once again. Every step he took made my heart beat faster. I felt like a gazelle waiting for a lion to pounce. Except I wasn't afraid. I was desperate. I trembled, my pussy already throbbing with need. I squeezed my thighs together, but that only made the sensations more intense.

"How much do you want me to fuck you?" he growled.

I swallowed, too aroused to think. "I don't know."

"You don't know? That's not a good answer. Try again."

I licked my lips. "You haven't even touched me yet."

"Who said you were in control here?"

Mac's big hand settled on the top of my head, guiding me to kneel in front of him. I could smell his scent inches away, making me salivate, desperate to taste him. But the man standing in front of me took his time. Finally, after a minute or two, I heard fabric rustle, and then I felt the smooth head of his cock brush against my lips.

"I'm the one in control," he said, his tone as hard as his cock. "Say it, Elodie. I own you."

"You own me," I whispered.

"Now, take my cock into your mouth like a good girl."

I licked the head and slowly took him into my mouth, savoring the salty taste. Mac dug his fingers into my hair as I began to bob my head and suck him off.

"You're so good at this," he crooned. "Do you love my cock in your mouth, sweetheart? Does that make your pussy wet?"

I nodded. I'd never liked blow jobs much—until I met Mac. Without even touching me, he managed to make them painfully erotic.

Mac tightened his grip on my hair and began to take control. He thrust harder into my mouth, going deeper and deeper until I gagged.

"That's it. Take all of me. Breathe through your nose." He groaned. "God, you're fucking amazing, baby girl."

Just as I finally started to relax into the feeling of having my throat filled, Mac pulled out. I gulped in a few breaths, but the break was short, and a moment later, he was feeding me his cock again. This time, he didn't go slow. He wrapped my hair in his hand and used it to keep my head steady as he fucked my mouth, going deeper into my throat, farther than I would've thought possible. I couldn't breathe, my throat burned, and my eyes watered, yet I had never been more turned on in my life. I'd never wanted to please someone more than at that moment. When Mac finally relented again, pulling back and allowing me to rest for a moment, saliva dripped down my chin. I was sure I looked like a complete mess, but I couldn't even care.

"God, Elodie," he rasped. "You look so beautiful with my cock in your mouth. Tell me how much you love it."

"I love it," I whispered. *I did.*

"Louder."

"I love it!"

"Do you want me to come down your throat?"

"Yes."

"Yes, what?"

"Yes, please."

"Good girl." I could hear the smile in his voice as he stroked my cheek. "Then no more stopping. You suck me until I come down your throat. Understand?"

"Yes."

He deep-throated me even longer this time. Tears ran down my cheeks as I struggled to breathe. But I loved every second of it. I was desperate to taste him. His grip on my hair tightened as he pushed deeper and let out a string of curses, then stilled as he pumped down my throat. He came in endless pulses, making me swallow all of it.

Mac sighed. He gently untied my wrists and took off my blindfold before lifting me into his arms. He carried me to the bed, and before I could say a word, he buried his face in my pussy.

I squealed as he licked me from ass to clit. He plunged his tongue into my sheath as his thumb worked my clit. It didn't take long before I was on edge.

"Mac!" I was ready to explode, and it was too much, too soon. "Slow down . . ."

He ignored my cry and kept eating me out, licking and sucking and fucking me with his tongue until I arched off the bed and moaned his name. When he sucked my clit into his mouth and plunged two fingers inside me, I came. I screamed through the orgasm, not caring if the entire club heard me. I could just make out Mac chuckling as I came.

Afterward, he gathered me into his arms, kissing me gently as he pushed my hair back.

"You good?" he asked. I could see the concern in his gaze. "Your throat okay?"

"I'm exhausted and sore. But in a very good way."

"I didn't push you too hard?"

"You pushed me, but I liked it. I promise you." I kissed him.

He sighed and wrapped his arms around me. "You're amazing."

I couldn't help but smile against his bicep. The infamous Cole Mackenzie, playboy hockey player, thought I was amazing at sex?

I would take that compliment with me for the rest of my life.

Chapter 17

Mac

My lawyer, Tony Williams, pushed a stack of documents toward me. "These all look good to me, but you read them over first."

Tony had been my lawyer since I'd first signed with the Blades. He and Andrea had always made sure I got the best deals and contracts. He was known in the industry as a bulldog, and his tenacity tended to piss people off. Despite his brutish demeanor, Tony was a total softie. He had photos of his wife and kids all over his office. He always showed them off to me, clearly proud of his family.

I scanned through the documents, but it was a struggle to pay attention to the legalese. "Why am I looking at this, again? Isn't that what I'm paying you for?" I joked.

Tony snorted. "Never sign on the dotted line unless you know what you're signing. Don't be a dumbass, Mackenzie."

"Aren't you always the one saying athletes never know their heads from their asses?"

"Oh, they don't. And don't think you're the exception to the rule. I've seen all those stories about you online." Tony's gaze narrowed. "Who's the married woman?"

I groaned. "You're worse than Andrea."

"My wife wanted to know. She's like a shark out for blood when it comes to gossip, that woman." Despite his words, Tony's tone was full of admiration.

If Tony was scary, his wife, Miranda, was downright terrifying. I'd met her once. She was a tiny brunette who had the scariest resting bitch face I'd ever seen. Her gaze literally cut a man to bits.

"That whole thing is over," I replied.

"Hmm. So what about that other woman? Did she sign the contract?"

Even though Elodie had signed the contract, I'd never sent it to Tony to make it official. Why? I didn't fucking know. Maybe it was because Elodie was different. She wasn't like all the other women I'd had arrangements with.

"She signed it," I said.

Tony raised an eyebrow. "And you, what, forgot to send it to me? Your lawyer? See, this is what I mean about athletes not knowing their heads from their asses. You see one beautiful woman, and you lose your damn mind."

I gritted my teeth. "It's not like that."

"Then get me the contract."

"I will."

Tony leaned back in his chair, his expression thoughtful now. "I think I should do a background check on her."

"What? No. That's not necessary."

"Let me do the thinking here. That's what you pay me for, right?" Tony grabbed a pen and a Post-it. "Name."

"You don't need to do a background," I repeated, frustrated at Tony's insistence.

"Dude, stop thinking with your dick and think with your head. If she has nothing to hide, then it'll come up with nothing. But you'll be pissed at yourself if she does have something and you were too caught up to do the bare minimum."

I knew Tony was right, even as it pissed me off. I got up out of my chair, feeling like Tony's gaze was pinning me to the floor like an insect.

"Name, Mackenzie."

"Christ, you're fucking relentless."

Tony chuckled. "Like I said, that's what you pay me for."

After a few more moments of indecision, I gave Tony Elodie's name. He looked triumphant, and it took all my self-control not to punch his smug face.

Why did I hire this guy again? I thought darkly.

"Good, I'll run that through today. I'll have the background check by Monday." Tony watched me pace, his expression amused. "What's going on? I've never seen you like this about a woman."

"Like what, exactly?"

"Cagey. Protective. Like you'd tear somebody apart for looking at her funny. You know, you remind me of myself sometimes."

That remark made me laugh. "You?"

"Yeah, me. You know, the second I met Miranda, I lost my ever-fucking mind. I had to have her, but she didn't make it easy. She told me to go to hell on more than one occasion. The first time I asked her out, she laughed at me. Laughed! Told me to come back when I'd finished law school. So I finished law school, passed the bar with flying colors, and then she told me to come back when I'd started my own firm.

"So I did, and she had no more excuses. We got married a few months later."

"Jesus."

Tony chuckled. "Yeah, we were fucking crazy. But I have zero regrets. The second she agreed to marry me, I had to lock that shit down. And she's told me since that she wished she'd said yes when I'd first asked her out."

I folded my arms across my chest. "What the hell does this all have to do with me?"

"Mackenzie, I'm telling ya, if this woman is special, don't let her go. You'll regret it for the rest of your fucking life. And do whatever she wants. That's what women do. Drive you crazy. But it's worth it."

I was about to counter that Elodie wasn't like Miranda in the slightest, but I also understood what Tony was getting at.

Intuitively, I knew that Elodie was different. She was special. She'd already burrowed herself into me, and I didn't know if I could get her out. Or if I even wanted her out. I started to feel guilty about giving Tony her name to look into. Was that really necessary?

The thought of never seeing Elodie again was like a punch to the gut.

Tony cleared his throat. "I'll get that background check in, then. And take that contract with you and actually *read* it."

I knew when I was dismissed. I gave Tony an ironic salute and headed out.

That weekend, we had a game up in Vancouver, Canada, which we lost—badly. It didn't help that my mind had been on everything but hockey. My mom had called last night and said that Caroline was deteriorating, and I hated to be away from Elodie. When I'd missed a goal, Coach had looked like he'd wanted to choke me out.

"Get your head in the game!" he'd yelled at me, his face red as a cherry.

The only upside—which was really not an upside at all—was that I hadn't been the only one distracted. Brady had missed a pass, while our goalie had also let an easy shot from the other team get through. I wasn't sure what was going on with either of them, but I'd been wrestling with my conscience all week long about whether I should visit Caroline. The debate ate away at me.

Our relationship had always been complicated. No one could understand it except the two of us. But I still cared about her despite everything. The thought of her dying without me seeing her at least once more made my gut twist. And that twist turned into a knot when I thought about how Elodie might feel if she knew I went to visit Caroline.

One of my teammates was from Idaho, and when I found out he was flying to Coeur d'Alene to visit his wife, I didn't hesitate to hitch a ride on his private plane. Then I drove to the hospital twenty minutes from the tiny airport. The entire ride felt like my heart was in my mouth—I had no idea what to expect, just how bad she was. Nor did I have a clue what I would say to her. Would she even recognize me? God, this sucked. But in my heart, I knew I was doing the right thing. I'd regret it for the rest of my life if she died and I never went to see her.

Walking into the hospital, I almost hoped they'd tell me visiting hours were over—make the decision for me. But when I asked for directions to Caroline's room, nobody stopped me. I stood outside her door for a long moment. A nurse slid past me, giving me a strange look, and I waited for her to leave again before entering.

Caroline's eyes were closed. She had multiple IVs, along with an oxygen cannula in her nose. She looked horribly thin—her cheeks were sunken in and her once beautiful blond hair thin and wispy. For the first time, she looked her age or maybe even older. It almost made it easy to pretend it wasn't her; maybe that would make this whole thing less painful.

Seeing the woman who'd basically controlled my life once upon a time was strange. Right now, she didn't look like she even had the strength to turn on the hospital TV, let alone tie me up, whip me, and make me beg for her mercy.

Her eyelashes fluttered open. "Who . . .?"

I sat down and took her hand. "It's Mac, Caro."

Realization dawned slowly on her face. She tried to sit up but didn't have the strength. It was devastating to see how weak she was.

"Mac," she kept saying. She touched my face, tears in her eyes now. "Is it really you? Or am I hallucinating again?" She let out a croaky laugh. "You know, these painkillers they give you—they mess you up. I keep seeing people in the corner of my eye, but nobody's there. But you seem real enough."

"It's me. No hallucination. I'm sorry I didn't come sooner."

"You should be careful. Dave has been staying the night with me. You don't want to run into him."

"I'll be careful." Even though I offered her assurance, I wasn't afraid of him. It didn't matter to me if he caught me here, but I didn't want to do anything to upset her in this condition, so for that reason, I hoped he didn't see me.

She let out a breath, then winced. "It hurts to breathe. They say the cancer has spread all over. Even with painkillers, there's still pain. How is that? I don't understand it. Aren't painkillers supposed to take away the pain? I guess I'm the lucky exception, or maybe I'm being punished for all the pain I've dished out."

She was rambling, and it hurt to see. Caroline had always been such a force of a woman. She'd done everything with confidence, including taking me under her wing and showing me the BDSM lifestyle at a time when I was desperate to understand myself. She never rambled or talked about hallucinations. *She was never dying.*

I realized now that cancer had left Caroline a shell of her former self. Selfishly, I almost wished I hadn't come. At least then my last memory of her wouldn't be this woman in a hospital bed who was at death's door. But this was life. And as tempting as it would've been to pretend this wasn't happening, I was glad I came.

"Mac, sweetheart," Caroline was saying. She touched my cheek. "I don't have much time left. I wanted to tell you—I needed to tell you something—"

She started coughing so hard that I almost called for a nurse. But Caroline forced me to sit back down. At that moment, I saw a glimmer of her former self and couldn't help but smile.

"That's a good boy. You know I'm still in charge, right?" She smiled grimly. "I wanted to tell you that I never stopped having feelings for you. Even after all these years. I told myself to forget about you, but I couldn't. And then when I got diagnosed, it was like a light bulb went off."

I stared down at her, shocked. Horrified. Confused. And angry, too. This was the first moment I started to second-guess having come here.

"What about your husband?" I asked hoarsely.

"What about him? He's never understood me. Never fulfilled me either."

"Then why did you stay married to him?"

It was our age-old argument: why she'd stayed with her husband despite her numerous affairs with other men. It had haunted me years ago. Now, though, it just made me feel pity for her.

"You know the reasons, Mac," she replied, sounding angry. "It wasn't that simple."

"Of course not." I patted her hand. It wasn't worth arguing about—not anymore. She hadn't been willing to give up the security her marriage had afforded her. And I'd been just a kid without a penny to my name. Back then, it'd stung. Now? I understood, even as I pitied Caroline, too.

"Tell me you feel the same," she said, her tone imploring. She was shaking now, clearly distressed. "I know you loved me once."

Guilt made me weak. "I still love you," I said, even as I felt the words to be a lie.

She took a deep, trembling breath. Then she closed her eyes, and I could tell my words—my *lies*—had given her peace. And for that, I couldn't feel guilty about saying them.

She was about to die. If I could give her this, I would. I needed to be the bigger person here. Even though Caroline's actions would leave me distrustful for the rest of my life, I still wanted to bring her solace. It was no wonder I'd doubted Elodie enough to give Tony her name. I'd been conditioned through Caroline to believe that a woman can really hurt you by lying to your face and cheating someone she claimed to love. The thing is, I knew Caroline believed she did love her husband. That was what made everything she did so fucking scary. She would try to justify it, because she claimed he couldn't give her what she'd needed.

Before I left, I kissed her on the forehead and said a silent prayer that she wouldn't suffer much longer.

When I was heading out to my car, I heard my name. Thinking it was a fan, I turned, only to see a fist coming straight at my nose. It was a hard enough blow that I was sent reeling.

"You son of a bitch! How dare you show your face around here? I should've shot you when I had the chance," said a voice I never thought I'd hear again.

It was Dave Bradford. And he looked like he was about to have a stroke.

I held up my hands. "I'm leaving," I said as I wiped blood from my nose.

"You better fucking be. Get out of here, Mackenzie, before I do shoot you."

Dave stalked inside the hospital. To my chagrin, a handful of people had caught the exchange, one of whom was holding her phone and filming it.

I briefly considered asking the woman who'd filmed me not to post it online, but that'd probably make things worse. And maybe she hadn't recognized me. It was dark out, and I'd made sure to wear a hat and inconspicuous clothes.

Despite the late hour, the last thing I wanted was to try to find a hotel room somewhere. I could always stay with my parents, but that thought was as bad as getting punched by Dave. Even with that altercation, I had no regrets about my decision to come see her.

I ended up going to a local bar that I'd often tried to get into using a fake ID back in the day. It was usually full of farmers and truckers—guys who didn't give a shit if a famous hockey star came around.

The interior was dark and dingy, which suited me just fine. It smelled like old beer and sweat. A TV was on in the corner with the volume on low. A few guys were scattered about, nursing their beers and not making conversation.

I ordered a beer for myself. The bartender gave me a strange look as he went to the tap and poured a Coors Light. I thought maybe he recognized me. Eventually, he delivered my beer with a chin lift. "Your nose is bleeding."

I winced. I grabbed a few napkins, wincing at how bruised my nose already felt. Dave had fucking decked me hard. Could I blame him? Not in the least.

I took my beer and napkins to a booth in the corner. On second thought, had I made a mistake going to see Caroline? The thought of Dave taking out his anger on his dying wife made me feel sick.

When I'd first met Caroline, I'd just been a kid. As the head pastor's wife, she'd seemed like a queen to me. She'd always dressed in designer clothes and worn a huge diamond on her hand that everybody had whispered had cost a fortune. And she was beautiful.

When she'd first noticed me at a dinner party my parents had hosted, I'd been an awkward, pimply-faced teen. I'd been tongue-tied, but she'd managed to make me feel like I was the only person in the world who mattered. When I'd told her that I wanted to play hockey instead of going into the church, she'd truly listened to me. Unlike my own parents, who'd told me I was wasting my time chasing an impossible dream.

The first time she'd kissed me, it had been like I'd been waiting for that moment my entire life. She'd been my sun, moon, and stars.

I grimaced, thinking about what a lovesick puppy she'd turned me into. It hadn't taken much longer to make me do anything she'd wanted.

And I'd loved her for it. I still did, in a strange, twist-ed way. Even when I'd been terrified of everyone finding out about our affair, I'd loved her. When she'd cried in my arms about how Dave ignored her, didn't love her any-more, wasn't a real husband to her . . . I'd wanted to fight her husband in her honor. Now, in hindsight, I could see how wrong it all was. How she might've been exaggerating things to justify her actions. Because after all these years, she was still married to him. That had to count for some-thing. The one thing I was certain of was that I'd never know the exact truth about their marriage.

Back then, though? If Caroline had asked me to kill Dave on her behalf, I might've done it. That thought alone made me shudder. The fact that I hadn't decked him back tonight proved that, on some level, I felt bad for him, both for what he was going through now and for my actions in the past.

A few hours later, I debated getting another beer when the TV in the corner caught my attention. To my disgust, the very video of Dave punching me was playing. Below that was the headline, *Playboy hockey star up to his old tricks again?*

Fuck. That was the risk of coming here. But I still didn't regret it, even though all my dirty laundry was now splayed out for all the world to see.

I waited for any of the guys in the bar to realize I was sitting in a booth. When they didn't, I let out a breath.

But then my phone sounded, and I looked down to read a text from Elodie that made my blood run cold.

I just got a CNN alert on my phone about you getting into a fight. Are you okay?

Chapter 18

Elodie

I tried not to let panic sink in when Mac wouldn't take any of my calls. I kept seeing that stupid video of him getting punched in the face. But what the video didn't show was what the hell happened in the end. Had it ended with that one punch? Or did more happen, leaving Mac seriously injured or worse?

What if he'd gotten a concussion? What if he was lying in a ditch somewhere? I called him for what felt like the thousandth time, but there was no answer.

I texted him a third time as well. My only bit of relief was that he had his read receipts on. The last text was soon marked as read.

But that was it. No return calls, no replies to texts. I only prayed that it was Mac himself who'd read those texts and not someone else. The thought of the latter made me shudder. What if he was dead? Panic and paranoia began to consume me. Because if he'd read those messages, he'd decided not to text me. That was troubling.

I knew Mac had gone to visit Caroline. Why else would he be in Idaho? I knew, yet I didn't feel any better. I felt like I was going to be sick.

It was nearing two in the morning now, and I couldn't sleep. All I could see was that man punching Mac, and Mac nearly falling to the ground.

I'd also been surprised that Mac hadn't punched the guy back. Though when TMZ had reported the name of Mac's assailant was none other than Caroline's husband, everything made a little more sense, even if it didn't take away the worry about what became of Mac after the punch.

I sat down on my couch, sighing heavily. The Caroline thing bugged me. Did Mac realize how strange it was that a pastor's wife would make him her BDSM pet? Did he not realize the level of manipulation that took on her part?

Something else niggled in the back of my brain. Mac had never told me when he'd started sleeping with Caroline, but I'd always assumed he'd been at least eighteen.

But what if he'd been younger? That would totally change things. My gut twisted at the thought. It was one thing if Mac had been an adult . . . another if Caroline had abused a child who should've been able to trust her.

I must've fallen back asleep because the next thing I knew, Mac was standing over me. I was so startled that I nearly had a heart attack.

"It's me," he said. One hand covered my mouth, stopping me from screaming. "I'm sorry. I needed to see you."

I'd given Mac a key to my place a few days before, but I'd never imagined he'd use it. Not yet, at least.

I sat up, my heart pounding so hard that I had to take a few deep breaths. "Jesus Christ! You scared the shit out of me."

He winced, then sat down, his expression grim. He looked exhausted, and his face was black and blue. When I touched his cheek, he winced again.

"Let me get you some ice," I said, hurrying to the kitchen before he could stop me.

I handed him an ice pack wrapped in a towel. When he didn't use it, I pressed the ice to his face myself.

"Ow, Jesus, Elodie. Not so hard," he complained.

"Then you hold it."

He did, his gaze amused now. "I never knew you could be so bossy."

"I can when you get into stupid fistfights outside of a hospital. And why didn't you return my calls? I was worried about you. You should probably go back to a hospital. What if you have a concussion—"

He took my hand and shushed me. "I'm fine. It's just a bruise. My nose isn't broken. And believe me, I know what that feels like."

We sat in silence for a while longer. Mac finally lowered the ice pack and handed it back to me.

"Are you okay?" I asked quietly.

He leaned against the couch. "No," was his honest answer.

"You went to see Caroline."

He nodded.

"And her husband punched you."

He nodded again.

"Mac . . ."

He held up a hand. "If you're just going to lecture me, then I'll go home."

I bit my lip. I didn't want to lecture him. I wanted him to be honest. I also wanted to know the truth about his relationship with Caroline. But would he ever admit that what she'd done to him was messed up?

"How was she?" I asked finally, deciding that was probably the most appropriate question to start with, given the circumstances.

"Dying. She's fucking dying. She looked like a skeleton. And then she . . ." Mac hesitated. "Never mind."

Never mind? He clearly didn't understand how invested I was in this situation.

"Tell me," I insisted.

He sat up, folding his hands together. "She told me she still loved me. That she'd always loved me."

His words were like a punch to the gut. At that moment, I hated Caroline Bradford. Why did she have to keep haunting Mac like this? Why couldn't she leave the poor man in peace?

"I told her that I loved her, but it was a lie." Mac groaned. "Is that terrible? Do you think I did the right thing?"

I could tell he was deeply conflicted. It took all my self-control not to burst into tears. Because Mac had told another woman he'd loved her—he'd never said those words to *me*.

Do you want him to say those words to you? I didn't know the answer. More likely, I didn't want to admit the true answer to myself.

"Mac," I said slowly, "how old were you when you and Caroline first . . ."

"What? Had sex?" Mac let out a gruff laugh. "I was old enough."

"You were eighteen?"

He shrugged a shoulder. "Almost. I was seventeen. Well, no, it started when I was sixteen, almost seventeen. But what difference is there, really?"

I gaped at him. "Are you serious right now?"

Now, he looked annoyed. "I didn't come here to be judged."

"I'm not judging you! I'm horrified for you. Mac, you were a kid. You weren't old enough to consent to sex!"

"I was old enough. I knew what I was doing. If I hadn't wanted to sleep with Caroline, I wouldn't have. Simple as that. What, do you think she took me to her lair and raped me?" He scoffed.

His voice rose with every word. I could tell by the tension in his body that he was angry with me. He got up and started pacing.

"Mac, it's not your fault," I said, trying to sound soothing. Calm. Controlled. "Don't blame yourself—"

"I'm not because there's no blame here. We had an affair. Caroline knew what I needed to experience. She gave me a purpose in life that no one else ever had. She showed me I didn't have to live inside the box my parents and everyone else wanted me to live in."

"Maybe that's true, but—"

"It is true!" He was yelling now. "What the fuck, Elodie? Are you seriously trying to tell me what I experienced didn't happen?"

Guilt assailed me. Was I wrong? But Mac had been sixteen. Underage. Besides, even if he'd been a legal adult, Caroline had still been in a position of power. She'd used that to groom him.

I could see that, clear as day. Why couldn't Mac? I guess that's what happens when someone is brainwashed.

But Mac was so distraught and angry that I knew I was getting nowhere. I went to him and put my arms around him. He was as stiff as a board, like he couldn't even tolerate my touch.

"I'm sorry. Okay? I'm just worried about you. That's all. I'm just trying to understand," I whispered.

It felt like an eternity, but Mac finally hugged me back. He put his chin on the crown of my head.

"I don't need you to judge me," he kept saying. "Not you."

"I'm not. I don't. There's nothing wrong with you."

"My entire life, I was never what anyone wanted me to be. I wasn't the good preacher's son. I wasn't the guy who wanted a vanilla marriage right out of high school. I'm not going to apologize for being different."

"And you shouldn't." I made him look at me. "You're incredible the way you are. I wouldn't have signed that contract if I didn't believe that."

His gaze roved my face. Then he pulled me into a hug so tight that I could barely breathe.

"Fuck, Elodie. Jesus fucking Christ." He breathed the words like a prayer into my hair.

We stayed like that for a long while until Mac finally said he needed to go home. He had practice later that day, and he'd barely slept. Although I tried to persuade him to stay, he wouldn't be deterred.

He kissed me, long and lingeringly, before he left. Only as I watched him drive away did I realize the sun was starting to rise. I yawned, suddenly exhausted, and returned inside to sleep.

But as I climbed into bed, I couldn't sleep. I couldn't stop thinking about Mac, or Caroline, or how fucked up the entire thing between them was.

Mac might not think it'd been wrong, but it was. Caroline had abused him. She'd used him for her own fucked-up desires and then had made him believe it'd been his idea.

But how could I convince Mac? I doubted he'd ever see himself as a victim. Besides, he still cared deeply for Caroline, even if he was no longer in love with her. No matter how tangled and devastating, that kind of bond was difficult to break.

Tears sprang to my eyes, and I let them fall. I realized at that moment that I loved Mac.

When had that happened? I didn't know. But I'd probably fallen for him the first time I'd seen him at the club. And as our relationship had changed and deepened, my feelings had deepened for him.

So I was in love with Cole Mackenzie. Even though we'd both promised each other that our relationship would be just sex. Oh, I was an idiot!

I started crying harder. I cried until my head pounded and my eyes ached. I cried because Mac was hurting, and I was afraid I'd made things worse. I cried because I loved him, but I could never tell him that.

I cried because I knew I'd get my heart broken, but I was too far gone to end things.

I buried my face in my pillow, punching my mattress for good measure. God, I'd really gone and fucked things up, hadn't I?

I waited until it was a reasonable hour to call Hannah. When she answered, she sounded groggy.

"Why are you calling me?" She yawned loudly. "Christ, what time is it?"

"I thought you'd be awake for your job."

"I have the day off. Emma and Ryan are taking the kids to Disneyland."

"I'm sorry for waking you up. I can call back later—" My voice broke.

"Wait, wait. Are you okay? What happened?"

I started crying again. I told Hannah everything about Mac and Caroline, and she listened without making any of her usual pithy comments.

By the time I'd finished, Hannah had fallen silent.

"Are you still there?" I asked.

"I'm still here. Sorry. I just don't know what to say."

That was a first. Hannah always knew what to say. "Am I fucked?"

"Well, maybe. Or maybe not. It's not like you've published any stories about Mac. Do you think he'd really freak out if he knew what your job was? Maybe just don't mention that you were trying to find dirt on him."

"I doubt he'd trust me if he found out I work for a tabloid."

"I mean, everybody in LA seems to work for Hollywood. Everybody knows somebody. But you know him better than I do."

"I mean, I did sign an NDA."

Hannah let out a surprised laugh. "Of course you did. Did you happen to mention that to your boss?"

"No. Of course not."

I could feel Hannah shaking her head through the phone. "Man, and here I thought you always played by the rules, Miss Elodie Andrews. You've gotten yourself into quite a pickle."

"So? What should I do?"

"Well, you can either never tell Mac what your job is, or you can tell him. Those are pretty much your two choices. I guess you could always quit your job, too."

I sighed loudly. "I can't. I have bills to pay. There's no guarantee I'd find another one quickly either."

"True. So it sounds like you're just not going to tell him about that part of your life." Hannah's tone turned sly. "I mean, isn't your arrangement just sex, anyway? Does he need to know everything about you?"

"Yes. I mean, I guess. Things have gotten more complicated."

Hannah made a noise. "Aw, shit, did you catch feelings for him?"

Now, I was annoyed. "It's not a joke."

"No, but be careful. That's all I'm going to say. You had an arrangement—don't think it's going to change. Mac might not want anything more than sex. I just don't want to see you get your heart broken."

I knew she was right, even as I resented her words. Mac had never alluded to us making our relationship official. I'd be wise to guard my heart in the meantime. The thought of us never being anything more than sex partners really hurt. I wanted him to fall in love with me. I wanted to heal the hurt from his past and grow along with him. But what I wanted didn't matter. Mac had so much going on in his mind right now that I doubted there was truly room to be falling in love with me on top of working through his regrets about the past.

I just hoped that someday I wouldn't become his *biggest* regret.

Chapter 19

Mac

"What the hell is the matter with you, Mackenzie?" Coach nearly roared when I missed another pass from Brady.

Coach Dallas was still an imposing presence despite being close to sixty, balding, and with a dad bod. He'd once been one of the best hockey players in the NHL, and he'd gone on to have an impressive career as a coach after an injury had derailed him.

I'd respected Coach since he never played favorites. If you fucked up, he'd tell you. If you did well—he might give you a shoulder slap paired with his famous lopsided grin. Once, when I'd scored a winning goal at the very last second, he'd even hugged me.

Today, though, Coach wasn't going to hug me. He might actually throttle me. He was beet red and beyond frustrated to the point that my teammates gave him a wide berth.

"Mac! You hear me? When are you going to get your head on straight? Did you fall and break your skull when you got punched or what?" Coach yelled as I skated past.

I scowled. Everybody had been ribbing me since that stupid video had been posted online. Coach had taken me aside to ask me what the hell was going on, but I'd lied and said it was just a misunderstanding.

"What? Did you screw another guy's wife?" Coach had demanded.

"No." *Not recently, at any rate.*

I thought about the irony that I'd been accused of sleeping with a married woman this year. While that allegation was false, it certainly wasn't unfamiliar territory for me, was it? Except the actual situation was far more scandalous than anyone could've ever imagined. I forced myself to try to concentrate. I couldn't keep letting thoughts of Caroline dying distract me. Or worse, the look on Elodie's face when I told her how old I'd been when Caroline and I had first started sleeping together.

She'd looked at me with pity. Pity! I didn't want her pity. I didn't want her judgment either. I tried to convince myself that she didn't understand, that the only people who truly understood were Caroline and me. I didn't need anyone telling me how I should feel about my own goddamn life. But Elodie's reaction to my age at the time of my affair with Caroline *affected* me. It made me doubt my own judgment. It made me think I should've been more traumatized, even if I'd never felt that way. At sixteen, I'd felt like a man, even if looking back now that seemed like a joke. And I'd never considered my parents' opinion to mean much because they were biased. But Elodie's shocked reaction was probably the first time I realized I *wasn't* a man back then at all.

I passed the puck to Brady, but I hit it so hard that it went up and then bounded off the side of the rink. Brady shot me an annoyed look.

"Dude, I didn't do anything," Brady joked. "Try not to break my face, okay?"

"Sorry," I grumbled.

I'd just managed to get back into Coach's good graces at the end of practice when our last scrimmage showed off our newest play to its advantage. Coach looked at me with narrowed eyes as I went to the locker room, but he didn't say a word. I would take that as a win for now.

I didn't want to go home, though. I also didn't want to go out with the guys or even go to the club. I texted Elodie, asking if she wanted to do something, but there was no reply.

Annoyed, I drove to her place without a second thought. I told myself I was just worried about her. She was always prompt in replying to my texts.

Didn't you just ignore her calls and texts when you were in Idaho?

I told myself that this was different. I even called her twice on my way to her place, but there was no answer.

Her car was in the driveway. I knocked, but once again, there was no answer. I peered through her windows, feeling like a total creep.

I was about to let myself in when the door opened. To my shock, it wasn't Elodie: it was a man I'd never seen before.

"Yes?" he asked me like he owned the place.

The guy was of average height and build. He wore glasses and looked like your average pencil pusher.

But why the hell was this guy at Elodie's house?

"Who the hell are you?" I growled, my blood pressure rising by the second.

The guy seemed surprised. "Uh, who the hell are *you*?"

That was when Elodie came to the door. When she spotted me, her eyes widened.

"Mac! What are you doing here?"

I scowled. "Who the hell is this guy, Elodie?"

The guy turned toward Elodie. "Elodie, who is this?"

Elodie sighed, shaking her head. "Mac, this is Todd, my ex-boyfriend. Todd, Mac is a . . . friend."

Todd, her ex? The man she'd broken up with before we'd gotten involved? *Was she back with him again?* A sinking feeling developed in my stomach.

I had the intense, sudden urge to punch Todd's teeth in. It didn't help that he had a smug face. Plus, he kept looking at me like I was a pest he'd found in the garbage.

It was only Elodie coming outside that kept me from getting into a brawl. Todd opened his mouth to protest, but Elodie shook her head.

Elodie folded her arms across her chest after she shut the front door. She walked me over to her car. Which meant she didn't want Todd to overhear our conversation.

"What are you doing here?" she asked.

"I wanted to see you. I didn't think you'd have company." I nearly snarled the word *company.*

I knew I was acting like an asshole, but I didn't care. Seeing a man at Elodie's door had ignited something feral inside me. I knew she didn't technically belong to me. But at the same time . . . *she belonged to me.*

"Todd just wanted to talk," she explained.

"I thought you two had broken up."

"We did. We *are* broken up. But he's still a friend."

I let out an incredulous laugh. "Baby, you think he just wants to be friends? Come on. He wants you back. He acted like your guard dog back there."

"So what? He's protective of me. We were together for five years. He was there for me after my mom died." Elodie tipped her head up, her jaw a stubborn line. "I'm not going to apologize for seeing a friend."

A friend? Was she serious? And I didn't want her to apologize. I wanted—what the fuck did I want? *If I could, I'd never let another man so much as look at her.*

We stared at each other, clearly at an impasse. I suddenly wished I hadn't come. It wasn't like our arrangement had meant we'd be monogamous. If Elodie wanted to get back with her ex, who was I to stop her?

Elodie reached out to touch my arm. "Trust me. This isn't anything to worry about. Todd is just here to talk."

I wanted to believe her. I hated that I didn't. I wished I didn't give a fuck. What was it about Elodie that made me feel like up was down, down was up, and that my entire life was a fucking mess?

"Does he know about us?" I asked.

"No. I didn't think he needed to know." She took a step closer to me. "What's between us is between us. Besides, Todd wouldn't understand."

"You mean he'd try to talk you out of it."

Elodie shrugged. "Maybe. I don't really care what his opinion would be."

I was slightly mollified by that statement. At least Todd wasn't so influential in Elodie's life that she'd let his opinions sway her.

"I'll call you later," she said. "Okay? Trust me."

I went home and opened a new bottle of whiskey. I didn't like to drink alone, but it seemed to have become a habit.

The whole thing with Caroline, along with my relationship with Elodie, had twisted me up inside and out.

I sighed, irritated with myself. I'd always prided myself on being rational. Logical. I didn't let emotions get in the way.

But it felt like they were constantly clouding my judgment lately. I needed to get control of myself before things got worse.

I drank one glass of whiskey and then another. I was considering having a third when my doorbell rang.

It was Elodie. I glanced at my watch. I hadn't realized it'd already been three hours since I'd been at her place.

"I thought you were going to call," I said, stepping aside to let her in.

"I thought it'd be better to talk in person."

I grunted and led her to the living room. I offered her a drink, but she declined. I decided to put the whiskey bottle away. I didn't need to get drunk with Elodie here.

She sat down and wiped her palms against her jeans. "About Todd," she began.

I raised an eyebrow. "You don't owe me an explanation, you know."

"I know. But I want to give you one. Like I said, we're friends. We talked for a bit, and then he left."

"He didn't try to make a pass at you?" I tried to sound like I was joking, but the joke fell flat based on Elodie's expression.

"No, not at all. He did ask me questions about you, though."

I grimaced. "And what did you tell him?"

"That my relationship with you was between you and me. And after that, he didn't ask me again."

I snorted. Todd was a better man than me. Then again, it didn't sound like he wanted to fight for Elodie, which pissed me off for some strange reason. What man in his right mind wouldn't fight for a woman like her? How fucking stupid was this Todd guy?

"I first met Todd in high school," Elodie said, forcing me to pay attention again. "We dated for a bit in tenth grade, then got back together after college. We've known each other for a long time." She sighed. "He was there for me after my mom died. I was just eighteen, you know. Barely an adult. Todd and his family were kind to me. I didn't have any other family around to help me."

"Didn't you say that your mom's family lives in the city?"

"Yeah, but I don't know them. Never did growing up. So I guess what I'm trying to say is that Todd represented a big part of my life. Our romantic relationship has ended, but it's not so easy for either of us to completely let go. We grew up together, in a way. Does that make sense?"

I suddenly felt guilty because my reaction earlier had clearly made Elodie feel like she needed to explain herself. I also realized I was being a huge hypocrite. I'd run back to Caroline's side after I'd found out she was dying, and we hadn't been together in a decade.

"I'm sorry," I said finally. "I was an asshole."

"A little bit." Elodie's lips quirked.

I took her hand, needing to feel her touch. "We both have baggage, don't we? Here I'm snarling about your ex-boyfriend when I went to see my ex in the hospital without telling you."

Elodie tensed. "Like you said, we never agreed to be monogamous."

I wanted to tell her she was wrong, which was insane. I didn't understand my own feelings. Me. I'd prided myself on always being in control, but I couldn't control my own emotions.

"I guess we just have to be patient with each other," Elodie mused.

I snorted. "That's too simple of a solution, clearly."

"Well, it's better than you breaking Todd's kneecaps."

"I wasn't going to break his kneecaps."

"Oh really? You were pissed, Cole Mackenzie. Don't even act like you weren't."

"I wasn't going to break his kneecaps, but I might've punched him," I joked.

"That's what I thought." She sighed.

"When some strange guy answered your door after you'd ignored my calls and texts? Yeah, I was pissed." I wrapped my arm around her waist, pulling her close. "You're mine. Even if it's just temporary."

Her lower lip started trembling. "What are you saying?"

"I'm saying that you don't get to see other men if you're seeing me."

She jutted her chin out. "And what about you? What about other women?"

"I'm not interested in any woman but you."

She inhaled sharply. I could see her breathing quicken, a flush crawling up her cheeks. In a moment, her nipples would harden like they always did. When I saw them peak and press against the thin fabric of her shirt, I smiled in triumph.

"What happens from here?" Elodie whispered.

I bent, my mouth a hairsbreadth from hers. "Fuck if I know," I said before I kissed her hard.

Chapter 20

Elodie

"**Y**ou did say you've been skating before, right?" Mac grinned down at me.

I scowled. "Yeah, once. On a field trip in the fifth grade. So it's been a second." I finished tying the laces on my figure skates and almost fell on my face when I tried to stand.

"Whoa there." Mac caught me in his arms, and I could tell he was trying not to laugh. "You good?"

I stuck my tongue out at him. "I'm good. I'm fine. This is fine."

Mac wasn't convinced, and honestly, neither was I. But I wasn't going to admit that the thought of learning to skate alongside one of the best hockey players in the NHL was intimidating as hell.

Mac had suggested we go on more real dates, take each other to some of our favorite spots and restaurants. This round was Mac's turn. When he'd suggested going ice-skating, I'd almost wanted to say no. But tonight, we were at a local ice-skating rink. Luckily, there weren't many people for me to injure.

I wasn't afraid of the ice. No, I was afraid of looking like an idiot in front of Mac. I said a silent prayer that I wouldn't break any bones out there. That would put me out of commission to do the far more important things he and I had planned.

I tentatively stepped onto the ice, very slowly gliding across its surface. I probably couldn't have been going any slower.

"It's not lava, baby," said Mac. "It's not going to hurt you."

As he said those words, he skated around me, smirking. I wanted to kick him in the shin. But there would be no kicking anything. Lifting my leg would surely mean falling flat on my ass.

Mac could sense my unease. He took my arm and gently started guiding me. As nervous as I was, I certainly didn't mind his touch.

"Don't stare at the ground. Dig the front of your skate into the ice to slow down and stop. Glide into it. There you go. You're a natural."

I laughed. "You're such a liar." I flailed a bit, but Mac caught me.

"Hey, I made you laugh." He grinned. "I'll take that as a win."

"You can't make me laugh. I'll fall."

"Pretty sure you have a high chance of falling without my sense of humor interfering."

We slowly skated a circle around the rink. Mac eventually let me skate on my own, but I had to grab the sides of the rink multiple times. I was worse than the little kids.

Had I been this awkward when I'd done this as a kid? All I could remember was falling on my ass a few times but getting right back up. I also remembered one of the girls had taken figure skating lessons. She'd spent most of the trip showing off. Considering she'd also loved to bully other students, including me, I'd been euphoric when she'd taken a tumble.

But I wasn't ten years old anymore. I had farther to fall. I wasn't going to give up, though. I gritted my teeth and kept moving forward, doing my best not to stare at my feet.

"Are you Cole Mackenzie?" A young girl and boy skated up to Mac, their faces alight with excitement.

Mac smiled down at them. "Yeah, I am."

A few more skaters, realizing who Mac was, came over, and soon, Mac was surrounded by kids asking for his autograph.

I watched in amusement as he asked each kid their name and their favorite hockey player. Most of them said Mac was their favorite. *Of course they did.*

"Did you always want to play hockey?" one boy asked Mac.

"Not always, but after I started taking lessons, I fell in love with it. Do you play?" Mac asked.

The boy nodded. "I'm a goalie. I want to play in the NHL someday."

Mac signed the boy's hat and returned it with a smile. "Then keep practicing. Every day, you'll get better if you put in the time and effort."

"My mom doesn't like hockey. She wants me to do figure skating," one of the girls said.

The boy next to her scoffed. "Girls aren't allowed to play hockey."

The girl's lower lip protruded like she was about to cry. Mac knelt in front of her. "If you want to play hockey, then don't let anyone stop you. Girls can definitely play hockey," he said, his tone completely serious.

The girl nodded, looking determined now.

Mac finally returned to my side. I couldn't stop smiling, couldn't help thinking what an amazing father he might be someday.

"What?" He looked embarrassed.

"You were so good with them." I smiled.

He shrugged. "It doesn't take much to be nice to a bunch of kids."

"Sure, but you could've just signed a few hats and hockey sticks and called it a day."

"If you think that means I'm getting soft, you're in for a rude awakening." He grinned wickedly, which made me blush and look forward to finding out what he meant.

We kept skating, and my skills improved marginally. My initial nervousness had faded, and by the time we'd finished, I'd started to thoroughly enjoy myself. I wasn't great at skating, sure, but I could see myself coming back.

"Did you learn to skate when you started playing hockey?" I asked, suddenly curious. "Or did you already know how to skate?"

"I'd skated some, but hockey is what forced me to get comfortable with it. But hockey isn't exactly figure skating." Mac's grin was wry. "We're not out there doing triple axles."

"Have you ever done figure skating?"

"Oh, fuck no. That shit's terrifying." He shuddered. "I saw a teenager trying to do a double something or other. She somehow twisted her leg right at the same time as she came down on it. Suffice it to say, everybody freaked the fuck out when they saw her bone sticking out of her leg."

I gaped at him. "Oh my God."

"I'm too much of a wimp for figure skating," he said, half joking.

I patted his arm. "It's good to know what your limits are."

He growled, and when no one was looking, he kissed me until I saw stars.

For dinner, Mac took me to one of his favorite wing joints. It was in a nondescript building that had been a gas station back in the fifties and sixties. It'd been turned into a restaurant thirty years ago and had flourished ever since.

The place was packed. When I saw the line out the door, I almost wished I'd brought a snack to tide me over. But Mac, being Mac, managed to get a seat within five minutes. I should've known.

"Nice to see you, big guy!" A middle-aged man walked over to our table. He and Mac shook hands. He then turned his gaze to me and said, "And who's this lovely lady?"

Mac shook his head. "None of your business, Vinnie."

Vinnie held up his hands, a wide grin on his face. "Whatever you say, boss." He handed me and Mac two very well-used menus and went to greet more patrons.

I chuckled. "Who was that?"

"The owner. He and his wife, Ramona, took over this place a few years ago from the previous owner. I also might've lent him some money to keep things afloat."

I raised an eyebrow. "You know them that well?"

"Kind of. Vinnie is a friend of a friend. Mostly, I loved this place so much that I hated that it might go under."

Now, I was intrigued. If this place was so impressive that Mac was willing to give the owners money, it must be worth trying. Mac ordered for us both, assuring me that I'd love it.

It didn't take long for our food to be brought out: crispy, perfectly golden chicken wings with a spicy peanut butter and jelly sauce. Alongside were french fries and onion rings and an assortment of other dipping sauces.

"Peanut butter and jelly wings?" I picked one up, intrigued. "That could either be incredible or terrible."

"They're fucking out of this world." Mac bit into his own wing and groaned.

I took a bite, and the taste of the salty but spicy peanut butter and the sweet jelly, combined with the crispy breading and moist chicken, was like heaven on Earth. I'd had my fair share of chicken wings—LA was famous for some fantastic chicken-and-waffle joints—but this?

"Okay, I get why you gave Vinnie money." I took another bite, quickly inhaling one wing and starting on another.

I didn't even care that my fingers soon were covered in sauce or that Mac reached over to wipe sauce from the side of my mouth. I didn't worry that Mac would judge me for having a healthy appetite.

When I'd first started dating Todd way back in high school, I didn't eat real food in front of him. Stupid, I know. But when we went out, I'd only order salads or tiny cups of soup. It got to the point that Todd asked me if I thought he couldn't afford to pay for a real dinner.

I'd fessed up and told him I was embarrassed to eat too much in front of him. He'd said I was being ridiculous. After that, I'd ordered more substantial meals. But even then, I never would've eaten wings like this with him. Todd had always been a stickler for eating healthy, especially as an adult.

I bit into the last onion ring and sighed happily. "You really outdid yourself," I said.

Mac grinned. "I'd take the credit, but I can't. I just know a great spot when I see one. Or taste one."

He then leaned toward me, his eyes heated. "And can I just say how fucking sexy you look, eating chicken wings?"

I burst out laughing. I didn't feel sexy. I was stupidly full, my fingers were greasy, and I barely restrained myself from belching after drinking a large Coke.

"You have a strange idea of sexy," I replied.

"Seeing a woman enjoying herself? That's always sexy. You know I just want you to enjoy yourself, right?"

I shivered at the look in his eyes. Fortunately for my stomach, the drive back to his place was long enough to digest all that spectacular food, although I found myself getting lulled to sleep as the sun went down.

I felt a gentle hand on my arm. "Elodie, we're home."

Although we were at Mac's, the words *we're home* resonated with me. His house had become comfortingly familiar. I'd even left a few toiletries there. Seeing my toothbrush in his bathroom made it seem like our relationship was serious.

Which is just silly of me, I thought. *A toothbrush is just for convenience, nothing more.*

"Oh, did I fall asleep?" I yawned, feeling sheepish. "I'm so sorry."

"Food coma. It happens to the best of us."

Before I knew what he was doing, Mac opened the passenger door of his car and lifted me out. I protested, even as a thrill went through me.

"I can walk!" I exclaimed.

Mac carried me into the house like I weighed nothing more than a feather. "But I like you in my arms," he said.

He placed me on the living room couch and then got me a sparkling water, which was what I usually drank. He sat down next to me, his arm around me, his warmth making my heart beat fast.

"Are you still tired?" he asked after some minutes of silence.

I wasn't sleepy in the least now. His mere proximity was like a flame to tinder. My body never failed to react to his presence.

It didn't help that he looked extra handsome, with his rumpled hair and blue T-shirt that defined his muscular chest and arms. I touched his cheek, the stubble rough against my fingers, and kissed him.

He kissed me back until I could've forgotten my own name. Any sleepiness I'd felt had melted away. Now, all I could feel was desire pulsing through me.

"No, I'm not tired," I replied, meaning it.

"Good. Because I have one last favorite thing to show you."

His grin was wicked. I nodded, my heart pounding now with anticipation. Mac then slowly undressed me until I wore only my bra and panties.

"Have you ever been edged?" he asked between kisses.

"Um, not really?"

"It's one of my favorite things. Let's see how long I can keep you from orgasming." He chuckled as he squeezed one of my nipples. "Because we both know it doesn't take you very long to come."

I snorted because I knew he was right. He played my body like a musical instrument. He seemed to know intuitively how best to bring me to climax. Even my trusty vibrator wasn't as good as Cole Mackenzie.

Mac sucked my nipples through the fabric of my bra, making me moan. I felt his fingers on my pussy, and he rubbed my clit lightly through the lace. But even as I tried to get him to rub me harder, he just shook his head and laughed.

"Patience, patience," he commanded. He slid down to the floor and parted my legs. "Pull your panties aside. Show me that sweet pussy."

I blushed. I couldn't hold his gaze while I did as he wanted. But I could feel his eyes on me, and it only made me gush with want.

"Show me that clit and pussy," he rasped. "Open for me."

I squirmed. "Mac—"

"Do as I say."

I obeyed, even as I blushed from head to toe.

"Finger yourself," he said.

I trembled as I pushed a finger inside. I was already sopping wet.

"Now fuck yourself," Mac commanded.

The sound of me finger-fucking myself filled the room. I felt Mac's fingers dancing along my labia, brushing my engorged clit, but not enough to bring me to orgasm. I shuddered when he licked my clit. His touch was feather-light—painfully soft—and I tried to add another one of my fingers.

He batted my hand away. "I didn't tell you that you could do that. Turn over."

I bit my lip. I turned over, and then Mac gave me three firm slaps on my ass cheeks. I squealed. That earned me two more slaps.

"Now, are you going to obey me?" he said.

I nodded, then quickly said, "Yes, yes."

Mac turned me back over and pulled my panties off. He put my legs over his shoulders, widening me until I had nowhere to hide, and buried his face in my pussy. He licked and sucked at a relentless pace until I was close to the edge.

But whenever I got close to coming, he'd back off, petting my thighs and making soothing noises. He drew me to orgasm, so close, and then would back off. Again and again, he edged me.

It felt like time had stopped. I was sweating, panting, arching like a madwoman in Mac's arms. He just pressed me down into the couch to keep me still.

"Please," I begged. "Please, Mac."

Mac lightly rubbed my clit with his thumb. "Keep begging, baby."

I did. I had no pride left. I felt my body tense, my climax just out of reach, but Mac knew exactly when to back off.

It was incredible. It was terrible. I didn't know the difference between pleasure and pain now.

"PleaseMacpleaseMacplease," I said in a rush. Tears streamed down my cheeks. I dug my fingers into the couch cushion.

"You want to come, Elodie?" He licked my thigh and then gave it a smacking kiss.

"Yes. I do. Please let me come."

Mac just watched me, his eyes dark and sultry. He massaged my thighs, my ass, touching every place that wasn't my pussy. I started sobbing in earnest now.

"Poor baby," he crooned. "Maybe I'll let you come now."

I nodded. "Please, please, please."

Then, before I could say another word, he parted my legs wide, latched his mouth onto my clit, and plunged three fingers into my pussy. I screamed. He fucked me hard and fast with his mouth and hands. The sounds of my squelching pussy filled the room. I arched and moaned and begged.

And then, I finally came so hard that I blacked out. Only the feeling of Mac petting my sides brought me back down to earth.

He pulled me down into his arms. I was as limp as a rag doll.

"Elodie? Can you hear me?"

I couldn't speak. Words failed me. "Um." That was all I could manage.

Mac kissed my temple. Then he gathered me into his arms and carried me upstairs.

When he put me to bed and climbed in beside me, I could only burrow into his embrace. I didn't think I'd ever recover from that session.

"Sleep," Mac whispered.

He didn't have to tell me. I fell asleep the moment I closed my eyes.

Chapter 21

Mac

The following Saturday, Elodie and I were in the car. I had no clue where we were heading because today was Elodie's turn to show me some of her favorite things. My phone buzzed, so I dug it out of my pocket. Finding a text from my lawyer reminding me to call him, I frowned. He'd left a message yesterday telling me he'd gotten Elodie's background check back. But I hadn't returned the call. I was busy and told myself it could wait. Or maybe I was just in denial that there could be anything I should be worried about when it came to Elodie.

But right now, I didn't want to think about background checks or contracts. I wanted to focus on the woman sitting next to me. So I stuffed my phone back into my jeans and tried to relax. Although when we pulled up outside a tiny theater in West Hollywood that looked like it'd seen better days, I was a little confused.

"Don't worry." She laughed. "It's nicer inside."

The theater was nicer inside—marginally. The old carpets were worn, and the floors creaked with every step.

When I used the bathroom before we took our seats, it had one of those weird endless towels to dry your hands. I had only ever seen those things on the Internet. And it was pretty much a miracle that anything flushed in that bathroom.

Elodie and I took our seats near the front. Tonight was a showing of *Hamlet,* but a modernized take on it. Elodie had explained that this theater troupe was one of the best in the city.

"I didn't know you were a theater geek," I remarked.

"I don't know if I would call myself that, but I've always loved *Hamlet*. Don't give me that look. Shakespeare is mind-blowing for a reason."

I could recall attempting to read *Romeo and Juliet* in high school—or the CliffsNotes version. English literature had never been my strong suit. I'd wanted to be out on the ice, not trying to understand plays over five hundred years old.

The play began, and despite the strange language, having it acted out made all the difference. I was sucked into the story: Hamlet and his faux madness; Ophelia and her real madness; the treachery of Hamlet's mother and uncle; Polonius's absurd speeches.

The actor playing Hamlet somehow managed to imbue the role with a tragic regality. At least, that was how Elodie put it. To me, the guy was just interesting to watch.

During intermission, Elodie said, "Do you have any favorite authors?"

My mind went blank. Grimacing, I admitted, "Uh, Dr. Seuss?"

She laughed. "Mac. Come on now. Please tell me you've read a book in the last year." At my expression, she sighed. "What about in the last five years?"

Now, I was offended. "Of course I have."

I failed to mention that the last book I'd read was a biography of Wayne Gretzky. I couldn't remember the last time I had read something willingly that wasn't about hockey.

"I think I liked *The Catcher in the Rye* back in high school," I said. "Is that the one with Holden Caulfield?"

Elodie smiled. "Good job." She patted my shoulder, which just made me growl at her.

When the play finished and we headed to our next destination, Elodie told me about how she'd fallen in love with writing after reading Shakespeare.

"His plays have everything in them: comedy, tragedy, romance, mystery. If you don't like one play, there's another one you will enjoy. His characters are complex. I mean, look at Hamlet. Was he just acting insane? Or was he truly going insane? I wrote an entire paper about that."

"Like I said, you're definitely a nerd, Elodie Andrews."

She shrugged. "Maybe. But I bet I could get you going talking about hockey for hours."

"I didn't mean that as a diss. I love that you're passionate about something. Too many people aren't passionate about anything. They just go through their lives not caring much one way or another."

Elodie seemed to accept that, and when she parked her car in front of the Central Library in nearby downtown LA, I had to restrain a chuckle.

"The library?" I shot her an amused look. "Really?"

"Have you ever been here? It's gorgeous inside. Come on."

Despite having lived in LA for years now, I'd never been to any of its libraries. The Central Library was an imposing white building in the classic Spanish design. After entering and going up a staircase, we stood in a large, colorful rotunda. In the center was an equally impressive chandelier.

"The ceiling?" Elodie pointed. "It's all painted motifs. Amazing, right?"

I nodded. "Cool."

We then wandered around, the quiet of the huge building rather imposing. We eventually went into a part of the library full of books and almost void of any human beings.

"I can't remember the last time I was in a library," I said, touching the spines of books as we passed through various aisles.

"Really? I love libraries. They're so calming."

I suddenly remembered my parents refusing to get us kids library cards when one of my sisters had asked for one. They'd claimed that libraries were filled with ungodly books. We could only check out books from our church's library. The selection there had been limited; there hadn't been any *Harry Potter*, that was for sure. It was no wonder I never got into reading when my parents led me to believe that most books were bad.

"Are you going to check anything out?" I asked.

Elodie's smile was sly. "Oh, I was planning on it."

The only thing I checked out was her. When she took me to a dark corner, she planted a heated kiss on my lips. I laughed once my brain connected with what the hell she was doing.

"Elodie Andrews, are you trying to seduce me?" I growled. "In a library?"

"Yeah. Is it working?"

I pushed her against the wall, thrusting my tongue into her mouth. She moaned as we kissed like teenagers. The thought of getting caught was enough to make me rock hard, even if it was just getting caught making out.

"You're a naughty girl, aren't you?" I whispered. I sucked on the lobe of her ear.

She shuddered. "You like me naughty, though."

"Oh, that goes without saying."

I reached under her shirt and fondled her breasts, careful to keep her from being exposed. Although we were alone, I didn't want to take any chances.

I kissed her neck as I played with her nipples. She never failed to respond to me playing with her tits. It was one of the many things about her that I enjoyed.

We kissed until I was half insane with lust. I was about to pull her shorts and panties down when she froze.

"Did you hear that?" she whispered, her eyes wide.

I stopped and listened. That was when I heard faint footsteps. I quickly pushed off her and grimaced as I tried to hide my erection. Elodie covered her mouth to keep from laughing.

"I'm glad you're enjoying my pain," I growled.

She looked mussed, her hair a mess, and her lips were kiss-stung. "Come on." She grabbed my hand, and we hurried off to another dark corner.

The day ended with a hike. I had to admit, I hadn't expected this last activity. Fortunately, Elodie had planned ahead and had packed us a picnic basket full of food. I had to steal a few things to eat before we got started on our hike, though, since I was absolutely fucking starving.

"That's for later!" Elodie protested, laughing at me.

"Baby, you don't want to see me hangry." I tossed some almonds into my mouth before we headed out.

Fortunately, it wasn't a long hike to the Hollywood

sign. Well, not for the experienced hiker. Elodie had chosen the more challenging climb, which took the least amount of time.

"I didn't know you liked hiking," I said.

"Oh, I do it when I can, but I'm usually too busy." She shot me a wry smile. "You good? Or do you need to take a break?"

I snorted. I'd just broken into a sweat. "Baby, I'm a professional athlete. I'm more worried about you."

"Don't worry about me. Worry about yourself."

I grunted. We eventually got to the section in the trail that made it difficult to keep conversation going. We passed handfuls of people going up and down, but there were sections where it was just us.

"You haven't taken me up this trail to murder me, have you?" I joked.

Elodie looked over her shoulder at me and just smiled evilly.

By the time we reached the top, I was starving once again. I downed an entire bottle of water, my muscles feeling the burn of the climb, but overall, I'd enjoyed the hike.

This was another classic LA thing that I'd never done. Did anyone who lived in the city care much about climbing up to see the Hollywood sign?

"It's not the sign," Elodie explained once we found a nice spot to sit. She motioned with her arm. "It's the view. And I just love watching sunsets."

The view was spectacular, I had to admit. Below us was the city, alight as always. And as the sun set, the sky color transforming from orange to red to purple, the moon peeking out from behind a few stray clouds, I couldn't disagree with Elodie.

We ate in companionable silence. Elodie had packed us sandwiches, fruit, chips, lots of water, and some homemade cookies.

I wrapped my arm around her as we watched the sunset together. "I think you might've won the challenge," I said.

"I didn't know our dates were a competition."

"Of course they were."

She smiled. "I don't know. Those chicken wings were pretty damn amazing."

We eventually packed up our picnic and made our way down the mountain. Elodie had packed flashlights, and by the time we reached her car, it was dark. Or as dark as it could get in a big city like LA.

Elodie took me back to her place. We burst inside, laughing like idiots, and began stripping each other's clothes off. I'd been tempted to seduce her on the mountain, but too many people were around.

"You've been fucking teasing me all day long," I said, unhooking her bra and tossing it into some dark corner.

She laughed. "Have I?"

"Yeah, you have. And you're going to pay for it tonight."

"You say that every time we have sex."

I spanked her, making her yelp. "Be a good girl, all right?"

Her eyes were wide with faux innocence. "I'm always a good girl!"

"No, you're not. In fact, you've been very bad all day long."

Even as I wanted to take control like I always did, I forced myself to hold back. This entire day had been about what Elodie loved. And if she had something particular in mind for tonight, I wanted her to feel like she could do whatever she wanted.

She took me to her bedroom. It was a small room, but it was neat and tidy. Elodie had even made the bed, and it was covered in throw pillows.

I picked one up covered in pink sequins. "What's even the point of pillows like this?"

Elodie clucked her tongue. "It's cute!"

"But you can't use it. Why have pillows you can't use?"

"It's for decoration." She rolled her eyes. "And you have no room to talk, Mr. I Bought A House And Didn't Even Buy Furniture For It."

"I was busy!"

"So says every bachelor."

That earned her a growl and a firm smack on her luscious backside. It took every ounce of my self-control not to throw her down on her bed and fuck her senseless.

She pushed me away. "I want to play a game," she said.

I narrowed my eyes. "What kind of game?"

"Who can hold off coming the longest."

I laughed. "Baby, you and I both know who'll win that one."

Elodie put her hands on her hips. "Who, you? Well, how about we play the game before we declare you the victor?"

"So defensive." I held up my hands. "How about we do this instead? Whoever gets the other person off the fastest wins."

Elodie narrowed her eyes. Then, to my amusement, she held out her hand. "Deal."

I shook her hand, forcing myself to keep a serious expression. Elodie had me strip naked, and then she was crawling up my body to kiss me.

"You're not going to get naked?" I asked, palming her ass.

She swatted my hand away. "No touching. And yes, I'm staying clothed."

I groaned, but I let her play. She kissed down my body, her mouth soft and sweet. She tongued my nipples, which just made me chuckle. When she poked me in my ribs, I nearly jumped out of my skin.

"Oooh, are you ticklish?" Elodie began tickling me in earnest.

I laughed, shouted, and then quickly overpowered her. Holding her hands captive, I growled, "New rule: no tickling."

She pouted. "That's boring."

"Elodie."

She thought a long moment, then sighed. "Fine, fine. No tickling."

I let her go. She kept her promise, although she looked a bit miffed. I just smiled darkly.

Then I was distracted because her mouth moved closer and closer to my cock. Her hair just brushed the tip, and when she finally gripped me in her hand, I sighed. I also made sure to glance at the clock on her nightstand. I wasn't about to let her win because I'd been too distracted to pay attention to how much time had passed.

Elodie stroked my cock, swirling her tongue around the tip. But she wasn't gentle for long. She soon had nearly my entire length in her mouth and throat. She sucked me hard at the same time she fondled my balls.

"Fuck," I hissed. There was a very good chance I could lose control.

She shot me a smile, even with me inside her mouth, and it only turned me on more. I could feel my balls already drawing up. Tightening my muscles, I willed my orgasm away.

How could this woman make me come this quickly?

I forced myself to think of anything else. England? No, something even more boring. Taxes. Coach Dallas. Worms?

I tried to keep my thoughts elsewhere, but then Elodie upped her game when she deep-throated me. She moved up and down my cock, her teeth just grazing the underside of my dick.

Her mouth was so wet and warm, her fingers gripping the base of me so firmly, that it only took a few more minutes for me to shout and start coming. Elodie swallowed every last drop.

And since I was never not competitive, I made sure to look at the clock right after I'd come. *Seven minutes.* I grinned inwardly.

No way in hell was Elodie going to last that long. I was pretty sure I'd always gotten her off in under five minutes, tops.

Elodie's eyes widened when she sat up. "I forgot to set a timer!"

"Don't worry." I winked. "I made sure to look at the clock."

Her eyes narrowed. "I don't trust you not to cheat."

"Me? I don't need to cheat, baby. Now, take off your clothes already so I can show you that I'm always a winner."

Elodie stuck out her tongue and made a show of starting a timer on her phone. For that, I grabbed her and ripped her clothes off for her.

Elodie giggled as I stripped her down. Then she was moaning within seconds after I put my mouth on her pussy. She was sweet and slick as always. I knew exactly how she liked it: two fingers inside, thrusting upward, with my lips sucking on her clit.

I could feel her start to tense within a minute. Her fingers grabbed at her comforter already. I smiled and increased the pressure on her clit.

"Oh!" Her eyes flew open. "Mac, that's not fair—"

I didn't care. I might not cheat, but I wasn't above playing dirty either. I finger-fucked her until she was arching off the bed. I could feel her orgasm coming with how tight her pussy got around my fingers.

I then pushed a third finger into her tight asshole, and Elodie screamed. A few moments later, she came hard, her juices flowing down my chin. I lapped them up, triumphant.

She was still trembling as I kissed my way up her body. I looked at her phone and grinned. *Three minutes.*

"I win," I crowed.

Elodie barely registered my words. "Whatever." She was breathing hard. "Do what you want with me. I'm done."

I just kissed her, loving how pliant she was in my arms. She was rosy and warm; a flush had covered her entire body.

She never failed to throw herself headlong into her own pleasure. It was one of the intoxicating things about her. I never had to worry that she was putting on a show for my benefit.

Although that hadn't happened since I was a teenager. As an adult, I knew my way around a woman's body too well. No woman needed to fake an orgasm when they were in bed with me.

"So what do you want?" Elodie asked.

"Want?"

"For your prize. You won, after all."

I kissed her palm. "Oh, I already won my prize. You, in my bed."

"Well, technically speaking, this is *my* bed."

"Sassy as always. I think that's something we should work on."

She just giggled, the giggles turning to moans when I started us on round two.

I woke up to the sound of my phone ringing. I picked up, groggy with sleep, barely registering who was on the other end. Elodie yawned next to me and turned back over to keep sleeping.

"Mac, sweetheart." It was Mom.

I sat up, any grogginess fading quickly. "Mom? What is it?"

She sighed. "Caroline died last night."

Chapter 22

Elodie

Mac barely spoke on the flight to Idaho. After he'd gotten off the phone with his mom, he'd told me that he needed to go pack.

"Let me go with you," I'd said before really thinking it through.

Mac had paused. Then he'd just nodded, told me he'd pick me up later, and left. I wasn't sure if he really wanted me with him or if he just didn't have the energy to fight with me over it.

I hadn't seen Mac shed a single tear. He'd been stoic, his jaw clenched, but surprisingly calm despite everything. On the flight, I tried to engage him in conversation, but he kept giving me one-word answers. I eventually gave up and tried to read my book, but I couldn't concentrate to save my life.

We were driven to a hotel in Coeur d'Alene right after landing. Mac had gotten us separate rooms, to my shock.

"It's just to keep the press from going insane," he explained, looking chagrined.

"But I don't think you should be alone tonight," I said.

"I'll be okay. Get some sleep. Tomorrow is going to be a long day."

We got up early and met in the lobby. It was an hour's drive to White Rock, and it was once again a silent trip. I wondered why Mac had allowed me to come at all.

But when he took my hand and squeezed it, I knew I'd made the right decision. He needed my support, even if it was silent support.

We arrived at the church and sat in the car for a few minutes. Mac breathed slowly and deeply. I imagined lots of thoughts floating around his mind at that moment. Memories of Caroline, good and bad. Having to face her husband. As bitter as my own feelings were about the Caroline situation, it was hard not to sympathize with him right now.

"It'll be okay," I said quietly.

His lips twisted. "Will it?"

The large and imposing church looked like any other building. It could've been a warehouse, for all I knew. Inside, the lobby was massive, and there was even a café at one end and a bookstore at another.

I was tempted to browse the bookstore, mostly out of morbid curiosity, but I couldn't leave Mac's side. We sat down on a bench and waited for others to arrive since we were a half hour early for the visitation and church service.

"Are we going to the graveside service?" I asked.

Mac shook his head. "I wasn't invited. It'd be awkward, anyway."

We sat and watched congregants slowly arrive. A few recognized Mac; some stared and whispered, while a few came up to him and shook his hand. I was thankful that soon enough, there were so many people that Mac and I could fade into the background.

When we entered the church, I felt dread fill me as I realized this visitation was an open casket. I'd only attended one open-casket funeral as a kid, and it'd freaked me out so badly that I'd had nightmares later.

Mac avoided getting in line to give Caroline's family condolences.

"Dave will probably punch me again," Mac said as we sat in the back of the church.

After the visitation, Mac's dad held a service. I held Mac's hand, but I didn't know if it was more for me than it was for him.

I could just make out Caroline's pale face inside her casket. The blond hair over her head looked like it might've been a wig—it was too perfect. I struggled to feel sad that she'd died. It was probably better that I couldn't see her clearly. I didn't want to remember what she looked like.

Didn't Mac understand that she'd used him? That she hadn't been a good person? I didn't understand his sadness. All I could feel was anger at the woman who'd abused a teenage boy who'd just wanted someone to understand him.

As Bob Mackenzie extolled Caroline's virtues, I felt my stomach twist. I whispered to Mac that I needed to use the restroom and got up.

I felt like I couldn't breathe. Despite the huge auditorium, the walls felt like they were closing in.

Was everyone in this place going to act like Caroline hadn't been an abuser? Or did they just think she and Mac had done nothing worse than have an extra-marital affair?

To my surprise, I spotted Judy on a bench near the café that had closed for the service. She had her hands folded like she was praying. When she caught me looking at her, she motioned for me to join her.

"It's nice to see you again," she said to my surprise. Her expression was sad. "I wish it were under better circumstances, though."

I didn't know how to respond. Did Judy know the whole story about Mac and Caroline? I couldn't imagine how she felt as his mother.

"I wish that too," I replied.

Judy looked at me, her gaze full of something I couldn't wholly define. "Take care of him, okay? And don't break his heart."

I let out a surprised laugh. "I don't think I could if I tried."

"You don't know my boy, then. He has a heart of gold, but he gives it out to people who don't deserve it." Judy looked stern now. "Don't be another person he'll regret."

She got up before I could respond. And then a few moments later, I heard people talking. The service was now over.

I returned to where Mac was sitting. Up at the front, I saw Dave turn to glare at Mac, his face visibly red. Mac was brave for showing up here knowing that Dave would make him feel badly for it.

"We should go," Mac said. He didn't look away from Dave, though. He just nodded tightly at him and then left with me.

I was hoping for a quick return to our hotel, but I knew that wouldn't happen when I saw the huge swath of photographers outside. Who had tipped them off? And who showed up at a visitation like that?

I was disgusted. Mac looked like he wanted to punch everyone there. It made me ashamed of my own involvement in the tabloid press. Being on the other side of it really brought home how tough celebrities have it when you can't even mourn in peace.

"Mac, when did your relationship with Caroline Bradford start?" one reporter asked brazenly, shoving a mic in Mac's face. "Did you know she was married?"

Mac's lip curled. "No comment," he spat.

Flashbulbs went off, and more reporters lobbed questions at Mac as we went to our car. When one guy asked why Mac only went for married women, I could feel Mac wanting to turn around to confront the man.

The last reporter asked Mac, "Did you punch anybody this time?"

Mac stopped in his tracks. For a moment, I thought he was going to lose it and show that last reporter precisely how he could throw a punch.

"Let's go," I said, squeezing his hand. Mac hesitated but eventually kept walking.

A few of the reporters tried to get me to answer questions. I worried that some of them would recognize me—or worse, that I'd know them—but I didn't see anyone I knew. I'd dodged my biggest nightmare. Once we got back into the car, Mac put his head in his hands. He groaned.

"What a fucking mess," he said. "Can you fucking believe those vultures? And who told them I was there? I thought I'd be safe in White Rock of all places."

I felt sick to my stomach. Not just because of what had happened but because those vultures had jobs just like mine. They were there because Mac was a celebrity, and they could make money off him. Because he was rich and famous, it meant that his humanity didn't matter.

"Showing up at a church, too," I said. "Pretty sure you'll go straight to hell for that."

That remark made Mac chuckle darkly. "We can only hope."

We returned to the hotel but only to change. Sitting on the bed, I watched Mac pace back and forth.

"We can get a flight out of here whenever we want," I said.

Mac shook his head. "I don't want to leave yet."

"Really?"

"I need to get out." He had a wild look in his eyes now. "Have you ever seen Idaho? I want to show you. Let's call it another date."

Despite how tired I was, I didn't have the heart to tell him no. I changed into comfortable clothes. Mac met me in the lobby, where he'd somehow gotten a car to drive us around.

"There's a place near Coeur d'Alene that I always loved as a kid," he explained. "I want to take you there."

After an hour's drive, we arrived at a national park. It was a beautiful, mild day. The initial cloud cover had disappeared, and the sun had begun to peek out from under the clouds.

"I always forget that Idaho is part of the Pacific Northwest," I commented.

"Northern Idaho is." Mac gestured at me to follow him.

We went to a nearby shop and rented a four-wheeler. Since I'd never driven one, Mac decided I'd sit behind him as he drove us.

We drove into the mountains, the trees getting thicker around us, the air cooling as we ascended. The scenery was gorgeous, and I felt a peace descend on me as we drove.

When we arrived at our destination—a waterfall surrounded by pine trees—Mac stopped the four-wheeler. We took in the sight, and I could feel the tension melt off him in a wave.

"It's beautiful," I said in awe.

Mac inhaled deeply. "I love this place. I haven't been here in years." His eyes sparkled for the first time since we'd gotten here. "You don't get to see things like this in LA much."

I smiled. "This much green? No way."

Mac took my hand, intertwining our fingers. We watched the waterfall and the birds flying to and from the surrounding trees. At that moment, I felt our connection deepening. And it scared me because I knew that our relationship was always meant to be temporary.

I thought of Judy's warning. Did I really have the power to break Mac's heart? I shuddered at the thought. I couldn't bear the idea that I'd hurt him. But wasn't I the one who should be guarding my heart, not Mac?

"Caroline never liked nature," he said quietly. "Once, I tried to get her to go hiking with me, but she refused. Told me it was a waste of time. I'm not sure that woman even owned a pair of hiking boots."

A tear snaked down his cheek. I leaned against him, hoping I could lend him some strength.

"I'm sorry." That was all I could think to say.

"We didn't even like the same things. Well, besides BDSM." His tone was darkly wry. "She was twenty-five years older than me, yet she had this hold over me. You know, when my mom told me she'd died, I felt relief."

His gaze caught mine. I could see the pain in his eyes.

"Does that make me a piece of shit?" he asked.

I shook my head. "Your relationship was complicated. And she was sick. I would bet she's relieved to no longer be in pain."

"That's the thing. It wasn't about her. It was about me feeling free." He shook his head. "Never mind. I'm talking bullshit. We should go."

When Mac decided that we should leave Idaho altogether, I didn't protest. I was also ready to get back home to LA. By the time we got on the private plane, I could feel the tension melting from my own body.

Mac, however, didn't seem to relax. Instead, he seemed to get even more agitated. He kept pacing on the plane; when he did sit down, he just stared out the window and drummed his fingers against the armrest. When I suggested he read or play a game on his phone, he just grumbled something and kept staring out the window.

It was like watching a caged tiger. I kept expecting him to pounce on me at any moment.

Despite his predatory behavior, I wasn't wise enough to avoid him. I went back to his house with him, but not before Mac warned me away.

"I'm not in the mood to be nice," he said, his eyes dark.

I swallowed and lifted my chin. "I'm not afraid of you."

He chuckled, but there was no humor in it. When we arrived back at his house, it was late. But neither of us was tired.

Mac took me straight upstairs to his bedroom. He opened the closet that led to all his BDSM things: whips, chains, ropes, dildos, vibrators, and a plethora of other things. When he came out with a flogger, I almost ran in the opposite direction.

He stared me down. "You have one last chance to leave," he said quietly.

"I'm not leaving."

He gazed at me long and hard, and then something came over his expression that made me shiver.

"Take off your clothes," he commanded.

I obeyed, my body responding to his eyes on me. My nipples hardened, and I saw him inhale sharply.

"Get on your hands and knees," he then said.

I hesitated a moment, only for Mac to use the flogger lightly on my ass. I gasped.

"Get on your hands and knees." His tone was unlike anything I'd heard before.

Although he'd warned me that I couldn't get away now, I still had the safe word. I knew without a doubt that Mac would stop if I asked him to. I just had a feeling that he needed me to take what he had to unleash. Perhaps it wasn't so much warning me as it was warning himself that he was at the point of no return.

I got on my hands and knees. Then I felt the flogger on my ass, harder this time.

"Don't move," he instructed. "Don't make a sound. This is your punishment, Elodie."

I nodded at the same moment he hit me once, twice, three times with the flogger. The strikes were sharp but brief, the pain intense yet pleasurable at the same time.

When he moved from my ass to my back and shoulders, I had to bite my lip to keep from crying out. Despite my best efforts, I couldn't help but make noise.

Mac's fingers trailed gently down my spine. "What did I say about making noise?" His voice was as gentle as his fingers now.

"I'm sorry," I whispered.

He whipped me harder for that remark. He flogged me until I was crying—whether tears of pain or tears of pleasure, I could no longer tell.

Through it all, though, I never once was afraid of Mac. I wanted him to use me. I wanted him to pour out all of his own pain and anguish onto my body.

I was sore, my back and ass stinging like crazy when Mac finally gave me a brief respite. But that was only to undress himself. His hard cock was already dripping.

When I tried to reach for him, he slapped my hands away. "Not tonight," he growled.

Then he kneeled and thrust inside me from behind. I dug my fingers into the rug as he pounded into my body, his fingers digging into my hips.

"That's a good girl. Take my cock," he crooned. He moved faster and faster, his cock relentless. I could only press my face against the floor and hide my moans as best as I could.

"Tell me you want my cum," he commanded.

When I didn't respond, he grabbed me by my hair, pulling me up. I yelled.

"Tell me, Elodie," he snarled.

"I want your cum," I sobbed.

He grunted and fucked me until I could feel his cock pulse inside me. Right before he pulled out, I came, my pussy clenching around his length.

He swore, and then I felt him coming on my back and ass cheeks. I could only shudder and moan, my entire body now total jelly.

I wanted to collapse, but Mac wasn't done with me. Not yet. He flipped me over and thrust back inside me, my legs hanging over his arms.

"Mac, oh my God—"

"You'll never get away from me. You hear me?" His gaze drilled through me, and I couldn't bring myself to look away. I'd never seen Mac this wild and uncontrolled. I pulled him down and kissed him. He grunted and kissed me at the same time he brought me to another body-wracking orgasm.

"Elodie," he groaned. "Fuck, Elodie."

He said my name like a prayer. At that moment, I knew that I'd never get Mac out of my heart. He'd invaded and conquered my very soul.

Mac collapsed on top of me, panting. We were both sweaty and exhausted. My entire body was sore. Mac had to help me up, even carrying me over to the bed.

He made sure to use a cool washcloth on my back, kissing the welts he'd left. Now that the adrenaline had dissipated from my body, I felt the full effects of the flogging.

Mac got up and returned with a glass of water and some pills. "So you can sleep," he explained.

I didn't even ask what he was giving me. I took the pills and sighed when Mac rubbed some cooling liniment into the welts. Although it stung at first, it felt like heaven a few moments later.

"You should get some sleep," he said.

I smiled and then yawned. "I'm getting there." My eyelids were suddenly heavy. "What did you have me take?"

"Something to put you to sleep," was his wry response.

I yawned a second time. Despite the heaviness in my body, though, my mind just wouldn't shut off. I couldn't stop thinking about the look on Mac's face when he'd brought out the flogger.

I wasn't mad at him for using it. But I was confused. Was it fair that he'd taken out his anger on me when he was angry with Caroline? Was it healthy? I didn't know. I didn't know how to process everything that had just happened. Although I'd told myself I'd wanted him to unleash all his feelings, I now wondered if I'd made things worse.

Or maybe you're just hurt that he used you like that.

It didn't help that whatever pills Mac had given me made me groggy. All I wanted was to fall asleep, but my brain wouldn't let up. I could see Mac in my mind's eyes, warning me. I saw the darkness there. I'd never seen Mac go to a place like that before.

What if that happened again? Was he going to punish me whenever he was angry about something outside his control?

I turned over, groaning silently, and stared at Mac's back. I could tell by his breathing that he was asleep.

Oh, Mac. What the hell are we doing?

When I'd signed that damned contract, I'd told myself this was just about exploring a kink. That we'd have some amazing, raunchy sex, and that'd be the end of things.

How could I have been so naive? Our lives had become intertwined to the point that I knew if we ended things, we'd feel the pain of that separation as much as I'd felt the pain of the flogger tonight.

Tears pricked my eyes. I didn't even know who to be angry with: Mac? Caroline? God? Myself? All of the above?

Caroline, I wish you could see what you've done to this man. Maybe then you'd have some remorse.

I couldn't regret helping Mac relieve some of his own pain. But I also knew I didn't have infinite strength to bear the brunt of his dark side either. Mac would have to deal with his past on his own. Otherwise, he would never be able to move on.

Finally, blessedly, the meds kicked in, and I fell into a restless sleep.

Chapter 23

Mac

I lay in bed staring at the ceiling, unable to sleep. Elodie had fallen asleep quickly—thank God—but I couldn't turn my brain off.

Anxiety crashed into me like a tsunami. Had I pushed Elodie too hard? She hadn't used her safe word, but she was still new to BDSM. Had she felt like she couldn't say no?

I grimaced, rubbing my forehead. The thought that I'd ruined everything between us because I couldn't keep my own emotions in check . . .

And I wasn't even angry with Elodie. She was innocent in all of this. But she'd selflessly let me vent my anger, hurt, confusion, desire, lust—everything.

I was angry with Caroline. I was pissed that she was dead, and I was pissed that she still haunted me, even in death. Did I need a fucking exorcism? Was that the only way to purge Caroline Bradford from my soul, once and for all?

I'd punished Elodie, flogging her like that. She'd assured me afterward that she'd enjoyed it, but would she

234

still feel like that in the morning? If she ran off and never talked to me again, I wouldn't even blame her.

I eventually fell asleep but woke to an empty bed. The sun hadn't yet risen; it was probably close to five a.m.

I went downstairs and found Elodie at the kitchen table, a mug of something in her hand. She was staring off into space. She didn't even hear me approach until I was right in front of her.

She jumped when I said her name. "Christ! You scared me."

"Sorry." I went to flip on the light above the oven. "It's pitch dark in here."

"I didn't want to disturb you."

I frowned. "From turning on a light downstairs? And how did you make something to drink?"

Elodie's smile was wry. "I could make tea with my eyes closed. What's funny is that I don't even really like tea, but I didn't think coffee would make sense. My mom was the one who loved drinking tea. When she was sick, I always made it for her. She always claimed that whenever I made her tea, she felt better. By the end, I knew she was just humoring me."

I sat down, unsure how to take Elodie's mood. "Are you okay?"

At the same time, she got up and said over me, "Do you want a cup?"

I nodded, only because it seemed like she was going to make me one regardless. What was ironic was that I hadn't even known there was tea in my kitchen. Had Andrea left it here? I rarely used my own kitchen beyond storing essentials.

Elodie eventually handed me a mug and returned to her chair. We sat in silence. I inhaled the scent of the green tea. I'd never been a big fan of green tea, but I wasn't going to mention that to Elodie right now.

I'd drink all the green tea she wanted me to drink if it meant she wouldn't run in the other direction.

I finally set down my mug, and that made Elodie's head swivel toward me. "I'm sorry," I said bluntly. "I shouldn't have taken out my emotions on you last night. You shouldn't have been punished for something that wasn't your fault."

She didn't reply for a long moment. Tapping her fingers against her mug, she replied, "It's okay."

Now, I was frustrated. "It's not okay. You have a safe word, but would you have used it last night? I told myself you would, but now I'm not so sure. You can always tell me to stop—"

Elodie held up a hand. "Stop. Mac. You don't have to punish yourself." Her lips quirked into a wry smile. "I had a good time, although it was intense."

"Then why did you come down here alone?" My mind was whirling.

"Because I needed to think." She chewed on her bottom lip. "Although I consented to everything you did, I agree that it wasn't . . . fair."

My stomach dropped. "Fuck, Elodie—"

"No, let me speak. Fair isn't the right word. I mean, you're clearly going through something." Now her gaze was direct, and it made the hairs on the back of my neck stand up.

She said, "What Caroline did to you wasn't right. I'm not going to act like it was. I don't care what you think. I know that's maybe hard to hear, but it's true. You're clearly going through something that isn't just grief." She reached out and took my hand. "Have you ever thought about talking to someone? Like a therapist?"

I didn't know what to say. I'd never even thought of going to a shrink. What would they do? Toss pills at me and call it a day?

"I think what happened last night was because you have trauma you need to work through," Elodie said.

I wanted to get defensive. I wanted to tell her she was wrong, that she didn't have a right to tell me how I should feel, that she didn't understand my relationship with Caroline. I wanted to say all those things, except something in her statement resonated. Something in her words spoke a truth that I'd been unwilling to hear for a very long time.

I swallowed, my throat dry. "I don't know."

"That's okay. I just want you to think about it, okay? That's all. Because if you're using sex and BDSM to work through your issues—well, I don't think it'll end well for anybody. And I know you don't want Caroline to keep coming between you and other people."

She didn't say the words *I don't want Caroline to come between us*, but I heard them all the same. I squeezed her hand back.

"I'll think about it," I said, my voice hoarse.

"Good." Elodie took her hand back, which made my idiotic heart twist.

Why did this woman have to affect me like she did? What had happened to keeping things businesslike? I'd never had this issue before. My previous lovers had come and gone, and I hadn't felt more than a pang. Besides Caroline, that is.

But Elodie was the complete opposite of Caroline. She was generous, kind, thoughtful. She also wasn't afraid to call me out on my bullshit. Even Caroline had never done that. Caroline had never wanted to have any hard conversations.

The only thing Caroline had wanted was to pursue her own pleasures, damn the consequences.

I had the sudden urge to show Elodie that I wanted to change. Or at least to make up for what I'd done to her last night. I finished the last of my tea and took her hand, leading her back upstairs.

I turned the water on for the bath, a huge Jacuzzi tub I'd used all of three times since I'd moved into this house.

When Elodie looked puzzled, I said, "I'm just giving you a bath. Unless you want it to turn into something else."

She shook her head in amusement but didn't protest. I wished I had shit like bubble bath, but my bathroom was sparse. I had toothpaste, an old bottle of body wash, and toilet paper. I'd only recently gotten a trash can after Elodie had teased me about it.

I had Elodie get into the tub before I got in. I winced inwardly when I saw the welts on her back. I loosely wrapped her in my arms and kissed those welts, willing them to disappear quickly.

"It's okay, you know," she said quietly. "I won't break. I'm pretty strong."

She didn't feel strong to me; she seemed small and fragile. I wanted to keep her protected. Safe.

Safe from me? I thought, angry with myself.

"No, really." She turned to look at me. "If I had wanted you to stop, I would've used the safe word. End of story. I'm more worried about you than I am about myself."

I sighed. "I don't deserve that."

"Now you're being stupid."

That made me chuckle. I then gave Elodie a gentle bath, and even as my cock rose in want for her, I didn't push for more. I'd meant it when I'd said Elodie would have to initiate if she wanted us to have sex again.

After the bath, I dried her off and rubbed lotion onto her back, telling myself that flogging myself internally wasn't going to help. If I wanted to show Elodie that I'd listened to her, I'd take her words to heart and really think about her suggestions. The thought of talking to some stranger about my history made me want to sprint to the hills. I hugged Elodie from behind, kissing the side of her neck.

"Do you have something in your pocket or are you just happy to see me?" she joked as she wiggled her ass against my cock.

I growled. "Keep teasing me and you'll find out."

She turned and wrapped her arms around my neck. "Oh, I definitely want to find out."

I kissed her. She tasted as sweet as always. I loved the way she made little mewling sounds when I kissed her.

I ran my hands down her warm, naked body. I palmed her breasts, and I made sure to tweak her nipples how she liked.

She broke the kiss, gasping already. I kissed the side of her neck and then took her to bed.

I laid her down gently. I almost wished I'd covered the bed in rose petals. Since when had I turned into some mushy romantic?

It was Elodie. Elodie made me sentimental. She made me want to be a better man.

Her gaze was hazy, her body flushed as I climbed on top of her. Normally, I'd seduce her fast and furiously, but not tonight. Tonight, I wanted to show her my tender side.

We kissed for what felt like an eternity. I turned so we were on our sides, facing each other. That also gave me access to her pussy, which was already dripping by the time I stroked a finger through her folds.

Elodie's cheeks were red now. "Mac," she said, her eyelids heavy.

I gently rubbed her clit, which made her moan. "Yes?" I asked, smiling.

"Go faster."

I chuckled. "I don't want to tonight."

"But I need you to." She arched when I played with her entrance.

I kissed her harder at the same time as I pushed my index finger inside her tight pussy. She shivered; I massaged her ass with my left hand as my right played with her.

I knew exactly how to make her come. Even then, I wanted to draw things out. I wanted to watch the pleasure rise and crest on her expressive face.

She was biting her lip as I circled her clit with my thumb. She kept trying to press herself harder against me. I shook my head and held her still against my gentle hands.

"Patience," I said.

She just groaned and writhed.

I watched as the orgasm slowly built inside her. Her nipples peaked; her body flushed a deeper red; her juices flowed down my hand with every stroke I made. When I pushed a second finger inside her and rubbed her clit just how she liked it, her eyes flew open.

"Mac," she panted. "I'm coming—"

I kissed her the moment she came against my hand, her sheath tight as a vise now. She moaned as I slicked my tongue against her own.

I only let her rest for a moment before I took hold of my cock and pushed it inside her still-contracting pussy. Elodie let out a cry of delight.

I fucked her as I held her close. I raised her leg over my hip, giving myself leverage. I returned to kissing her as I thrust inside her.

I knew I wasn't going to last much longer. It didn't help that Elodie was wild in my arms, her second orgasm building quickly and with more intensity than the first.

I shoved hard inside her, going as deep as I could, and then I let out a long groan as I came hard. Elodie yelled my name, her fingernails digging into my shoulders as she shuddered.

I didn't want to part from her. I kept kissing her, half-hard cock still inside her, loving the way she wrapped around me.

When had I become completely obsessed with this woman? I had a feeling it was the moment we'd first met. She'd made a home for herself and the thought of letting her go was now unbearable.

"I think I'm falling for you," I said, stroking her cheek.

Her eyes widened. "But that's not part of the contract."

I couldn't tell if she was joking. I just shook my head, kissing her nose. "Does it matter?"

She didn't say anything, but she didn't pull away either. She just wrapped her arms around me and kissed me. I took that to mean she felt similarly.

Were we making a huge mistake? At that moment, everything felt right. But I also knew that I wasn't the type of man Elodie needed.

She craved stability. She craved a man who wanted to marry her and give her children. She deserved the white-picket fence.

Could I give her that?

I didn't know. But as I rolled on top of Elodie, still kissing her, I couldn't help but hope that I could be the man she needed.

Chapter 24

Elodie

I awoke to my phone ringing. And ringing. I thought it went to voicemail, but it kept ringing. Mac groaned and rolled over in his sleep. I grabbed my phone and grimaced when I saw that it was Roy.

"Andrews!" he barked, making me jump. "What the fuck is going on?"

"Uh, care to elaborate?"

"Yeah, I'll fucking elaborate. I just saw you all over social media. You were spotted with that hockey player, holding hands and everything. I thought that story was dead! What aren't you telling me?" I had to hold the phone away from my ear since Roy was practically roaring at me. I scurried downstairs in the hopes that Mac hadn't heard any of the phone call. That would be a nightmare.

"Roy, I'm sorry, I should've told you." I scrambled to find an explanation, but my sleepy brain was struggling. For some stupid reason, I'd never thought Roy would care who I saw outside of work.

You're an idiot, I thought to myself.

"Told me what, exactly? You told me there was nothing on this guy, but now you're seeing him? Or are you just getting information from him? Tell me, Andrews."

"There's nothing to tell. There was no story, but Mac and I have become . . . friends."

I could hear Roy huffing and puffing. "Friends," he deadpanned. "Huh."

"Yes. Friends. That's all there is to it." I blushed. "Hey, I'll see you later, okay? And we can talk."

"You're not getting out of this that easily. I'm going to get to the bottom of this." Then he hung up on me.

I sighed, feeling a headache beginning to form between my temples. How had this situation turned into a hot mess? And was I going to lose my job over it? *Roy can't fire you because you're dating a celebrity,* I reasoned. But that didn't mean Roy wouldn't fire me when he discovered there were plenty of stories to be written about Mac . . .

I went back upstairs, but I stopped when I heard Mac speaking to someone. I felt the floor melt under me when I heard Mac say, "She's a reporter? You're sure about that?"

I went into the bedroom, a frozen smile on my face, and hoped that Mac wasn't talking about me. But when he met my gaze, I knew the jig was up. Mac was stone-faced. "Okay. Thanks. I'll talk to you later." He put his phone down, and we stared at each other.

I didn't know what to say. The room was swaying. Did I lie? Did I tell him everything? My heart pounded so hard I felt a little faint.

"That was my lawyer," Mac said slowly. He kept staring at me, like he was trying to see all my secrets. "Is it true? Are you a reporter?"

I sat down on the bed, feeling like I was going to piss my pants. "It's true. But I can explain."

That made Mac laugh darkly. "You can't be fucking serious. Elodie—are you telling me the truth? You're a fucking reporter?"

When I tried to touch him, it was like I'd triggered an explosion. He got out of bed and started pacing, energy coursing through him now. He looked wild-eyed. If I didn't know him as well as I did, I might've been afraid of him at that moment.

"I am, but everything between us has been real, I swear it," I began.

Mac held up a hand. "Start from the beginning."

I told him everything: being assigned to dig up dirt about him and his supposed affair with a married woman, discovering he was using a decoy, following him to The Scarlet Rope, and everything after that.

Mac stared at me in silence, his arms folded across his chest, his brow furrowed. I couldn't tell what he was thinking as I unloaded onto him.

"So you did know who I was when we first met?" he accused.

I blushed. "I did. I'm sorry."

"And then when I told you about my interests, how I wanted you to sign a contract with me, was that just for a story?"

I nearly catapulted myself off the bed now. "No! No. I haven't told my boss anything. Once we started to get involved, I told him that there was no story. Look me up. I haven't published anything about you."

"That doesn't mean you won't."

"I signed multiple NDAs, Mac. Why would I do that if I meant to break them?"

"People break NDAs all the time." Mac raked his fingers through his hair, tugging at the strands. "And given who you work for, I'd bet they have great lawyers if push comes to shove."

"You have a lawyer, too."

"Because I need to protect myself. Your company is only interested in profiting off others' personal information. It's different."

I chewed on my lower lip, tasting blood. "What can I do to prove I'm not doing this for a story?"

"You can't."

I felt those words like a blow. My chin started quivering, to my humiliation. *I'm not going to cry. I'm not going to cry.*

"I told you from the very beginning that I needed to be able to trust you, and vice versa. But you lied to me from the start. How do I know anything you've said is the truth? Why would I be different from any other person you've gotten dirt on?"

"You are different!" I grabbed his arm, but he just stepped away from me. "I've never cared about any of the people I've written about. I've never become friends with them, or had sex with them, or fallen in—"

I stopped myself. Mac stilled. The moment and silence lengthened until the tension was painful.

"Don't," he murmured, his tone harsh. "Don't fucking tell me shit like that when I can't know if you mean it."

Now, I was crying in earnest. "I'm sorry." That was all I could say, over and over again.

"BDSM is about trust. I told you that. Even my fucked-up relationship with Caroline was based on trust. I told you things in confidence that I never would've told a goddamn *reporter*—"

He started pacing again. I could only sit back down on the edge of the bed and try to stem the flow of tears. I sniffled and sobbed, hating myself for seeming weak, while also wishing I could make Mac believe me.

"I didn't tell my boss anything. I promise you. You have to believe me," I said.

"Why should I?" Mac's voice rose. "Why should I believe you? You've lied to me from the start! I don't fucking know who you are."

"You do know me. I'm no different from when we first met. I just didn't know how to tell you what my job was." I wiped away the tears, but they kept coming relentlessly.

"I thought I had feelings for you," he was saying, almost to himself. "I can't fucking believe this."

I stood, lifted my chin, and forced myself to stop crying. "What do you want me to do? Name it."

He stared at me, but his gaze went straight through me like an arrow. It was like the Elodie of just an hour ago no longer existed in his eyes.

"You can get out of my house," he said finally.

I swallowed, a huge lump in my throat. I knew I wasn't going to convince him. Not when he was too hurt to hear what I wanted to say.

"I'm sorry. I'm sorrier than you can ever know," I said.

He gave me a sad but almost wry look. "I know. That almost makes it worse."

Chapter 25

Elodie

A few days passed. I hadn't heard from Mac since I'd left his house. Roy also hadn't called me again, which could be a good or a bad thing. The morning I decided to go into the office, I took a hot shower but only ended up crying again.

I'd been crying off and on since Mac had told me to leave. I'd decided to give him space, but it'd been difficult not to contact him to see how he was doing.

Was he still angry? Would he hate me forever now?

The guilt was going to eat me alive. What was worse was that I deserved to feel like this. I'd lied to Mac. I could've had the courage to be honest, but I'd avoided it. I'd just naively hoped that it would all work out in the end. Now Mac hated me, my boss was pissed at me, and I was probably close to getting fired.

I forced myself to get dressed and go into the office. As I drove onto the freeway, I got another phone call, this time from my coworker Darren.

"Roy assigned me to follow that hockey guy," Darren was saying. "The one you were seen with."

My blood ran cold. "Roy assigned you to Mac?"

"Roy is sure that there's a story there. He also gave me the address you gave him. I'm staking it out. It's this ugly office building. Is this really the place you saw Mac go in? Because there doesn't seem anything interesting to me here."

"It's a dead end," I lied, wincing internally. "I already looked into it."

Darren was silent. "You sure about that?" He sounded skeptical.

"Yes, I'm sure. It's one of the reasons I told Roy there was no story there. I don't know why he would've assigned you to Mac."

"Probably because you were out with the guy, so now there's a conflict of interest." Darren sounded amused.

"There's not. I promise you. We just got to know each other. He's a really interesting guy."

Darren made a noncommittal noise. "Elodie, you know I like you. I also know you pretty well."

"I like you, too," was all I could think of to say in reply.

Darren said nothing for a long moment. Then I heard him sigh. "Well, okay. I'll keep staking out this building for another day or two until Roy is convinced there's nothing here."

I felt like I was going to jump out of my skin once I got off the phone. Darren wasn't stupid. He could probably tell I wasn't telling him the entire truth.

If he figured out that Mac was a member of an exclusive sex club *and* that I'd signed a contract with Mac . . . my career would be over. Roy would never let me write another story again. And knowing my boss, he'd also make sure

I didn't write again in this city. Because what good was a reporter who got personally involved with her stories?

I knew it was a long shot, but I called Mac. I needed his advice. I also wanted to hear his voice, because I missed him. Desperately. To my frustration, he didn't pick up. I wound up leaving him two voicemails.

Before I could think about it, I did something rash. I got off the freeway, turned around, and went straight to Mac's house instead.

When I arrived an hour later, I was able to get through the security gate with the code Mac had given me. I knocked on the front door, but there was no answer. I peeked inside Mac's garage, and his usual car was gone.

"Fuck," I muttered to myself, at a loss. I called Mac a fourth time, but he still wouldn't pick up.

"Mac, I need to talk to you," I said in my third voicemail. "I know you're mad at me. But this is important. I wouldn't be calling you if it wasn't."

I stood in Mac's driveway, staring at the asphalt, my brain moving a mile a minute. What if Darren got into The Scarlet Rope tonight? And what if Mac was there?

I had to warn him. I didn't care if he hated me. I wasn't going to sit around and wait for shit to hit the fan if I could prevent in.

I heard footsteps. Looking up, I saw one of Mac's landscapers. I waved him over.

"Have you seen Mac?" I asked.

I'd only spoken to Josh one time when I'd had trouble getting through the security gate. He'd barely said two words to me. Now, he shaded his eyes and looked me up and down, like he didn't recognize me.

"I'm Elodie. Mac's friend," I explained.

Josh grunted. "Yeah, I know."

"Have you seen Mac?"

"No."

I stared, waiting for any more information.

"Okaaay," I replied, frustrated. "Do you know where he could be?"

Josh shrugged. "Nope."

I restrained myself from throttling the guy. "Well, if you see him, tell him I need to talk to him ASAP. It's important."

I was about to get back into my car when Josh said offhandedly, "Rosa saw him."

Rosa was Mac's housekeeper. "She did? Is she here?"

"Nope." Josh paused. "She told me she saw Mac with a bunch of suitcases."

I froze. "She did? Do you have her number?"

"Yeah, but she lost her phone. Dropped it in the pool, so you can't call her."

I gritted my teeth. "Okay. Well, thanks. Can I give you my number?"

Josh agreed, although I doubted the guy would message me again. He sauntered off, clearly not distressed that Mac had up and left LA without telling anyone, at least as far as I knew.

I got back into my car and drove to The Scarlet Rope. When I arrived, I circled around for Darren's car, but to my relief, I didn't see him. All the same, I parked a few blocks away and wore my hoodie and sunglasses just in case.

I got inside and ran into Serena. She raised an eyebrow at my attire.

"I know, I know. I'm looking for Mac. Have you seen him?" I asked.

Serena furrowed her perfectly waxed eyebrows. "Mac? No, I haven't. He hasn't been here for a week. Maybe longer." She shrugged. "We don't keep tabs on our regulars."

I sincerely doubted that, but I took Serena's word for it. I returned to my car and tried to gather my thoughts, wondering who else I could call.

I ended up calling Brady. He picked up on the second ring. "Well, isn't this a nice surprise?"

"Brady, it's Elodie. Mac's . . . friend."

"Yeah, I know. Caller ID and all."

"Have you seen Mac? Or talked to him?"

"No. He wasn't at practice today."

"I've called him a bunch of times and went to his house, but he's not there." I decided not to mention that Mac had also not been at The Scarlet Rope.

"Shit. Let me go ask Coach something."

I waited, tapping my foot with impatience, when Brady finally returned to the phone. "Okay, sorry. Coach says that Mac didn't call in sick or anything. Just was a no-show. We have an away game tomorrow, and he's supposed to be here in the next two hours."

I felt anxiety make my gut twist. "Shit. That's not good. His housekeeper saw him leaving home with a bunch of suitcases. Would he have gone to your away game early?"

"No, and he never misses practice. We get fined if we don't show up without an excuse. Hell, Mac came to practice once with a raging fever. Nearly passed out on the fucking ice."

"I'm worried about him. Can you call him? He might pick up for you."

Brady was silent for a long moment. "Did you guys have a fight?"

"Kind of. It's complicated. Can you just call him? And let him know I need to talk to him?"

"I don't like getting involved with couples' spats but . . ." I could almost hear Brady shrugging. "I'll try."

I thanked him and hung up, my heart pounding. Now I knew something was wrong.

Was Mac okay? He wasn't the type to disappear without telling people. The fact that he hadn't shown up for practice today was deeply concerning.

Had I pushed him over the edge?

I forced myself not to panic. Mac was a grown man who was more than capable of taking care of himself. This wasn't some macabre true crime case either.

Even as I tried to keep my panic at bay, I also felt so guilty that I almost threw up. None of this would have happened if I hadn't lied to Mac in the first place. I should've just had the courage to be honest with him.

I took a few deep breaths. All I could do was hope that Mac would contact me or, at the very least, talk to Brady.

Please be okay, I prayed.

Chapter 26

Mac

I shouldn't have come here.

But here I was, standing in front of Caroline's grave as if her ghost would give me the answers I needed. To make things more obnoxious, it was a gorgeous, sunny day without a cloud in the sky. I felt hot in just jeans and a T-shirt.

Shouldn't it be pouring rain? Or storming? That would match my mood at least. But no, the sun just had to shine; the universe just had to remind me that life could be warm and beautiful.

I snorted as I drank from the bottle of wine I'd brought with me.

"You'd laugh at me, wouldn't you?" I said to Caroline's gravestone.

On it was written *Caroline Miller Bradford. A devoted wife and mother.* Below that was a verse from Proverbs: *Who can find a virtuous woman? For her price is far above rubies.*

"What a crock of shit," I said, shaking my head. "Did you approve this headstone before you died? Because I really can't imagine you did."

I had a feeling Dave had chosen that verse as one last jab at his wife's cheating. Why the man hadn't divorced her years ago, I didn't know. Did he have no self-respect? Because I knew for a fact that I wasn't the only man Caroline had cheated with.

"God, I fucking hate you." I slurred the words, but I didn't even care that I was already drunk. I kept drinking, needing the burn of alcohol to banish every bad feeling that wanted to overwhelm me.

I'd thought I could trust Caroline, but she'd betrayed me. I'd thought the same about Elodie, and look where I was now. A pathetic heap of a man, drinking in broad daylight at his ex-lover's gravestone.

I would've laughed, but I had a feeling I'd only start crying instead.

"I always defended you, didn't I?"

If she were still alive, Caroline would've told me she'd loved me. That I was the only person who'd ever truly understood her. The first time she'd kissed me, I'd been shocked. Aroused. Terrified. This gorgeous older woman, the pastor's wife, wanted *me*.

"Do you know how sexy you are?" she'd said to me, her voice sultry and low.

I was a gangly, tall teenager with acne. The last adjective I would've used for myself would've been *sexy*. But I wanted to believe Caroline.

She'd pulled me into an unused office at the church when I'd found her crying one evening. I'd found her crying before. She'd told me all about how Dave was cruel to her, how her kids wouldn't listen to her, how lonely she was.

That night, she'd taken my hand, and we'd been in the dark together. I'd been sure that my heart would explode out of my chest. Then she'd kissed me.

I'd kissed girls before. I'd had a girlfriend my freshman year, and we'd had sex a few times. But sex with Caroline? That had been entirely different. She knew what she was doing. And she knew what she wanted. I didn't have the strength to tell her no.

"Could I have told you no?" I asked her gravestone. "Because I don't think you would've let me."

After we had sex the first time, she'd begged me not to say anything. Dave would kill her. "He has guns," she'd told me with tears in her eyes. "I don't want you to get hurt."

Considering everyone in Idaho had at least one gun, I had no reason not to believe her. I also didn't want her husband to hurt her. What if he killed Caroline because he found out about me and her?

I'd kept her secrets. I'd kept the sex, the confessions, the tears, the arguments, the BDSM—all of it, I'd kept it secret. And I'd convinced myself that I was desperately in love with her. I'd decided that I was going to convince Caroline to leave her husband and run away with me.

I was eighteen by that point. I'd take care of her. I didn't know how, but I'd figure it out. Wasn't that what true love was about? Figuring things out just so you could be together? I'd shown up at Caroline's house to tell her about my plan. It was Friday, which meant that Dave was down at the church. Caroline's kids were at their friends' houses.

I went inside, listening, when I heard groans. I rushed to Caroline's bedroom and found her in bed with none other than her own husband. All three of us stared at each other. Then Dave jumped out of bed, red as a tomato, while Caroline laughed.

Laughed! I couldn't believe it. The only thing that came into my stupid brain was to say, "I love you, Caroline."

That just made Caroline laugh harder. Dave grabbed me by the arm and nearly yanked my shoulder out of its socket.

"Get the fuck out of here," Dave snarled.

I couldn't move. I had to make Caroline understand. "You didn't have to do this," I said.

She gave me a pitying look that felt like an arrow through the heart. "Oh, Mac, go home."

Dave still held my arm. I pushed his hands off and shoved him to the floor so hard that he stumbled back.

Then I ran, Dave roaring behind me, the sounds of Caroline's insane laughter making me wonder if I'd been the one who'd lost my mind.

Now, over a decade later, I was talking to a gravestone. *I might be the crazy one after all*, I thought darkly.

I wiped my mouth and returned to my rental car. But I knew I was in no fit state to drive, so I dozed in the front seat until I sobered up. Once I was good to drive, I headed out. When I parked in front of my parents' church, staring up at its austere steeple, I wasn't even sure why I'd come.

Did I think this place would give me the answers I'd always sought? I doubted it. I'd twisted myself into knots, trying to fit into the mold religion and my parents wanted, but it'd never been enough.

I went inside. I told myself it was to get a bottle of water from the vending machine, but when I wandered upstairs to the church offices, I wasn't surprised to find

Mom up there. She didn't look surprised to see me. She just clucked her tongue and pointed at a chair. "You look terrible," she said.

She was handing me water and a granola bar before I could even ask for them. I drank and ate in silence, Mom standing over me, a resigned expression on her face.

"Your coach called me," she said after I'd finished.

"What?"

"You have people who are looking for you, Mac. What are you doing here in Idaho when you have a game today?"

I let out a pathetic laugh. "I thought maybe you could tell me."

"You can't run from your problems. You know that." She'd always said that to me. *You can't just leave. You can't just run away. You have to face what you're afraid of.*

But was leaving always due to fear? I'd left Idaho because there'd been nothing for me here. I'd left my family because they'd never understood me.

"I went to see Caroline," I admitted.

"I figured." My mom shook her head. "That woman. I won't say out loud what I think about her, but let's just say if I did, I'd be losing treasures in heaven." That made me smile a little. Mom had always refrained from saying aloud her worst thoughts for that very reason.

"Mac, I'm not going to say that what you and Caroline did together was right," Mom said slowly. "I still don't understand it. Your dad definitely doesn't."

At the mention of Dad, I tensed. "I didn't come here to get lectured."

"You seriously came to church and didn't expect a lecture?" Mom let out a laugh. "Cole Mackenzie, you always were a special kid, I'll give you that."

I scowled. "You know what I mean."

"I know you're hurting. I know you're confused. I know you thought you loved that woman."

"I did love her."

"I'm sure you did." Mom let out a sigh. "'Love does not delight in evil but rejoices with the truth. It always protects, always trusts, always hopes, always perseveres,'" she quoted.

I groaned. "Please don't quote Bible verses at me."

"You're in a church. Do you see how many Bibles are sitting right behind you?" I glanced over my shoulder. There were too many Bibles to count. I felt the weight of them, staring at me, judging me.

"If Caroline had loved you, she would never have tempted you," Mom was saying. "Real love would've meant understanding that an affair would hurt everyone."

"I'm not saying our relationship was healthy—"

"Relationship?" Mom let out a sad laugh. "You were just a child. Yes, a child. I didn't see that at first, and I'm sorry for that. More sorry than you'll ever know. You were always so mature for your age."

Tears started in Mom's eyes. Guilt hit me like a punch to the chest. "Please don't cry," I pleaded.

"I love you so much, Mac. I'm sorry you're hurting. I just want you to be happy." Mom wiped her eyes, but the tears kept coming. "You know, all those times I called you after you left? I couldn't tell your dad. I had to use Glenda's phone here in the office so he wouldn't catch on. He'd forbidden me from contacting you, and I just couldn't do it."

I'd had no idea. More often than not, I hadn't even picked up the phone when Mom had called back then. I'd seen an Idaho number, and I'd ignored it.

"Real love doesn't hurt people. Love is about respect. Do you think Caroline ever respected you? Because I'm not sure she did," Mom said.

I didn't know what to say. I'd been so caught up in the emotions of our relationship that I might've mistaken lust and obsession for love. My brain felt like it was complete mush. Mom got up and put a hand on my shoulder. "I hate to see you like this, son," she said quietly.

"I'm sorry I'm such a fucking mess."

She clucked her tongue. "Language. And everyone is a mess. By the grace of God are we saved from our own messes." She made me look up at her. "If you care about this Elodie girl, you'll tell her how you feel."

I gaped at my mom. "Elodie?"

"Yes, Elodie. I saw how you looked at her when we went to dinner. And a woman who attends the funeral of a man's . . ." My mom's mouth twisted. "I hate the word 'girl-friend,' but I guess that's all we got. A woman who attends the funeral of her guy's ex-girlfriend is a special person."

"She is special. I've always known that," I said, almost to myself.

"Then tell her. Don't hope that she just knows."

I shook my head. "It's not like that."

"Well, it could be if you talked to her. Are you in love with her? Because she should at least get a chance to re-spond to your feelings."

I hardly recognized my mom at this point. When I'd been growing up, she'd always deferred to my dad. She'd rarely taken us aside and given us talks like this. She'd ei-ther tell us to talk to our dad or to pray about it. I must've looked confused because my mom chuckled. "I've been go-ing to therapy lately. Can you tell?"

Now my eyebrows rose. "Seriously?"

"Seriously." She squeezed my shoulder. "And maybe you should, too."

I nearly burst out laughing because Elodie had suggested that exact thing. But I wasn't about to tell my mom that. She'd just tell me to listen to the women in my life because ninety-nine percent of the time, they were right.

I got up and hugged my mom tightly. "Thanks."

"I love you, Mac. And I'm proud of the man you've become. I hope you know that."

For the first time in a long while, I believed her.

Chapter 27

Elodie

I wasn't sure if I had the courage to get out of my car. I stared at the outside of the brightly colored restaurant, the Filipino flag on full display, and wondered why the hell I'd agreed to this meeting.

My uncle had reached out again. In a fit of desperation, because I was lonely and I missed Mac, I'd agreed to see him. Mac telling me that I should be grateful for any family who wanted a relationship with me had made an impression. So now I was going to lunch with my Uncle Jose and Aunt Maria at a restaurant that was apparently one of the best in the city for Filipino cuisine.

After another deep breath, I finally got out of my car. The restaurant was bustling, and I could hear sounds of Tagalog and English mixed. The smell of lumpias reminded me of my mom so much that I nearly turned around and ran.

"Elodie!" A man beckoned to me. "Over here!" It was too late to run now. I smiled awkwardly and sat down at a table with a man who looked like the male version of my mom. His wife was tiny and gorgeous.

Uncle Jose gave me a brief hug, while Aunt Maria just nodded at me. My uncle was in his midfifties, his hair silver at the temples. He had a big smile that seemed to take up his entire face. But it was his eyes especially that reminded me of Mom. It hurt to look at him, because it made me miss her even more.

"Have you been here before?" Jose asked me as I sat down.

I shook my head. "It's been a long time since I've had Filipino food," I admitted.

"Your mom was really good at making lumpia. Even better than our mom."

Before my mom got sick, she'd make lumpia often. I remembered coming home from school to the smell of fried dough and pork. I'd always end up being too impatient to wait for the lumpia to cool, and I'd burn my tongue biting into them. My mom would scold me, even as she piled my plate with more of the fried rolls.

"She was," I said.

We fell into silence. I didn't know what to talk about, and it seemed like my aunt and uncle didn't know either. I was grateful when our server took our orders, although my uncle ordered for our entire table when I hesitated on my choice.

"Their sinigang is amazing." He kissed his fingers.

"It's too hot for soup," Maria complained.

"It's never too hot for sinigang. Besides, it's good for you. Clears out all the bad juju." He winked at me. "At least that's what my mom always said."

It was too hot for soup, but I wasn't going to tell Jose no. As we bit into our plate of lumpia, I wondered if this had been a wasted trip. Had my uncle just wanted to talk about food? Why had he been so intent on seeing me?

"You know," Jose said, "you look just like your mom. When I saw you come in, I thought for a second that you were Ana."

"I never thought we looked alike," I said, surprised.

"Oh, you do. Doesn't she look like Ana?" he asked Maria.

Maria shrugged. "I guess so."

Jose shook his head. "Don't listen to her. She only met your mom a few times before . . ." He grimaced. "Well, before everything happened."

The familiar anger returned. "After you disowned my mom, you mean?" I snapped.

Jose looked sad. "I never agreed with Mom doing that, you know."

I folded my arms across my chest. "Yet you only just started caring about me now? What about when I was a kid, or when my mom could've used your help?"

Jose gave me a strange look. "You didn't know?"

"Know what?"

He glanced at Maria, but she didn't seem inclined to assist him. He said finally, "I reached out to Ana when you were a kid and tried to help her, but she wouldn't take any help. She thought I was on Mom's side, I guess. I finally had to give up after a while."

I stared at him, shocked. "Mom never told me that."

Jose's smile was wry. "My sister had a lot of pride so that doesn't surprise me. She hated accepting help from anyone. And yeah, maybe I did try too hard to keep both sides happy. I should've told our mom off, but Ana also wouldn't bend either. They were too much alike, those two."

Our server served our bowls of sinigang, the scent of tamarind making my mouth water. When I had my first sip, it almost felt like my mom was right there with me. I told myself that the tears that filled my eyes were from it being so hot, and not from sheer nostalgia.

"Good, isn't it?" said Jose.

I nodded, because I couldn't trust myself to speak right then.

We ate in silence, which I was glad for. I needed a moment to process Jose's revelations. If what he said was true, then he hadn't abandoned my mom. He'd tried to help us. My mom hadn't had to struggle like she had.

Why, Mom? You couldn't have accepted help from your own brother?

"Why do you think my mom told you no?" I asked aloud.

"Why?" Jose shrugged. "Like I said, your mom was very proud. It probably didn't help that our mom was sure that my sister couldn't be on her own without our help. My sister never backed down from a challenge."

Although I wanted to judge my mom, I couldn't. I probably would've done the same thing. Sometimes you needed to prove to yourself, above everything, that you could succeed. And my mom had everything stacked against her: a husband who'd left her; a family who'd judged her. She'd also been an immigrant, and she'd had to learn a new language, raise her daughter, and work multiple jobs.

She'd been a warrior. I just wished we'd had more time together.

"I took care of her when she was dying," I said, staring at my soup. "It was just us. I didn't understand why her family didn't want to help us."

"I wanted to be there. I know you have no reason to believe me, but I did." My uncle leaned toward me, his expression intent. "But Ana wouldn't hear of it."

To my surprise, Maria finally said, "He really did try. I had to tell him to leave her be."

"Really?"

Jose looked sheepish. "Ana might've told me to buzz off."

"That's the polite version," Maria added, deadpan.

I shook my head, stifling a laugh. "I'm sorry. Mom could be so stubborn, like you said. It was hard to get her to rest, even after her chemotherapy and radiation appointments. I'd catch her making dinner like she used to, and I'd basically have to threaten her to sit down."

Jose chuckled. "That sounds about right."

I finished the last of my sinigang, my belly full, and my heart even fuller. "I guess we have a lot of lost time to make up for," I said.

"I would like that." Jose took my hand and squeezed it. "I've always wanted to get to know my only niece."

"She's not your *only* niece," Maria protested.

"She's my only niece by blood, then."

Maria rolled her eyes and waved a hand at her husband. Jose just took it and kissed the back of her fingers, making Maria laugh.

"How long have you two been married?" I asked.

"Thirty-three years," replied Jose proudly.

"No, it's thirty-two," said Maria.

"Thirty-three! We just had our anniversary a month ago."

Maria tapped her chin. "Oh. You're right."

Jose's mouth dropped open. "Did you just hear that? My wife never says 'you're right' to me. Ever. This is a miracle."

I laughed at their antics. Jose's expression turned sly. "What about you? Do you have a special somebody?"

That question made me blush like a teenager. Then I wanted to cry, because Mac still hadn't talked to me. Brady had finally gotten ahold of him—thank God—so I knew he was okay. But him going off to Idaho so suddenly, without telling anyone, worried me deeply.

"It's complicated," I hedged.

Jose and Maria glanced at each other. "So you do have someone?" my uncle probed.

I let out a sigh. "Kind of? But I screwed things up. He won't talk to me. I don't know if he'll ever forgive me."

Jose leaned back in his chair and folded his hands. "You know, when I first started dating this one, I screwed up. Big time."

"He kissed another girl," Maria interjected.

"Another girl kissed *me*," Jose said. I had a feeling this was an old argument. "But that's besides the point. Maria saw a girl kissing me, and she broke up with me. Told me to go to hell and wouldn't talk to me for weeks."

Maria looked annoyed. "You make it sound like it was some random girl." She turned to me. "It was his ex-girlfriend. His ex! She still had feelings for him, and he was too nice to tell her to get lost."

"Anyway," said Jose, "I knew in those weeks when Maria wouldn't talk to me that she was the one. I was a mess. I tried to forget her, but it didn't work."

I cocked my head to the side. "So how'd you get her back?"

"I went to her work—she was a server—and I begged her to forgive me in front of the entire restaurant. Didn't I, sweetheart?" he said.

Maria smiled. "It was so pathetic. I told him to get lost, but he wouldn't take no for an answer. But I needed him to grovel for a bit longer."

Jose rolled his eyes. "At any rate, I was honest with her. Told her that I loved her, I needed her, and I wanted to marry her. And after she'd made me suffer, she finally relented. And we've been married ever since."

I wasn't entirely certain how to take this story. "So you're saying I should humiliate myself to get my—friend—to forgive me?"

"Be honest with him," said Maria. "And if you really care about him, don't let him go without a fight."

I chewed on my bottom lip. Would Mac want me to fight for our relationship? I didn't know anymore. He'd told me he was starting to have feelings for me, but that didn't mean he still cared. Trust had been so important to him. And I'd broken that.

After we finished lunch, we hugged. Jose told me that he was going to invite me to their son's birthday party if I wanted to come. Although the thought of being around even more extended family was intimidating, I said yes. Getting to know the family that I'd thought for so long wasn't interested in me or my mom felt nice.

Mac, would you be proud of me today? I thought to myself. *Because I'm proud of myself.*

Even if I couldn't get Mac back, even if I couldn't show him that our relationship had always been real to me, at least I had more people in my corner.

Chapter 28

Mac

Coach eyed me up and down. "That's all you have to say then, Mackenzie?"

I nodded tightly.

To my dismay, Coach didn't look pissed this time. He looked disappointed. He folded his hands and then cleared his throat.

"You know, you can always talk to me. If you need to, that is," he said. Even as he said the words, he looked like he wanted to be anywhere else.

I had to restrain a dark laugh. When Coach had called me into his office to reprimand me for missing practice, he'd reamed me a new asshole. But then he'd asked me what the hell was going on with me, and I'd shut my mouth.

I wasn't about to spill all my dirty little secrets to my coach. Besides, none of that had anything to do with hockey. My personal life was just that: personal.

"I'm sorry I missed practice and almost missed the game," I repeated. "It won't happen again."

Coach gazed at me for a long moment. "You look like shit. Have you been eating? Taking care of yourself? There's a counseling service you can use—"

I held up a hand. "I'm fine. Thanks for the concern. Like I said, I won't miss practice again without calling in."

"Hmph. Well, if you're sure . . ." Coach cleared his throat again. "Um, you can go, then. Just—take care of yourself, okay?"

Coach had never been the type of guy to show anxiety for his players. He preferred the gruff approach, where he told you get your head out of your ass and stop fucking around. The fact that Coach spoke to me gently was enough to make me run away.

I took the back way through the stadium, mostly because I didn't feel like running into my teammates. I'd already had Brady calling me nonstop, asking me what the hell was wrong. And then of course Elodie, who'd finally stopped calling after I'd ignored her long enough . . .

When I'd finally called Brady back, he'd told me that Elodie had been worried about me. I wanted to believe Brady, but I couldn't let myself. Elodie was just worried that she'd completely alienated her nice, juicy story. I needed to keep reminding myself of that.

When I saw her standing by my car, I couldn't even feel surprised. Worse, I felt excited. Hopeful.

Don't be a fucking idiot. Don't let your guard down.

Elodie looked frazzled. Her hair was in a messy bun, she was wearing wrinkled sweats, and she looked like she hadn't slept in days. Worry struck me, even as I pushed the feeling down.

"Mac," her voice made my heart jump. "I'm so glad to see you. Are you okay?"

"What do you want?"

She flinched. I forced myself not to care.

"I wanted to see if you were okay. Are you? Okay?"

I folded my arms. "I'm fine. Don't worry about me."

"I get why you didn't want to call me back—"

"So you showed up to my practice instead? Pretty sure that's classified as stalking."

Now she looked pissed. "Mac, if you'd just let me explain."

"There's nothing to explain. You lied to me. Unless you lied about lying?"

Elodie's expression fell. "I know. I did lie to you. I should never have done that. The guilt has been eating me alive. I know our relationship started out on the wrong foot, but everything between us was real. My feelings for you—they're real. They've always been real, I promise you."

I looked away; I couldn't stand to see the tears in her eyes. "Is that why you came here? To tell me what you've already said?"

"No. I came to warn you. My boss took me off the story about you, but he's assigned another reporter. Darren is a total bloodhound. He can track dirt in a snowstorm."

"And what? You'll get a byline in Darren's story? Congrats." My tone dripped with contempt.

"No, listen to me!" Elodie hissed. "Darren has the address to the club. He's been watching it. He's been watching *you*. You need to stay away from there."

"And let me guess, you gave him the address? Sweetheart, if you're trying to do the right thing here, you suck at it."

"I did, before I got to know you." Elodie hung onto my arm, her gaze intent. "I wish I never had. But I'm telling you what I know before it's too late. You'll keep a low profile if you don't want the whole world to know about the club."

I stared down at her. I had a feeling that in this instance, she was telling the truth. I could hear the regret in her voice. But it was too late for regret. The damage had been done.

I gently moved her hand from my arm. "Thanks for telling me," I said quietly. "I'll be careful. Now, I need to go."

Elodie looked frantic. "Mac, please. I'm so, so sorry."

"You've said that already."

"Do you believe me, then?"

I sighed. "I believe that you feel guilty and are doing anything you can to make yourself feel better."

"It's not that! I want to help you." Tears spilled down her cheeks now. "Mac, I love you. I know I wasn't supposed to fall for you, but I did. I love you so much. I hate that I hurt you. I'll do anything to make it up to you."

"Elodie . . ."

"You said you had feelings for me. Are those gone now?"

I didn't know what my feelings were anymore. Everything had gotten so fucked up that I didn't know where to begin to untangle everything.

"You know, I've heard those words before," I said. "Caroline would always tell me she loved me and couldn't live without me when I tried to end things."

I shook my head. "Christ, I should've called Tony back. I'm such a goddamn idiot."

Elodie looked confused. "Tony?"

"My lawyer. He pulled a background check on you, but I didn't want him to do it. It seemed unnecessary. I guess he was right after all."

"I'm not a criminal! And I'm not Caroline either."

"You might not be a criminal, but you and Caroline are both liars, that's for sure."

Elodie flinched. "Mac—"

"You're both liars. You both use love as a weapon to get me to do what you want. Now that I think about it, you ladies are two peas in a pod. I guess I have a type." I laughed, but it was hollow.

"I'm not using my love as a weapon. I'm just telling you that I'm doing this, trying to make things right because I love you," Elodie protested.

"Whatever makes you sleep at night."

Elodie's expression shuttered. "Now you're being cruel."

"Am I? I told you to go. You're the one intent on keeping this going."

"What can I do? What can I do to make you believe me?"

"Nothing. It's over, Elodie. We're over. Don't you get that?" I brushed past her and opened my car door. "Just leave me alone, Elodie. Go home and move on with your life."

She wasn't crying anymore. She raised her chin, her fists clenched, and she looked like a warrior. Like she'd beat down the gates of hell to get to me. But it was too late for that. Her lies had ruined everything between us. I'd told her that trust was the most important thing to me, and she'd betrayed my trust.

"This isn't over," she vowed.

I gave her a sad smile. "Sweetheart, it never even began in the first place."

Our home game the following weekend was a disaster. We lost by three points, and Coach was pissed and looked apoplectic. What was worse was that I couldn't muster the energy to care. I'd fallen into a pit of pathetic, self-pitying despair ever since I'd seen Elodie. I'd spent my nights drinking, my days hating the world, and with little interest in what I thought I'd care most about in the entire world.

I also didn't care that my brother Brian wasn't around as my decoy. He'd bailed at the last minute, telling me he had to go to the East Coast. Whether it was for work or for a woman, I didn't ask.

So when I exited the stadium, I expected the usual crowd. What I didn't expect was a literal mob of people.

"Mac! When did you join The Scarlet Rope?" one reporter yelled as he tried to shove a mic in my face.

Another reporter asked, "When did you get into BDSM? Are you a sub or a Dom?"

It felt like time slowed down. I couldn't get through the mob of people fast enough, like I was being pulled back toward them by an inexorable current.

How had they found out? Had Elodie's coworker gotten someone to squeal? Or was it Elodie herself?

"How does your dad the pastor feel about your interests?" another reporter asked me.

I felt ice drip down my spine. The reporter asked the question snidely, like they couldn't wait to see my reaction. It took everything inside me not to grab the guy and punch his lights out. I pushed through the reporters and paparazzi, pulling my hat down over my face as far as I could. But the questions wouldn't stop. Even as some of my other teammates came outside to see what all the commotion was, I was the only player they cared about.

"What made you get into something like BDSM?" a woman asked me. She had a wide smile on her face, her expression almost deranged.

I just looked at her and shook my head. "No comment," I growled and continued to push my way through the crowd.

They followed me, even as I could hear Brady and some of my other teammates tell them to back off. They stalked me to my car. One even tried to open my passenger door, like he'd get into my car with me.

I was shaking now. Rage beat at me, wanting to take it out on this mob of assholes who thought my private life was fair game. These people who thought they could dig up dirt on me and then get me to talk about it against my will. They mobbed my car as I tried to drive away. Only when I heard shouts did the mob break up enough for me to pull out and drive away.

I sweat, my head pounded, and my gorge rising. I kept checking to see if anyone had followed me, and of course, there were multiple cars on my tail. Only when I got on the freeway and started driving way above the speed limit did I lose them.

I barely registered that I was home when I arrived. I practically fell out of my car, and I realized I was shaking. With horror. And with such an intense, all-consuming rage that I could barely see straight.

I was about to go into my house through the garage—I parked my shit Corolla outside since my garage was full of my nicer cars—when I heard rustling in the bushes. I paused, listening, knowing that I was acting like a paranoid crazy person.

I heard a voice then. *Not a raccoon.* I didn't stop to think about what I was doing. I stalked to those bushes and grabbed a man from them, hauling him to his feet and then punching him in the face before he could say a word.

The man fell to the ground, yelling and cursing. His camera equipment fell all around us, and before the reporter could blink, I was smashing his camera against the wall of my house.

"Hey!" the reporter cried out, scrambling to his feet. "Hey, what the fuck! That's my camera!"

"Get the fuck off my property!" I snarled.

"You don't have a right to destroy my stuff!"

"The fuck I don't! You're trespassing, and you think you have any rights here?" I grabbed the guy by his collar, enjoying how he struggled to breathe. "You have a lot of fucking nerve."

The man tried to loosen my grip, but I was twice his size. I let him dangle for a long moment before I finally let him go. He gasped for breath.

I tossed him his broken camera. "Who are you? How did you get past my gate?"

The man was wheezing. His nose was bleeding from where I'd punched him, and the sight filled me with satisfaction.

"Your gardener left the gate open," he finally replied, coughing. "Blame him."

"That still doesn't give you a right to hide in my goddamn bushes!"

"Look, I didn't come out here to be assaulted." The man held up his hands. "I'm just doing my job."

"That's not an excuse."

"No, but it's not worth killing me either." He wiped his mouth. "If I would've known you'd go berserk, I wouldn't have come here. Elodie never mentioned that little detail that you're fucking crazy."

I froze. "Elodie?"

"Yeah. She's my coworker. We work for the same paper. I was given you as my assignment when she dropped the ball."

Darren. That was the name Elodie had given me. "You've been watching me?" I asked.

"Obviously." Darren inspected his broken camera. "You didn't have to fucking break my camera," he mumbled.

"Did Elodie tell you about the club?"

Darren looked up. "What? No. She told me that was a dead end. She was wrong, of course. I knew she was wrong or just straight-up lying." Darren kept fiddling with his camera, which prompted me to take it back from him.

"Focus," I growled. "What all did Elodie tell you? About me?"

Darren stared. "Nothing. Why? Does it matter?"

"Yeah, it fucking matters."

"All I know is that she got offered a big check to write a story about you."

"Did she accept it?" I demanded, my heart pounding.

"Dunno." Darren picked up the rest of his camera gear. "Uh, I need to go. I'd rather you not decide to kill me after all."

I almost admired his sass even as I wanted to punch him again. "Get out of here before I have you arrested. No, wait. I'll escort you myself."

"Oh, goody," Darren retorted.

Once I finally got rid of him, I went inside. I collapsed onto my couch, the adrenaline of the past hour making my stomach roil.

Had Elodie taken the money that Darren had mentioned? I knew she was tight on cash. If she had taken it, I almost couldn't blame her.

Almost being the operative word.

I sat up, groaning. What the fuck was I going to do? My secrets were out. Everything was out in the public to consume, judge, and comment on. What did this mean for the team? And for my career? And what would my parents say?

I picked up a bottle I'd left on my coffee table and threw it at the wall. It smashed, glass scattering everywhere. But the satisfaction was short-lived.

What the fuck am I going to do now?

Chapter 29

Elodie

I was a basket case when I saw the news about Mac. I'd been at the office, and Darren had come in to my cubicle with a strange expression.

"What is it?" I'd asked, instantly worried. I also couldn't help but notice his face was bruised.

Darren grimaced. "Here. I thought you should know before it's published." He handed me his tablet, and I stared down at the screen, unable to comprehend what I was reading.

Hockey star is a BDSM enthusiast? Blades player Cole Mackenzie apparently loves whips, chains, and sex clubs.

I felt sick. I just looked up at Darren with wide eyes. "How . . . ?"

"I did my job," he said, surprisingly gently. "I knew that office building had more to it. I'm sorry, Elodie. But it was surprisingly easy to get people to talk."

"You bribed them."

He shrugged. "We pay anonymous tipsters all the time. This isn't a new thing." He took his tablet back and stuffed it into his bag. "But I wanted to give you a heads-up."

I nodded. I couldn't fault him for doing his job. Because he was right; this was just an assignment. Mac was a celebrity, and we wrote about celebrities.

Oh, Mac. What are you going to do?

The story was published and all over the Internet by the end of the day. Roy was ecstatic, although he kept giving me dark looks. I was sure he knew I'd lied about being unable to find any dirt on Mac.

I called Mac multiple times, but he wouldn't pick up. I left him three voicemails. I tried to explain that I wasn't the one who'd published the story, but did it matter? I'd been the one to give Roy the address to the club in the first place.

The following day, I was working from home, but Roy called me, telling me to come to the office ASAP. *Is he going to fire me?*

I drove into the office, almost not caring what happened to my job, even as I'd gotten a bunch of bills that morning that were overdue. The water company was threatening to turn off my water by the end of the month if I didn't pay. *Who needs running water anyway?* I thought in despair.

I went to Roy's office right after I arrived, steeling myself for the inevitable.

But to my surprise, Roy wasn't angry. He looked like he was at a complete loss.

"Sit down," he said gruffly.

I sat and folded my hands to hide their shaking.

"I got an interesting call this morning," he said, shaking his head. "From Cole Mackenzie's publicist."

Now I was the one who was confused. "His publicist?"

"She wanted to schedule an interview. Now, here's the kicker. Mackenzie wants *you* to interview him. Nobody else would do." Roy's eagle-eyed gaze pierced straight through me. "Now, why would that be?"

I gaped at Roy. "There must be some mistake."

"Oh, there's no fucking mistake. I made the woman clarify three times. Apparently, Mackenzie wants to 'address the rumors head-on' or whatever bullshit." Roy scowled. "We don't do interviews. We're a gossip rag. Have you ever done an interview?"

"A few. It's been a while."

Roy grunted. "Well, that's better than none. They want to do the interview on Friday. I told them you'd do it."

I didn't understand. Why would Mac want me, of all people, to interview him? Was this some kind of revenge scheme?

"I'm assuming they want to vet my questions beforehand?" I asked.

Roy chuckled. "No, they don't. They said ask whatever you want. Fuckin' crazy, right?"

I told Roy I'd start preparing my questions right away. Although he confirmed that Mac's team didn't want to see the questions ahead of time, I planned to send them anyway. At the very least, I wanted Mac to know I took this assignment very seriously.

I knew I shouldn't, but I tried calling him again. I realized, rather wildly, that this interview might be the last time he'd ever speak to me.

I have no choice, do I? I thought to myself as I stared at my laptop that evening. I didn't even know where to begin. It didn't help that I already knew a lot of the answers people would want me to ask.

How did you get into BDSM?

Why did you join a sex club?

Are you a sub or a Dom?

Have you ever had a normal relationship?

Were you always like this? When did this all start for you?

I felt a headache coming on. Even as exhaustion hit me like a freight train, I felt a sense of resolve.

Mac clearly believed I could do this. He also wanted to set the record straight. The least I could do was make sure my interview was thoughtful and insightful. No gotchas, no attempts to back Mac into a corner.

I love you, Mac. But what is your endgame here?

When I arrived at Dawn's pottery studio in Malibu, she didn't seem surprised to see me again. I was impressed that she remembered my name.

"I saw online that you and Mac are an item," she said with a wry smile.

I blushed. "We're not an item."

"Really? Did you break up?"

I sighed. Where did I even begin? *Had we even been dating in the first place?*

Dawn saw the look on my face and ushered me inside. "I'm just cleaning up from my last class. You can help me out."

I wasn't about to protest if it meant Dawn would talk to me. When she handed me a broom and dustpan, she pointed at the front of the studio.

"Get cracking," she said.

I did as she asked. I couldn't help but wonder how Mac had managed to be friends with her, only because he liked to be the bossy one. Had he and Dawn butted heads as teenagers? They both seemed like people who always had to be in control.

Dawn began watering plants near where I was sweeping. "So," she said, "why are you here?"

"I should tell you that I'm a reporter," I said.

Dawn paused and set down her watering can. "Is this an interview?"

I shook my head. "No. This is all off the record. I'm here for a personal reason."

"Because of Mac?" Dawn started watering a large Monstera that took up nearly an entire window. "I heard about Caroline, you know."

"He won't talk to me. I keep trying to call him, and he won't pick up. I tried to warn him but I don't know if it just made things worse." I realized I was babbling, but Dawn just waited for me to clarify.

I forced myself to start from the beginning. I blushed bright red when I told Dawn about The Scarlet Rope and the contract I signed with Mac, but Dawn seemed unfazed. All she said during my storytelling was that I needed to keep sweeping.

"And now he won't talk to me," I ended, throwing up my hands. "Except he wants me to interview him. Make it make sense!"

Dawn frowned as she handed me a trash can to empty the dustpan. "You know, I only ever wanted Mac to be happy when we dated. We each had our secrets. But I could never get behind him dating Caroline. Or whatever the fuck it was. Caroline used him for her own selfish ends," said Dawn.

"He kept defending Caroline, even to me," I replied, sighing. "He only seemed open to hearing that maybe their relationship was wrong after Caroline's funeral."

Dawn's eyes widened. "Did you go to the funeral?"

"I did. Why?"

Dawn seemed to look at me with new eyes. "I'm surprised, is all. Mac was always so closed off. Even when we were dating—well, fake-dating—and he was seeing Caroline, he never let me meet her. I mean, I knew who she was. White Rock is a small town, and I'd gone to the Bradfords' church a few times as a kid. But Mac never let me be around Caroline. When I asked him about it, he'd get super defensive."

"I'm not sure that I follow . . ."

Dawn shrugged. "I guess what I'm saying is that it sounds like Mac trusts you."

That statement made me wince. "He used to trust me. He doesn't anymore."

"I think he still does if he's asking you to interview him. He could've gone with any reporter in this city and beyond. Why you? Because he knows you. And I'd bet my bottom dollar that he has feelings for you, too."

Those words made my heart soar. But even as I wanted to believe Dawn, I knew it would be dangerous to do so. For all I knew, Mac had decided to have me interview him to enact some weird revenge. There was no way I could allow myself to get my hopes up only to have them be shattered again.

"Mac would never have let me come with him to Caroline's funeral," Dawn said, breaking through my thoughts. "The fact that he let you come with him? And you met his parents?" She let out a whistle. "Yeah, that's a whole fucking sign right there."

Dawn scrubbed the tables and chairs where students worked on their pottery. She seemed agitated now. "Mac's parents never let him just be himself," said Dawn. "His dad, especially. I remember when Mac and I went to prom. Mac wore a red velvet coat—he looked fucking amazing— but his dad threw a shit fit. Said that Mac looked like a—"

She paused, wincing. "Well, you can guess the word. His dad never accepted him, and his mom just stood by silently and did nothing. When they found out Mac was with Caroline, his dad pretty much kicked him out of the house. Mac only survived because he had hockey to fall back on."

"What's ironic was Mac's dad calling Mac the f-word, when I was the gay one," said Dawn wryly. "He never liked me, though. I had a feeling he knew I was into girls. He'd give me this cold look whenever I came to see Mac."

I took in all this information, and my heart hurt for young Mac. His parents hadn't protected him, had they? They'd only judged him and found him wanting. And when he'd been preyed upon by Caroline, they'd blamed him for it.

"I hate that you lied to Mac," said Dawn, her gaze direct. "But it sounds like you're trying to make amends, at least. Mac isn't an aberration, though. His private life shouldn't be used for gossip fodder."

"I know that. And I agree."

Dawn stared me down, and I had to restrain myself from fidgeting. "Does he know there's nothing wrong with him? That he isn't some freak of nature?"

"I'm not sure. I think he still judges himself," I replied quietly.

Dawn shook her head. "I only ever wanted him to be happy. I still do. We lost touch years ago, but I've followed his career. I'd always hoped he had let go of all that guilt and shame."

"I think with Caroline dying, he's starting to," I said.

"Good. And good riddance to that hag. She used a kid and never faced any consequences for it. May she rot in hell."

I blinked, a little taken aback. But I couldn't disagree with Dawn either. I also hoped that wherever Caroline was, she was finally feeling all the pain she'd inflicted on other people.

When I was about to head out, Dawn gave me a fierce hug. "Take care of him, okay? And tell him I'm thinking about him."

I nodded, feeling tears prick my eyes. "I'm not sure he'll talk to me after this interview."

"He will. He's in love with you. I saw those pictures of you together, and he's let you in to his deepest, darkest secrets. No guy does that if he's not in love. He'll come around."

I hugged her back and prayed that Dawn was right.

I didn't sleep the night before the interview. Couldn't remember the last time I was this anxious. When I got out of my bed and looked at myself in the mirror, I winced. I looked terrible. I had dark circles under my eyes, and I looked pale. I put on more makeup than usual just to make myself seem like less of a zombie.

I was all nerves when I arrived at the hotel where Mac's publicist Olivia had scheduled for us to meet. I'd sent over my final draft of questions the night prior, but Olivia replied that Mac didn't need to see them beforehand.

I was early, so I waited in the lobby for Mac. I got a latte from a nearby café but couldn't even drink it. My palms were sweaty, and sweat had broken out on my upper lip. I just hoped I wasn't sweating through my dress. The last thing I wanted was Mac to see me as a complete mess.

When he arrived, I didn't even need to see him to know he was at the hotel. I heard a commotion near the entrance, and then suddenly, it was over before it'd even begun.

One of the hotel workers came over to where I was sitting. "Come with me," he said. When I hesitated, he gave me a look over his shoulder that seemed to say, *I don't have all day.*

I followed him into the restaurant attached to the hotel. To my surprise, it was completely empty even though it was lunchtime. Then I saw Mac sitting at a table near the back, away from any windows. He wore a button-down shirt and had his hair slicked back. When he saw me, his gaze pierced straight to my soul.

I started shaking. I swallowed and took a deep breath. *This isn't a date. This is work. Act professional.*

When I went to Mac's table, I held out my hand. "Nice to see you," I said. It was hard not to reach out and hug him. But I had to remind myself yet again of the boundaries he'd set. Mac raised an eyebrow. He stood and finally shook my hand. The feel of his palm against mine was electric.

"Nice to see you," he drawled.

Although the restaurant was empty, that didn't mean we weren't being watched. There was staff all around us.

When we sat down, I said, "Now, let's get started."

Chapter 30

Mac

The moment Elodie walked into the restaurant, I wanted to fall to my knees and beg her for forgiveness. It didn't help that she looked absolutely gorgeous. She wore a simple gray dress with her hair up in a bun, but it was the prettiest I'd ever seen her.

Damn, was I deep in it.

I couldn't keep my eyes off her when she sat down across from me. I drank her in like a man parched.

Andrea, along with my publicist, Olivia, had been the ones to suggest that I do an interview. At first, I'd balked at the idea. My private information was already out there—why make shit worse?

"Wouldn't you rather get to set the record straight?" Olivia had asked me.

Andrea had nodded along. "You should get to tell your side of the story. Otherwise, the speculation will continue."

"So should I call the guy I caught in my fucking bushes?" I shot back.

"I think we can do better than the guy who wrote the first story," Andrea said dryly.

I had started pacing my dining room. Although I'd wanted to tell these two women to go to hell, I knew that deep down, they were right. I needed to set the record straight. I needed to stop running away from my problems.

"I'll do it," I'd said finally. "But only if Elodie interviews me."

Olivia's eyes bugged out. Andrea let out a surprised guffaw.

"Oh shit," said Andrea, "you're serious."

I folded my arms across my chest. "It's either her or nobody."

"Mac, you can't have your ex interview you," said Olivia.

"Why not? Is there some law against it?" I asked. "It's not like she isn't an actual reporter."

Andrea rolled her eyes. "No, but it seems sus all the same. And it could also backfire spectacularly. Will Elodie even talk to you now that you've ended things?"

"She's the one who warned me that her paper was onto me," I pointed out. "I'm certain she'll take the assignment."

Olivia sighed. Andrea sighed. I had just waited impatiently.

"Do you think he knows?" Olivia asked Andrea.

Andrea glanced at me. "Maybe?"

Now, I was seriously annoyed. "What do I not know?"

"I mean, you've never acted like this about a woman before," Olivia said. "The few times I suggested that you take your relationship public, you've acted like I'd asked you to set yourself on fire."

"And now you want this woman to interview you?" Andrea said. She raised her eyebrows. "That's a big step. People might think you've got actual feelings for Elodie."

I scowled. I wasn't about to spill my guts to these two women, but I wouldn't disagree with them either. I missed Elodie. I wanted Elodie. I *loved* Elodie.

I'd realized it after she'd come to warn me about Darren. No—I'd probably loved her long before that. It just took me way too long to get my head out of my ass. Even worse, Olivia called me after setting up the interview with Elodie to tell me that Elodie had apparently put in her notice at her job.

"So she's not doing the interview?" I'd asked.

"She's doing it as her last assignment. Her boss told me all about how she agreed to interview you, but she didn't want money for it. She's just doing it as a favor? I don't know. Her boss sounded pissed."

I had stared out my living room window, at a loss for words. I knew how much Elodie needed her job. How was she going to make do without it?

"Why would she agree to interview me for free?" I asked aloud.

Olivia had snorted. "You know what? You think long and hard about that one, my dear. But I'm pretty sure it has something to do with her having feelings for you."

Now here I was, sitting across from the woman I loved, and I had to restrain myself from yanking her into my arms and kissing her. Showing her how much I loved her and wanted her and *needed* her.

"Can you tell me about growing up with your dad, the pastor?" That was her first question.

I could almost believe she didn't know the answer. I felt the familiar shame and anxiety creeping up my throat. But I wasn't going to let my past dictate my future. Not anymore.

I told her what she already knew: about how my dad had always been strict and had expected me to follow in his footsteps. How I'd struggled to be the perfect Christian boy. How I'd never lived up to my parents' expectations.

Elodie then asked me about my dating history, and specifically about me dating married women. It was strange talking to Elodie about these subjects. Maybe it was because I'd already told her everything. Or perhaps it was because she didn't seem like the Elodie I knew.

This was Elodie, the reporter, in front of me. She had a job to do. Seeing her work made me fall even harder for her at that moment. When we got to the end of the interview, Elodie folded her hands. "Why did you want to do this interview, Mac?" she asked quietly.

"Because I want to take back control of my own life," I said finally. "I'm tired of running away. It only creates more speculation anyway. So I'd rather give my side of the story and take the reins of the narrative."

"Is there something specific you want people to know?" she pressed.

I swallowed. "I wanted to say that the rumors are true. I am a member of a sex club. I like BDSM and have for a long time. And you know what? I'm not ashamed of that fact. Not anymore." I leaned forward, my gaze intent on Elodie. "I'm not going to apologize for what I like to do in private with other consenting adults. Nobody else should either. Everybody spends too much time and energy judging what other people do. And you know what? Fuck that. I'm tired of it. I'm tired of being a prisoner of other people's opinions."

Elodie smiled. "Off the record, are you sure you want me to include all that?"

"If you don't print it, I'll sue you."

She chuckled, shaking her head and scribbling something down on her notepad. I waited for her to look back up at me.

"This is also on the record," I said. I kept my gaze glued to her beautiful face. "Most of all, I wanted to do this interview because I wanted to apologize to you. I wanted you to trust me, but I couldn't do the same for you. I'm sorry, Elodie."

Her eyes filled with tears. "Mac . . ."

"No, let me finish." I took her hand. "You're everything, baby. You're the most incredible woman I've ever met. You gave up your job for me. You're doing this interview pro bono, even. The only thing that's your fault is making me fall in love with you."

Her eyes widened. "What?"

"I love you. I know I said we weren't supposed to fall for each other, but I did. Do you still love me? Because if you don't, I'll spend the rest of my life proving to you how much I love you and to make you fall back in love with me."

Elodie laughed and then sobbed. She was just shaking her head over and over again. "Of course I still love you, you idiot." She wiped her eyes, laughing again. "How did you know I'd quit my job?"

"Your boss told my publicist. He sounded pretty annoyed about it."

"Roy is annoyed about life in general."

Seeing her there with tears spilling down her cheeks broke my restraint. I got up and pulled her into my arms.

"Do you love me?" I demanded.

"Yes, I still love you. Do you love me?"

"Didn't I just say I did?"

She poked me in the chest. "Say it again. I forgot."

"I love you. I love you. I love you." I wrapped her tightly in my arms. "I'm never letting you go, Elodie Andrews. And you can put that on the record, too."

Epilogue
Elodie

I lightly slapped Hannah's hand away from the tray of cookies. "Those are for tonight!" I admonished.

Hannah stuck out her tongue. "I've only eaten one!"

"Try three, going on four. Those are Mac's favorites."

"Oh, well, we can't make Mac mad." Hannah winked. "He might take me out back and spank me."

I rolled my eyes, even as I laughed. Mac might be into spanking, but Hannah and I both knew he was only interested in spanking *me*.

Hannah and I had been preparing for the house-warming party all afternoon. Mac had been helping us, but his agent had called him as he'd been cutting up veggies to talk about something that sounded important. Although I couldn't help but wonder if Andrea had been asked to call him so Mac could get out of party preparation duties . . .

"How many people are coming tonight?" Hannah asked. She gazed at the huge spread of food on the dining room table. "Because I'm pretty sure this is enough to feed an army."

"Hockey players are pretty much an army. They inhale food like Pac-Man." I reviewed my list for the thousandth time, ensuring I hadn't missed anything. "Shit! The hummus!"

"I'll get it." Hannah went to the kitchen and returned with three different tubs of hummus. "All of these?"

"Yeah." I began opening them. "I wasn't sure what flavor people preferred . . ."

Hannah stopped me, squeezing my upper arm. "Babe, it's gonna be fine. Great even. It's just a housewarming party, not a wedding."

I knew that. I'd told myself that, but I still wanted to leave a good impression with all of Mac's teammates and friends. Even though he'd assured me that everyone would be happy with just chips and beer, I hadn't been so optimistic about the whole thing.

"But what if people get bored and leave early?" I asked, almost talking to myself. "Should I have made it a dinner party instead? Maybe finger foods aren't enough."

"Oh my God, Elodie, chill." Hannah rested her hands on my shoulders, forcing me to face her. "Go get a glass of wine and sit down. I'll finish up here."

I didn't have the energy to protest, so I nodded and followed Hannah's instructions. After one and a half glasses of wine, I felt a tiny bit calmer.

"Is Mac still on the phone?" Hannah asked as she dipped a carrot in one of the tubs of hummus.

"I guess so. I should go check on him."

Hannah waved a hand. "It's fine. I wanted to have some time with you alone." She sat down in a chair and pointed at me to sit, too. "I like what you guys have done with the place."

I smiled. I'd moved into Mac's house—now our house, of course—about a month ago. Although he'd added more furniture since we'd started dating, the place still lacked character. When I'd started putting up photos and artwork, Mac had protested a bit until I'd reminded him it was my house now too.

Behind Hannah was one of my favorite pieces. It was a red ribbon on a dark background. One end of the ribbon was floating in the wind, while the other end was twisted into a loop that would fit around somebody's wrists. It was a subtle nod to our BDSM lifestyle, but not so in your face to make people uncomfortable. When I'd first brought it home, Mac had just raised an eyebrow and then chuckled.

"It looks more like a home, right?" I said, nodding. "What is it with guys and not decorating?"

Hannah shrugged. "No idea. They save up thousands for a down payment for a house, and then only buy a bed, a TV, and maybe an air fryer if they're feeling fancy."

I laughed, shaking my head. "What's the worst place you've been to?"

"Oh God. Um, probably the guy who was using cardboard boxes for all of his furniture? With the mattress on the floor, just to add to the ambience. Best part? The dude was the CEO of a multibillion-dollar company."

"No! Seriously?"

"Seriously." Hannah wrinkled her nose. "I had one drink and ditched him when he proudly told me he washed his sheets once a year."

We giggled like teenagers. Ever since moving in with Mac, I hadn't had as much time to see Hannah. I didn't even know if she was dating anyone.

"Brady is supposed to be here tonight," I remarked, trying to sound sly.

"That's nice," Hannah replied. "Is he still single?"

"As far as I know, yeah."

"Well, I'd imagine he's not the type of guy to commit to one woman. So his definition of 'single' might be pretty loose." Hannah shrugged a single shoulder. "What about Mac's parents? Are they coming? I know you mentioned you invited them."

I winced inwardly. Mac had reached out to Bob and Judy Mackenzie to let them know we'd moved in together and to extend an invite, but they were noncommittal at best—said they'd *think* about attending. We hadn't heard from them since, which was close to a month now. I'd tried to get Mac to follow up with them, but he'd been too hurt by their lack of interest. I suspected they weren't happy about our living together out of wedlock, considering their religious beliefs.

"I doubt they're coming." I sighed.

"I thought Mac and his parents were working on their relationship?"

"I mean, it's better than it used to be. But they're still not close. I've tried talking to them on Mac's behalf, but Mac got pissed when I told him. So now I just stay out of things."

"That sucks." Hannah frowned. "But I do agree with Mac that you should probably let them figure it out themselves. You're still the outsider, after all."

"Thanks," I said dryly.

I was about to press Hannah on her dating life when my phone rang. *Roy Fink* flashed on the screen. My old boss had called me twice earlier this week already. I'd been dodging his calls because I didn't want to deal with him. What was there left to say, anyway? I'd quit and moved on. So I didn't understand why Roy kept trying to get ahold of me.

"Are you going to answer that?" Hannah asked, pointing at my phone.

"No. Why should I?"

"Has he been calling you before now?"

I avoided Hannah's gaze. "Maybe."

"Elodie. Come on. Bite the bullet."

Before I could react, Hannah grabbed my phone and answered the call. "Elodie's right here," she said before holding out the phone to me.

I cursed her under my breath and took a deep breath before bringing the cell to my ear. "Hi, Roy."

"Elodie!" His voice was so loud that I didn't even need to put my phone on speaker to hear him. "Finally! I thought you were dead in a ditch somewhere."

Hannah snort-laughed.

"Nope, still alive. Just busy," I replied.

"Well, you got time for me, or not? I have an offer you can't refuse." He chuckled.

"As long as you aren't going to put a horse head in my bed when I say no," I joked.

"Why would you say no? This is an amazing chance for you. I want you to come back to *The Tea*. I'll pay you double. You'll get the best assignments. You can interview whoever you want."

I hadn't expected that kind of offer. I stared at Hannah. Her eyes widened in surprise as well.

I'd gotten a handful of offers from other tabloids after the Mac interview, but I'd turned them all down. Quitting *The Tea* had been such a weight off my shoulders. I'd realized that following around celebrities to find dirt on them had been too stressful for me. And it wasn't what I wanted to write about, anyway.

"That's very nice of you," I started to say. "But . . ."

"*Nice*? It's amazing." Roy grumbled. "I've never offered anybody a job like this, not even close."

"Be that as it may . . . I'm still not interested. I'm sorry, Roy."

"Why not?" he snapped. "Why the hell not?"

I thought about it for a moment. Was it worth being honest? Hannah gestured at me to speak.

"Roy, I never liked writing for tabloids," I said, sitting up straighter. "It's a huge emotional drain. I always felt icky doing it. Sure, these people are rich and famous, but don't they deserve their privacy, too? I always felt like I was compromising my own morals, and I was tired of it."

Roy was quiet for a long moment. Eventually, he sighed. "You know, I think that might be the most honest you've ever been with me."

I made a face. "Your tone isn't making that sound like a good thing . . ."

"Maybe it is. What the hell do I know? Not much, except it's fuckin' annoying being turned down. Though I appreciate your honesty nonetheless. And if this job isn't what you like, fine. I'd rather hire somebody who wants to hustle."

"Thank you. I think."

"But if you change your mind, just give me a call."

"Okay."

We hung up after that, and I stared down at my phone, nonplussed. Even Hannah didn't say anything.

"Well, that was . . . interesting," she finally said.

I shook my head. "I think I need another damn glass of wine."

Hannah laughed and went to the kitchen. She poured two glasses of pinot grigio and passed me one. "So . . . what *are* you going to do for work now? I don't see you living off Mac's dime either."

"I'm writing a romance novel, actually."

Hannah's eyes widened. "Seriously?"

I blushed a little. I hadn't told anyone besides Mac that I was writing fiction. I'd been apprehensive at first, but as I'd gotten started, I'd realized how much I'd enjoyed it. "It's the romance-novel version of my story with Mac," I said.

"Ooh, whips and chains and all?" Hannah asked.

I laughed. "Of course. Do you see me writing some sweet and clean romance with closed-door sex? No way. Lots of fucking and all the details."

Mac finally came back downstairs. He apologized for having been on the phone for so long. "Andrea would not shut the hell up," he said, grimacing. He kissed my forehead, and his eyes roamed my face. "Your cheeks are pink. How much wine have you had, baby?"

"Enough to enjoy this party now." I chuckled. The doorbell rang, and I shot up. "Time to get this shindig started!"

People began arriving in quick succession. Before long, the house was filled with most of the Blades, along with Coach Dallas and his wife. Although there were only fifteen players, they were such big guys that it felt like twice as many people were packed in our huge house.

"How are you two doing?" Elise Dallas, the coach's wife, walked over. She looked around. "This place finally has some warmth to it. The last time I was here, the house was so sparsely decorated that I thought Mac was moving."

Elise was tall, thin, and blond, but she had warm eyes that belied her icy beauty. When I'd first met her, I'd thought Coach had married a woman half his age. It was only later that I learned she and Coach were actually the same age. I'd been tempted to ask Elise about her skincare routine because whatever she was using clearly worked.

Coach Dallas, on the other hand, looked his age. He had a handsome face, but he was balding and had a bit of a pot belly. Despite that, everyone could tell he and his wife still adored each other.

Mac came up and slid his arm around my waist. "We're doing great."

"What was it like moving in together?" Elise asked, her lips quirking. She turned toward her husband. "I remember when we first moved in together. That was after we got married, of course. My parents would have had a heart attack if we'd done it any earlier. But I remember wondering if I'd made a huge mistake, marrying a guy who couldn't put his socks in the hamper."

Coach Dallas grunted. "I'm well trained now. You've taught me the error of my ways."

I laughed. "Fortunately for me, Mac knows where the hamper is." I patted his chest. "Now, the dishwasher? We're still working on that one."

Mac protested. "I just unloaded the dishwasher last night!"

"After I *asked* you to three times." I patted him again, which earned me a growl that made everyone else laugh.

"God, you're so damn whipped now." Mac's buddy Brady joined our group. His gaze was on Mac as he shook his head. "I never thought I'd see the day."

"You mean that I'm happy and in love and not bouncing from bed to bed?" Mac replied, his tone wry.

Brady shrugged. "You make it sound like that's a bad thing."

Mac's gaze turned to me. "Someday, you'll understand. You don't know what you're missing until you've found the person you're meant to be with."

I blushed, pleased with my man's response. Brady groaned, and Coach and Elise looked amused.

"I heard your daughter is returning to town," Mac said to Elise. "You must be happy about that."

"Grace? Oh yes, we're thrilled. We've missed her so much," said Elise.

I couldn't miss the change in Brady's normally cool expression. His grip tightened on his beer bottle to the point that I could see his knuckles whiten.

"Was she away at school or something?" I asked.

Coach nodded. "She just graduated from college. Summa cum laude. Luckily, she takes after her mother when it comes to brains. She's moving back to LA to do an internship for the team."

"Seriously?" Brady said. "For the Blades?"

Elise raised an eyebrow. "You don't sound pleased. Do you have a problem with that?"

Brady rubbed the back of his neck. "Me? No. No problem. Grace has nothing to do with me." He looked around the room. "I'm gonna grab another beer. I'll catch you later."

Not long after, Mac and I had a moment to chat alone in the kitchen while everyone else was in the living room or outside on the deck. "What was that about?" I asked. "With Brady?"

"What about him?" Mac popped some chips into his mouth.

I put my hands on my hips. "Seriously? He looked like he was going to have a stroke when Coach mentioned Grace was interning at the Blades."

"I didn't notice."

I rolled my eyes. Men never noticed these things. "Brady looked pissed. Or upset, or something. Do they have a history?"

"I have no idea." At my expression, Mac chuckled. "Babe, I really don't know. Guys don't talk about this shit with each other. But"—he ate one more chip and then continued—"if there is something, I'll find out and tell you as soon as I can, okay, my little gossip-hungry queen?"

I was somewhat appeased. Maybe I'd been imagining things. But now that Mac knew to look out for any information, I knew we'd get to the bottom of whatever this was sooner or later. I guess it was the old reporter in me.

Actually . . . this would make a great story for a romance novel, player and the coach's daughter. But only if my hunch was wrong about Brady's interest in Grace. The last thing I wanted to do was piss off Mac's best friend and his coach by getting too close to the truth again.

The doorbell rang. Mac and I looked at each other.

"I thought everyone was here?"

He shrugged. "I lost track after the third time the bell rang."

We went to the door together. To our shock, we opened to find Mac's parents.

"Dad. Mom," Mac's voice was hoarse. "You're here?"

"Hi, sweetheart." His mom smiled. "Sorry we're late."

Mac's father had his arms crossed over his chest, and based on his expression, he didn't seem too pleased to be here.

"I didn't think you were coming," Mac said.

"You invited us," Bob scowled. "It wasn't like you gave your mother a choice."

Judy elbowed her husband. "We're delighted to be here. And we also came to say something. Didn't we, *Bob*?"

Mac and his father stared at each other. I could feel the tension hovering around all of us. Eventually, Bob sighed and uncrossed his arms. As if it weren't shocking enough that the man gave in first, Mac's father reached out and pulled his son into a bear hug.

I could tell Mac didn't know how to react. Judy had tears in her eyes. When Mac finally relaxed and hugged him back, I was relieved. *Maybe this is the real start of a new beginning*, I thought.

The two men pulled away, but Bob still had his hand on Mac's shoulder. "I saw your interview," Bob explained, glancing at me. "I was impressed, son. I realized that life is too short to stay away from family. I knew I couldn't refuse your invitation to come. I'm just sorry we're late."

Mac swallowed. "Dad . . ."

His father held up a hand. "I'll never totally understand your lifestyle, and I'll always pray for you. But you're my son, and I just want you to be happy." Bob wiped his eyes and stepped back a little. "You know that, right?"

"I know that now." Mac pulled me toward him, and I hugged him close. "Elodie is the one who gave me the courage to be my authentic self, though. She was also the one who wanted me to invite you guys today."

Judy smiled at me. "Then she's clearly a good influence on you. Family is everything."

Bob stuffed his hands into his pockets. "Thank you for loving our son."

I had to dash a few tears from my eyes. After, I hugged both Mac's parents, and then I hugged and kissed Mac, which made our little foursome laugh, breaking the tension from earlier.

"Come on, Pop." Mac swung an arm around his dad's shoulders. "You should meet the team."

Mac and I made the rounds, introducing his parents to all of our guests. Coach Dallas and Elise were speaking with them both when our doorbell rang—*again.*

"What the hell?" Mac said. "Who's left?"

I laughed. "I don't even know anymore."

We went to the door, and now it was my turn to be shocked. My uncle Jose and aunt Maria stood there, both holding platters of food.

"Elodie!" Jose shouted my name. He tried to hug me, but the platter in his hands made it awkward. "We're here! Sorry we're late."

"Traffic was terrible," Maria bemoaned.

Mac leaned to me and whispered, "I invited them. I hope that's okay."

I hadn't seen my aunt and uncle since I'd had lunch with them. We'd texted a few times, but I hadn't known how to proceed with the relationship. I'd considered inviting them to the party, but I hadn't found the courage.

"No, it's okay. It's great." I turned to my aunt and uncle. "I'm so glad you're here."

A little while later, a few of my cousins showed up, too. Our house was filled to the brim with people. Jose and Maria made sure everyone tried the lumpia they'd brought. Everyone raved about them, and it didn't take long for the two huge platters to empty.

Even Bob and Judy couldn't help but fall under the spell of my aunt and uncle. Jose and Maria were so warm and welcoming, asking Bob and Judy all kinds of questions about Mac and their family.

"Your parents are great," Jose said to Mac. "Your dad is a funny guy."

Mac blinked. "My dad? Funny?"

"He's hilarious. He told us all about the time you and your brother nearly lit your house on fire." Jose chuckled. "Great storyteller, that guy. He sounds like he could be a great public speaker."

I had to stifle a laugh. Mac shook his head, amused.

"You have no idea," Mac said wryly. "No damn idea."

Jose and Maria found me alone later and peppered me with questions about moving in with Mac. I shared that I was writing a novel, and they were so thrilled that they told me I had to send them the completed draft immediately when I'd finished it. They also vowed to tell everyone they knew that their niece had written a book.

"It's not even done yet!" I laughed.

"So what? You'll finish it," Aunt Maria said proudly. "And it'll be a bestseller. I bet I'll see it at Walmart."

"And your aunt will buy up every last copy." Jose winked at me.

As I watched everyone at our party mingle, talk, and laugh, I couldn't help but wonder at the nature of forgiveness. I'd been reluctant to know my extended family because I'd been holding on to the past. I'd thought I was being loyal to Mom. But had I kept them at arm's length because I'd just been afraid of rejection?

Seeing Mac start to forgive his parents made me realize that I could forgive my family, too. I was already looking forward to getting to know them, and starting anew. Wasn't that what made life amazing? The ability to start fresh, not letting your past define your future? I could've stayed with Todd instead of taking the leap into Mac's arms. What a tragedy that would've been.

My heart filled as I watched Mac on the other side of the room. Sometimes I felt like I didn't deserve him, but I wasn't letting him go either. I could only be grateful that we'd found each other.

I collapsed onto our bed, sighing with exhaustion. "Is everyone gone?"

He grinned. "Yes, dear. The house is empty."

"Finally."

"I never knew you were such an introvert."

"It's been a long time since I've hosted a party with this many people."

Mac lay down next to me. "You did an amazing job, baby."

"You too." I brushed the hair out of Mac's eyes. "Were you happy to see your parents?"

"Yeah. I think we actually might be able to start over. I didn't think that'd ever happen." I could see a variety of emotions shining in Mac's eyes. Before I could respond, though, he climbed on top of me, his grin devilish now.

"I've been waiting all evening for people to leave." He began to pull my blouse over my head.

I laughed. "Aren't you tired?"

"For you? Never."

My own tiredness disappeared quickly. I let myself fall under Mac's spell. He stripped me naked, kissing and sucking all of my sensitive spots, before turning me onto my stomach. He then tied my wrists and blindfolded me.

I inhaled sharply, excitement bubbling in my stomach. I heard Mac get off the bed. A few seconds later, he returned, and the touch of a feather traced a line down my spine. After, Mac smacked my ass with the feather whip, making me gasp.

"I've been wanting to paint your ass red all night," he growled. Mac whipped me again, and again, and I groaned, letting him have his way with me. He alternated between soft touches and harsh smacks. One second, I only felt pleasure; the next, the sting of pain. The variety of sensations made me squirm, and I grew desperate for Mac to touch me.

"*Please*. Please, Mac. I want you."

But Mac ignored my begging. Instead, he pulled me up by my hair and kissed my neck. When he bit the sensitive skin, I moaned and writhed.

"Spread your legs," Mac commanded.

I did so eagerly. His fingers danced down my back, spreading my ass cheeks. When he reached between my legs, he cursed.

"So fucking wet for me. I bet I could make you come in ten seconds. But I don't think I will . . ."

"Mac . . ."

I could feel the edges of an orgasm building quickly, though Mac wasn't going to let me get off that quickly. He danced around my clit, dipping a finger into my pussy before pulling out again. I pushed against his hand, desperate to get more pressure against my clit.

For my insolence, Mac slapped my ass three times, hard and fast. "Behave," he growled.

I loved it. I wanted him to smack me more. I wanted him to fuck me. I buried my face in the duvet and moaned.

Mac moved, then suddenly, his tongue was inside my pussy. I squealed. Mac had to hold me down, which only made me thrash harder. He suckled my clit, thrusting two fingers inside me and fucking me until I couldn't breathe.

My orgasm hit hard and fast. Mac drew it out until I was sure my bones had liquefied. He flipped me over and pushed his cock inside my still quivering pussy. I wrapped my arms around his shoulders as he buried himself in one deep thrust.

"Fuck, Elodie," he groaned. "You feel like heaven." He kissed me, lifting my hips to get a more intense angle. Before long, a second orgasm was building. Mac increased his speed, and it was all I could do just to hold on. He swore as he came inside me. Hot cum filled me up, and I gasped and writhed my way through another release.

After, Mac held me close as we both came down from our orgasms. He kissed my forehead, then my lips, telling me how much of a good girl I was, and he untied my wrists and kissed my hands. I reached up to take off my blindfold, but he stopped me.

"Keep it on." I heard the smile in his voice. "But from here on out, you're not my sub anymore. You don't have to do anything if you don't want to."

"Okay . . ."

He gave me one last quick kiss and left the bed. I shivered, the cooling sweat on my body making me cold without Mac's heat to keep me warm.

Mac returned and helped me sit up. I waited, my heart beating with anticipation.

"Elodie Andrews," he said, his tone suddenly serious. Something cool slid up my ring finger, then Mac moved off the bed. "Take off your blindfold, babe."

I did. And found Mac down on his knee. A giant diamond ring sparkled from my finger.

"Will you marry me?" he asked, his eyes shining.

I didn't hesitate, didn't even have to think about the question. I wanted nothing more than to spend my life with this man. I threw my arms around Mac's neck and cried out, "Yes! Of course I'll marry you!"

Mac kissed me. "You're mine forever now."

I smiled. "The ring is just a formality. I've been yours since the moment we met."

THE END

Guess who is getting his own story? Brady Carmichael! The ***Breaking Point*** is coming October 6th!

Pre-order
www.amazon.com/dp/B0D6LFQFP7
your copy to read more about the men who visit
The Scarlet Rope!

Connect

www.facebook.com/people/
Fallon-Greer-Author/61553397643622/

www.instagram.com/fallongreerauthor/

https://www.tiktok.com/@fallongreer

Sign up for my mailing list
https://fallongreer.com/
to stay in touch!

About the Author

FALLON GREER is a twentysomething lover of romance novels, coffee, and bookish t-shirts, of which she has far too many. She lives in Miami with her Persian cat, Mortimer, who loves to sit on Fallon's laptop when she's trying to write.

Fallon first discovered her love of reading when she'd steal her mother's Lisa Kleypas novels. That led her to start writing the types of books she loves to read.

When she's not daydreaming through conversations with people and pretending to listen, she's putting those daydreams to good use, writing novels as hot as the Florida sun.

Printed in the USA
CPSIA information can be obtained
at www.ICGtesting.com
LVHW050902110724
784715LV00001B/1